KEEP YOU CLOSE

KEEP YOU CLOSE

CLOSE

A Novel

Karen Cleveland

Doubleday
Canada

Doubleday Canada and colophon are registered trademarks of
Penguin Random House Canada Limited

Library and Archives Canada Cataloguing in Publication

Cleveland, Karen, author
Keep you close / Karen Cleveland.

Issued in print and electronic formats.
ISBN 978-0-385-69093-5 (softcover).—ISBN 978-0-385-69094-2 (EPUB)

I. Title.

PS3603.L483K44 2019   813'.6   C2018-906408-0
                                              C2018-906409-9

All statements of fact, opinion, or analysis expressed are those of the author and do
not reflect the official positions or views of the Central Intelligence Agency (CIA) or
any other U.S. Government agency. Nothing in the contents should be construed
as asserting or implying U.S. Government authentication of information or
CIA endorsement of the author's views. This material has been reviewed
by the CIA to prevent the disclosure of classified information. This
does not constitute an official release of CIA information.

Keep You Close is a work of fiction. Names, characters, places and incidents are
products of the author's imagination or are used fictitiously. Any resemblance to
actual events or locales or persons, living or dead, is entirely coincidental.

Book design: Virginia Norey
Cover design: Carlos Beltrán
Cover photograph: © Benakiba/Getty Images
Printed and bound in the USA

Published in Canada by Doubleday Canada,
a division of Penguin Random House Canada Limited

www.penguinrandomhouse.ca

10 9 8 7 6 5 4 3 2 1

Penguin
Random House
DOUBLEDAY CANADA

For B.J.W.

The truth is rarely pure and never simple.
—OSCAR WILDE

KEEP YOU CLOSE

Prologue

The woman jolts awake, gasping, heart pounding. Gunshots echo in her head, ones conjured in sleep. She reaches for the other side of the bed, finds it empty. Only an indentation in the sheets, now cold.

She slips out of bed and shrugs on a robe. Pads quietly into the darkened hall, bare feet cold on the wood floor. She peers through the first open door. A boy sleeps soundly, his features barely visible by the light of the moon. On to the next door. A little girl asleep in a rainbow-colored room, a night-light casting a muted glow on her innocent face. Third door now. Twin boys, asleep in twin beds. One has a thumb in his mouth. The other is snuggled up with a tattered stuffed bear.

Faint sound from downstairs draws her onward. Television, the volume low. She glimpses the screen when she's halfway down the stairs. News, the twenty-four-hour kind. Russia. Election interference. The sort of story her husband can't stand, always shuts off.

A few steps more and the rest of the room comes into view. The living room, cluttered with plastic toys and board games, mantel full of family pictures. And a figure in the center of the room, bathed in flickering blue light from the television. Perched on the edge of the couch, watching the screen intently. The unnatural light distorts his features. For a moment, he looks like a stranger.

He seems to sense her presence. Turns toward her, and his face breaks into a familiar, comforting smile. He mutes the television. "Another nightmare, sweetheart?" He extends an arm, an invitation to sit beside him.

She doesn't move, only nods in response to his question.

He stands, aims the remote at the television, and the picture disappears. They're plunged into darkness. "Let's go back to bed."

He walks toward the stairs, toward her, but her eyes haven't adjusted, and he's nothing more than a hulking shadow. He lays a hand gently on her back.

She shrinks away from it. "I'm going to stay down here."

He hesitates, then stoops to kiss her cheek, brushes past her up the stairs. She watches him until he's gone.

Alone in the darkness, she cinches her robe tighter. Looks into the living room, at the television screen, now black. In her mind she sees that expression on his face. Almost a smile, a twisted one. But it couldn't be, because it looked nothing like the man she knows, the man she loves.

She tries to convince herself it was just the light. That unnerving blue flicker from the television. They don't have secrets, not anymore.

Still, a shiver runs through her. She wraps her arms around herself.

What if he's not who she thinks he is?

How well does she really know him?

Chapter 1

Nighttime's always been my favorite time to run. I like the stillness. The quiet streets, empty sidewalks. It's not the safest time to be out, sure. But in running gear, it's not like I have much to have stolen. And as far as assault: I'm tougher than I look. Trained in defense tactics, able to hold my own. It's the nonrandom crime that worries me more. But if someone's coming after me, they'll find a way to do it, regardless.

The Reflecting Pool's off to my left, dark and glassy. Mile six of a planned ten, all under seven and a half minutes so far. A solid pace tonight, better than usual. It's the looming storm that's spurring me on. We've had a week of early spring, unseasonably warm temperatures, the kind that coax buds from bare tree branches, tulip stalks from the soil. But the weather—it can turn on a dime here in the District, and the forecast says we're due for one last blast of winter. Wind's already picking up.

I pass the World War II Memorial, start up the incline to the Washington Monument. I'm in my element here. Muscles working, stretching, strengthening. Pushing myself. I'm in a light jacket, running pants that hit mid-calf. My head's bare, hair pulled back, tied up away from my neck. Eighties rock in my earbuds, but quietly. Soft enough that I'd hear someone approach, that I'm fully aware of my surroundings.

At the top, I catch a glimpse of the White House. Off to my left, glowing bright. Still gives me a thrill to see it, even after years in the city. A constant reminder that I'm close to the highest reaches of power. And where there's power, there's a need for what I do.

Past the monument now, heading down the incline, picking up speed. The Capitol dome is ahead, illuminated against the night sky.

A memory fills my mind, just for an instant. Me, in that wood-paneled office, all those years ago. Him, standing up from behind his desk, coming toward me . . .

Focus, Steph.

It's that damned case at work that's doing it, making me think of the past. I force my legs to work harder, push harder, move faster. Listen to the slap of my feet hitting the pavement, the staccato rhythm.

The National Mall stretches out in front of me. A straightaway, a chance to test my speed.

My legs are straining. There's pain in my knee, but I push through. Not giving up now.

The dome looms large ahead. I see his face in my mind, once again. I can feel his hand on my arm, squeezing tight. . . .

Faster still, almost a sprint.

I can't change the past, can't do anything about him, not without jeopardizing everything that matters. But I can do something about the future. I can stop someone else.

I glance down at my wrist. Five-and-a-half-minute mile. I can feel the smile come to my lips.

I've got this. Tomorrow power gets policed.

• • •

Four in the afternoon, and Hanson's already at the bar. I'd never pegged him as a drinker, back at Quantico. Maybe he changed. Or maybe he hid it well.

A bell chimes as I open the door, a tinny ringing echo. The place is a dive, narrow and dark, neon signs on the walls, a couple of pool tables, both in use. Journey's playing on the sound system. "Don't Stop Believin'." I let my eyes adjust for a moment. He's toward the far end of the bar, a glass in front of him, nearly full.

I walk over, feeling stares, ignoring them. I know I'm a fish out of water here. Black pantsuit, high heels, tailored wool coat. Plenty of bars in D.C. attract that sort of crowd; this isn't one of them.

"Hey, Hanson."

He turns. He's thicker around the middle than last time I saw him, thinner on top. A smile spreads across his face. "Maddox. Well, I'll be damned."

He half stands, leans in for an awkward hug. Awkward because we haven't seen each other in years, and because I can't think of a time we'd *ever* hugged. Back at the Academy, he'd probably have greeted me with a slap on the back.

His face colors, like he knows it was the wrong move. Like it dawned on him, too late, that we're not equals anymore. Not colleagues, not really. Onetime friends.

I avert my eyes from the flush, slip off my coat, slide onto the stool beside him. A bartender walks over almost as soon as I'm sitting.

"What can I get you?" she asks, resting her hands on the bar, leaning forward. There's a tattoo on the inside of her wrist, a heart wrapped in spiky barbed wire. My eyes travel from that to her face, innocent looking.

"Just water, thanks."

She walks off, and I turn back to Hanson.

"It's been too long," he says, recovered now.

"Long time indeed."

"I heard you were at headquarters, but our paths haven't crossed."

"Till now."

"First in our class to reach the big leagues, huh?" He lifts his glass, takes a long sip, his eyes on me the whole time.

"Guess you could say that."

A handful of classmates are supervisory special agents, like Hanson. But I'm the first to advance beyond that. Chief of a division at headquarters, albeit a small one. Internal Investigations Section.

The bartender sets down a glass of water, wordless, and moves off.

"How've you been?" Hanson asks.

I take a sip of my water, then place the glass back on the bar, carefully. I turn to face him. He's aged in the past decade, no doubt about it. But I can still see the guy who sat next to me in Criminal Evidence, who sparred with me at the gym. Who brought me soup from the cafeteria when I was laid up with the flu. *Shit.*

"Are you aware you're being investigated for allegations of sexual harassment?"

The pleasant look fades. His lips part in surprise, then quickly close. His face hardens. Like a light switch, flipped. "*That's* why you're here?"

"She's your *subordinate*, Hanson."

"It's a bullshit claim."

"It's the truth. You and I both know it."

He averts his eyes, and his jaw tightens. There's a long lull. Behind the bar, I can hear the clink of glass.

"My word against hers," he says.

I can feel anger spark inside me. "Yeah?"

"You can't fire me for that shit."

"How about for time and attendance fraud?"

His mouth twitches, just the smallest bit. I can see him fighting to keep his face impassive.

"I've had an agent on you for the past week. I know exactly how many hours you've worked. And how many you've been *paid* for working."

His eyes are burning now, but I can see the worry behind the fire.

"I also know that you're still carrying." I nod toward the bulge at his hip. "I know that you drove your government vehicle here, and that you're on your second glass of bourbon."

"What the hell, Maddox?"

I don't say a word.

"We used to be friends."

"That's why I'm here."

He waits. He's breathing hard, his nostrils flaring slightly with each breath.

I lean toward him. "Here's what's going to happen. You're going to hand over your badge, and your gun, and your keys. And first thing tomorrow, you're going to walk into headquarters and re-sign."

He snorts in contempt. "And if I don't?"

I glance toward the door, nod in the direction. "See those two guys over there?" McIntosh and Flint are standing on either side of it, watching us. "They work for me. And they're prepared to make a scene. Right here, right now. Breathalyzer, cuffs, the works."

"That's bullshit."

"Wanna bet?"

He looks back at the door, then down at his drink. His glass is nearly empty now. His fingers have tightened around it. Left hand's bare, but I can see the indention where the ring usually lies.

"Your career's over, Hanson. I'm giving you the chance to get out quietly. Face the consequences for the harassment, and this"—I nod toward the bourbon—"doesn't become an issue. Neither does the fraud."

"I have a family," he says. "A wife, kids. A *mortgage*. You can't fuck me over like this."

Bon Jovi's playing now—"Livin' on a Prayer." Fitting. "It's your choice how it goes down."

He glares at me. Then he pulls off his badge, slams it down on the bar between us.

Chapter 2

The cherry tree outside my brownstone is starting to bud, dozens of pink knobs closed tight like tiny fists. In a few weeks, it'll be in full bloom, and the city will be bursting with pink blossoms. Hordes of tourists, too; they'll clog the usually quiet sidewalks around the Tidal Basin. And then before I know it, the flowers will wilt, the color will disappear, and the sidewalks will be empty once again.

My heels click against brick as I climb the steps to my front door. Slowly, heavily, feeling spent.

I turn my key in the first lock, then the second. Step inside, shut and lock the door behind me, pause for a moment in the hall. The alarm console on the wall is lit green. *Disarmed.* The house is silent. I listen for some sound, any sound, but hear nothing. *Might as well get used to it,* I tell myself.

"Zachary," I call up the stairs. "I'm home." He's Zach to his friends, has been for years now. But to me he'll always be Zachary. I said I wouldn't do it. Wouldn't be like my mom, the only person who still calls me Stephanie. But when I look at him, I don't see a teenager. I see my little boy. *It goes so fast,* everyone warned, and I didn't believe it at first. Now I know truer words have never been spoken.

I wait another moment, listening, but all is still silent. I hang up my coat, toss down my keys and work bag on the table in the entry-way, and walk into the kitchen, flipping the switch on my way in. Light floods the room from the fixture above the center island, bounces off dark granite, stainless steel. It's a chef's kitchen, re-modeled when Zachary was in middle school. Perfect for home-cooked dinners. Rarely used.

I set a brown paper bag down on the island. Thai takeout, his favorite. I'd texted him earlier, let him know I'd be bringing it home. Otherwise he'd have eaten before I arrived, like he does most nights now. *I was hungry, Mom,* he'd say. *I couldn't wait.* And I'd have had just a few precious minutes to talk with him, standing in the doorway of his room.

It's bribery. That fact isn't lost on me. I'm an FBI agent, bribing my son with Thai food. But it's time with him. Precious, precious time.

I head for the fridge, open it. Sparse contents, mostly drinks. Bot-tled water, arranged in neat rows. Amber bottles below, all IPAs. I take one, the hoppiest of the bunch. Close the door, pop the top, take a long drink. I can already feel some of the tension start to drain away. Hanson had it coming. Black-and-white, no question about it. Power, policed.

I hear Zachary's bedroom door open, his footsteps in the up-stairs hall, then pounding down the stairs. He used to barrel down when he was younger, like he didn't have the time to tread carefully, like he was in a hurry, always in a hurry. His pace slowed as he grew, but it still sounds like he's thundering down. Maybe it's his size now, the fact that he's bigger than me. Or maybe I'm just remem-bering the way it sounded when he was young.

In any case, I'll miss that sound. He swings around the corner, one hand on the banister. In jeans and a grubby T-shirt, bare feet. There's a hint of stubble on his face, just the smallest bit, and it looks like it doesn't belong, like he's a boy pretending to be a man. I have to keep reminding myself that he *is* a man, or almost is, anyway.

"Hi, honey. How was your day?" My voice sounds falsely bright, like I'm trying too hard. I *am* trying too hard.

He catches the tone, recognizes it. He glances at me with a hint of suspicion, a realization that the takeout is pretext for forced bonding. "Fine."

I wish I could take back those words, try again. I focus instead on taking off my suit jacket. Fold it neatly in half, lay it on the back of one of the barstools, smooth out the front of my blouse, adjust the holster at my hip.

When Zachary was young, locking up my gun was the first thing I'd do when I got home, even before I'd give him a hug and a kiss. I'd secure the Glock in the gun safe in my bedroom closet, because I didn't want him to see me with it, never wanted weapons to be part of our lives. Then I'd peel off the clothes that I wore in the presence of criminals, like somehow that would keep them at a distance.

But he's older now. He knows I carry, and he couldn't care less. He's never had the slightest interest in guns. And criminals can find a way in, no matter the defenses against them; haven't I learned that one the hard way?

I pull plates from the cabinet and set them down beside the food. "School okay?" I ask, aiming to keep the words sounding neutral, conversational.

He heads for the island, digs into the paper bag. He pulls out a clear plastic container, then another. Pad Thai and Panang curry. Our usual.

"Yeah."

One-word answers. It's about all I get from him these days. All

I've gotten for a while now. And on the rare occasions we *do* talk, he's invariably sullen.

It'll get better. I keep telling myself that. This is just a rough patch; the teenage years always are, right? We were close once, and we'll be close again someday. Things would probably be easier if I were mother to a girl, or father to a boy. Maybe he'd be more himself around me, less guarded, less uncomfortable.

I've watched Zachary with his friends, all those kids who are strangers to me, even if I knew them once, when they were young. In the parking lot at school, in pictures on social media. My son's different with them. Expressive, happy. Engaged, too; he's president of the Computer Club, a student government representative, a member of various honor societies. Works hard for a tech start-up after school, does all their coding, excels at it. But you'd never know any of it, the way he acts around me.

He scoops rice onto his plate, three messy spoonfuls. Then he glances over at me. His hair's skimming his eyes in the front; he needs a haircut, but I'm not going to say anything, not now. "You? Work okay?"

"Yeah. You know, the usual." I too aim for breezy and short. He doesn't want to know details of my day any more than I want to discuss them. I want to talk about *him*, hear about *him*. I scoop noodles onto my plate, while beside me he layers curry onto his rice. Then, wordlessly, we switch containers. We've got this routine down; years of practice.

"Did you hear anything today?" I ask. He's in the waiting phase now, college applications all submitted. I'm waiting, too. Waiting to see how far away he'll end up. Dreading the day it all becomes real, and I become a thirty-seven-year-old empty nester.

"Nope." He sets down the pad Thai container and walks around me to the dining room with his plate and two forks.

I grab two bottles of water from the fridge and join him. "Any day now." I slide into the chair across from him, set my work phone down in front of me, and we start eating in silence.

The table's too big for just the two of us, and mostly bare. It's a nice table, heavy mahogany, eight chairs around it. Still looks brand new, even though we've had it for years. Don't know for the life of me why I bought such a big table. For a brief moment I miss the old one, the scratch-riddled oak. I can picture the art projects and homework that used to clutter it, the plastic trucks and soccer balls that used to litter the floor in here, the chairs that were unfailingly askew.

I used to hate the constant state of chaos we lived in when he was young. The perpetual disarray, the noise, the mess. *You'll miss this one day,* my mom had warned, and I'd rolled my eyes. Well, she was right. I miss it. Because the house was lived in, then. I have the house I always thought I wanted, the one that's magazine-perfect, and I'd trade it for the clutter in a heartbeat.

He's eating too fast, shoveling it in. I should say something, tell him to sit up straight, remind him of his manners. It's my job as his mother, and besides, at this rate he'll be done in minutes, back to his room for the night. But this time we have together seems fragile. I don't want to break it by scolding.

I take a bite of curry and try to think of what else to ask, what to say to keep alive the conversation—or what passes for conversation these days. "Which school do you think you'll hear back from first?" I ask.

"Maryland," he mumbles, mouth full. He doesn't look up and meet my eyes. University of Maryland. I'd love it if he went there, stayed near D.C., close to home. But we both know he only applied there to make me happy. Berkeley's his first choice. *Berkeley.* On the other side of the country. He wants to get away from here, make a fresh start somewhere. And I can't blame him—I just can't bear the thought that he might stay there, never move back.

After college he wants to go to law school. Become a defense attorney. Wrong side of the law, in my opinion, but I have time to talk some sense into him. In any case, it's nice to see him following in my footsteps, at least a little.

A lull follows, each of us chewing our food quietly. I need to try something else, a new topic of conversation, something that might elicit more than a one-word answer.

"How's Computer Club going?" I've never understood that club. Such a solitary pursuit. Why make it social?

"*Programming* Club." His tone's exasperated. But I swear the focus of the group keeps changing. Freshman year it was all about robotics, then at some point it switched to coding. He even mentioned hacking at one point. *Ethical* hacking, whatever that is. *No such thing—hacking is wrong,* I remember telling him. *It's a gray area,* he'd replied, his eyes flashing.

"Programming, then. How's *Programming* Club?"

"I quit."

"You what?" I ask, because I must have misheard.

"I quit."

My fork is still suspended in front of me. "Today?" I ask, because I don't know what else to say. I don't understand this news.

"Couple of months ago."

A couple of *months* ago? How did I not know this? "Why didn't you tell me?"

"You didn't ask."

How was I supposed to know to ask? I stare at him, but he's not looking at me. He's focused on his food, takes another sloppy bite. I feel like wheels are turning in my head, spinning idly, not making any forward movement. "But you loved that club."

A wry smile twists his lips, almost a smirk. "I'm a good actor."

A strange sensation runs through me, the dizzy feeling that I don't know this person in front of me, even though he matters more to me than anyone ever has, than anyone ever will. I watch him take another bite of his food. "Why?"

He shrugs, and I can feel the anger rising in me. This is something that deserves more than a shrug.

"*Why*, Zachary?"

He looks up. "I just did it for college applications. Once they were all submitted . . ." He shrugs again.

I realize my fork is still hovering above my plate. I lay it down slowly. I'm almost afraid to say the next words. "What about everything else? What about student government?"

He shrugs and avoids my eyes, but the answer's clear.

"Zachary," I breathe. I've taught him better than this. Surely I have. "You can't quit like that. You have an obligation. A responsibility."

"It's not a big deal, Mom."

"It *is* a big deal."

His plate's almost empty now, and I can tell from his posture, the way he's poised to spring out of his chair, that he's ready to escape to his room. He's not going to get seconds. Dinner's almost over.

"What if the colleges look into it?" I ask quietly.

"I didn't lie. I *was* in everything when I applied."

"Zachary, this is serious."

He holds my gaze, almost defiant, and says nothing.

"You could be turned down for this," I say.

"School's almost over."

"You're jeopardizing everything you've worked so hard for."

Silence crackles between us. Finally he looks away, and the instant before he does, I think I see a hint of sheepishness. In my mind he's a preschooler again, and I see him in the kitchen on a stepstool, milk spilled all around an overturned paper cup on the countertop. I can picture those round, sad eyes, the quivering chin. I can hear his little voice. *I'm sorry, Mommy.*

"We'll talk to the advisors, ask them to reinstate you," I say firmly. Same reaction as when he was young, when he'd make a mess or break a toy or forget his homework, and he was crushed by the mistake. *It's okay, Zachary. I'll fix it.*

"Will they?" His eyes land back on me. I don't see the sheepishness anymore. Was it ever there? Or was I just expecting it to be? What I see is frustration, like he doesn't want my help, but knows he doesn't have a choice.

"We'll do whatever we can."

"I'm gonna go do homework." He pushes his chair back from the table.

"Okay," I murmur, but by the time the response leaves my lips, he's already out of the room.

I hear the faucet turn on in the kitchen, the clang as he slides his plate into the dishwasher. Moments later, his footsteps racing up the stairs. The bedroom door closing.

Then everything is quiet, once again.

Chapter 3

An hour later, the kitchen's clean and the dishwasher's humming softly. Pantsuit's been traded for workout clothes, and I'm headed back downstairs, into the living room. It's a light-colored room; white sofa and loveseat, plush white rug over the hardwood floor, glass coffee table and end tables, a treadmill in the corner. There's an antique chess set on the coffee table, one that belonged to my grandfather. A game in progress. It's Zachary's turn—at least, it *was*. The board's been like this for two weeks now.

We used to play quite a bit. It was sort of our thing. But games have become fewer and farther between. I've lost the last half dozen. And he's lost interest. Told me he'd rather play the game online. Started talking coding and the merits of computerized play, lost me with the technical jargon.

I really need to win this one.

I step on the treadmill, start it up, the usual settings. Slow jog at first. I stare at the chessboard, like I've done for weeks now. He'll move his rook, I decide. Even though he'll lose it. His bishop's in a better position. It's what I'd do, anyway.

I pick up the remote and turn on the television, mounted to the wall above the fireplace. The news is on; a story about Russia. It's always something about Russia, ever since that big disruption of sleeper cells a couple of years ago. This one's about potential election interference. Seems to be the topic *du jour*.

The shot switches to a Senate hearing room. Halliday leading the questioning, Jackson testifying. I can't watch them, not now. I increase the speed on the treadmill, change the channel. It's a cooking program. I change it again, and it's one of those dating shows. At that I turn it off altogether, increase the speed once again. The only sound in the room is the whir of the motor, the pounding of my feet.

The conversation from dinner creeps back into my mind. Zachary should know right from wrong; I've taught him that. A vague sense of dread settles over me. If he hasn't learned it by now, isn't it too late? There's nothing else I can do. He's almost gone.

I increase the speed again, make myself run harder, faster. I know I'm not handling it well, the prospect of Zachary leaving. Kids leave for college all the time; parents become empty nesters. It shouldn't be this difficult. Maybe it'd be different if I had a partner, someone to make the nest feel less empty. Or if I had someone else to confide in—family or close friends. But Mom's the only real family I've got, and I can't talk to her about this, can't let her know I'm struggling. I can just see the disapproval on her face. *I knew you couldn't do it, Stephanie.*

And I've never been close to the women I should be friends with, contemporaries at the Bureau. The ones with kids are in the throes of young motherhood, days I'm long past. The rest seem to be reveling in couplehood, that exclusive club that's closed to singletons. Add to that the fact that I investigate the investigators, and other agents tend to keep their distance.

Years ago, I'd have confided in Marta. Longtime friend, an analyst over at the CIA, one of the few people I trusted—and the only one I almost shared my biggest secret with. But those days are done. That's what I got for insisting on doing the right thing. Lost my closest friend. *Stop it, Steph.* I force the thought from my mind.

I've thought about seeing a professional. Sitting in some psychiatrist's office, on some couch, a tissue box at my side, and just spilling everything while she nods along, scribbles down notes on a legal pad. Tells me it's okay to feel that way, gives me ways to cope. But I've heard the stories at work, agents who've sought help and then promptly had their careers stagnate. Or worse, implode. Getting help would be tantamount to sacrificing my career. And God forbid I ever took an antidepressant. How would it look on the stand to admit I'm under the influence of a drug, even a legal one?

Anyway, it doesn't matter. I can figure out exactly what a psychiatrist would say. I play the game sometimes; I imagine I'm on the couch, across from her. She talks with me, dispenses advice, says things like *You're not losing him forever* and *Your relationship will improve* and *There's still so much to look forward to.*

I focus on the pounding of my feet. The rhythm is comforting, predictable. Running's my escape lately, the best way to keep my mind from drifting to places I don't want it to go. Today, it doesn't seem to be working. *Zachary's almost gone.*

I press the stop button, hear the beep in response. The motor slows, my footsteps slowing in unison. Down to a slow jog, then a fast walk. I hop off just before it comes to a complete stop, wipe the sweat from my forehead with a hand towel. There's a familiar feeling running through me, a current of anxious restlessness, a worry that everything's out of order.

That face, on the news. Zachary's smirk, the one that made him look like a stranger. I give my head a frustrated shake, but the images stick in my mind.

I head for the kitchen, open the cabinet under the sink. There's the plastic tub of cleaning supplies, perfectly organized. I reach for the canister of disinfectant wipes, pull out a wet cloth, start scrubbing the countertops. They're clean, sure. But an extra pass won't hurt.

It's on to the appliances next, inside and out. Then the floors. Sweep, then Swiffer. It's what I do when life seems out of control, try to make my house perfect. The psychiatrist would have a field day with that one.

I head to the living room next, duster in hand. At the entryway I catch sight of the chessboard and pause. If anything in here needs dusting, it's probably that.

I could ask him to come down, finish the game. He might. But I don't want him to say no. And I don't want him to think I'm pushing. It's better to let him come to me, tell me when he's ready.

But he's not coming to me. It's been two weeks. Isn't it time I go to him? So what if he says no?

At least I'd have tried.

I set down the duster on the coffee table and walk upstairs before I can change my mind.

His bedroom door's open, but across the hall the bathroom door's closed. I hear the shower turn on, and I feel a rush of disappointment. His showers take forever. It was a battle years ago, until I finally threw in the towel, stopped pounding on the door.

There goes chess. It was probably a bad idea anyway.

I turn around to head back downstairs, and I catch sight of his room through the open door. Overflowing laundry basket, a pile of clothes on the floor. Unmade bed. McDonald's cup on top of the bookcase, no coaster, probably leaving a ring.

It's the cup that does it. I walk into the room, breathe in the faint, unmistakable reek of teenage boy. Over to the bookcase, pick up the cup, wipe off the ring of condensation with my other hand. No stain at least. Something else catches my eye—a crumpled Chipotle bag on the floor, over near his bed. I scoop that up, too, tuck it under my arm.

I take a last look around. I can still hear the shower, and who knows what other fast-food remnants are in this mess. I bend and check under the bed. No sign of trash. I move some of the clothes on the floor, just to see if anything's buried there. Nothing, thank God.

I head to the closet next, a large walk-in. There's a row of hanging clothes, collared shirts and button-downs and a suit. Shelves off to one side, with stacks of clothes in varying states of disarray. The top one holds everything he wears on a regular basis—jeans, a handful of solid-colored T-shirts, hoodies—all barely folded. The lower shelves are more organized—summer shorts and swimsuits on one, clothes he's outgrown below that.

The bottom shelf catches my eye. It's stacks of his old T-shirts, soccer and Little League and basketball. He'd added them once to a pile of old clothes I was going to donate; I noticed them and put them back in his closet. I'm not even sure why I did it. Maybe I didn't want to concede that those days were over, that there was no going back, no finding the time to attend the games I'd missed.

There's something on top of one of the stacks. A brown paper bag, the fast-food type, or smaller maybe—the kind I used to pack his lunches in, that year he didn't want a lunchbox. It's pushed to the back, almost against the wall, nearly hidden from view.

I bend for a closer look. The bag's folded and creased, something inside.

I reach for it without thinking. There's weight to it; it's not trash. And the feel of it, the shape of it—I know instantly what it is.

There's a terrible sensation bubbling inside me, like I know what's about to happen and I'm powerless to stop it. Like my world is intact but it's about to be shattered.

I unfold the top of the bag. My fingers are trembling.

I pull the edges apart.

I look inside. And then I see it.

A gun.

Chapter 4

It's a Glock 26. Like mine, but smaller. A subcompact, easier to conceal.

Zachary has a gun in his closet.

A memory fills my mind, one I haven't thought of in years. We were at the park, Zachary and me, back when he was in preschool. I sat on a bench, reading a report, keeping one eye on him. He was wearing corduroy pants and a bright blue shirt. He was waiting for the big twisty slide, the one he loved, and a little girl in pigtails cut in front of him. An instant later he shoved her out of the way, hard; she toppled to the mulch and burst into tears. I bounded off the bench, grabbed him by the arm, led him away. *Never do that!* I'd yelled, my voice brimming with fear and desperation. I glanced back and she was still on the ground, sobbing as if her heart would break; her mother was by her side, comforting her, brushing mulch off her knees. I bent to Zachary, furious with him, scared at the same time. *How dare you try to hurt someone like that?* And then his face twisted, his eyes filled with tears, his bottom lip quivered. *I'm sorry, Mommy.*

Another memory takes its place. Rushing into the principal's office when Zachary was in sixth grade, seeing him sitting there, stone-faced, kicking his heels against his chair. Beside him, another boy, another mother. The boy's nose was bloodied, one eye already swollen shut. The mother was glaring at me. *What happened?* I breathed, my attention firmly on my son. He shrugged, no emotion on his face, none whatsoever. And all I could think of was his father. *What if he's like his father?*

A shiver runs through me.

Why the *hell* does Zachary have a gun in his closet? There's absolutely no good reason my seventeen-year-old son has a handgun hidden in his closet.

Is he being bullied? Does he feel like he needs to protect himself?

I look down at the gun again, more closely this time. Find the chamber indicator, that little square bump, protruding ever so slightly from the slide: the gun's loaded. My hands are trembling.

He's been distant lately, sure. A stranger, almost. But this? *This?*

What if I don't know him, not anymore?

I take a shaky breath, then another, try to marshal the thoughts swirling inside me.

I have to turn him in.

I have to call the local police, tell them I found a gun in my son's closet. What other choice do I have?

My son's going to jail.

The shower falls silent. The sudden absence of sound makes me freeze.

I fold over the top of the bag. Move, as quickly and quietly as I can, out of his room, down the hall. Into my own bedroom, ease the door shut behind me. Then into my closet, shut that door, too.

I unlock the safe, drop the bag inside, lock it again, then sink down to the carpet.

Zachary has a gun.

A loaded gun.

Shock and disbelief slowly start to give way to anger.

I stare at the keypad on the safe until my eyes blur. Then, abruptly, I get to my feet. Leave my bedroom, walk blindly to his. Rap on the closed bedroom door, harder than I have to, fist clenched tighter than it needs to be.

How dare you do this?

"Yeah," he says, his voice muffled through the door. It's the same syllable I always hear from the hallway, the intonation that means I can come in.

I open the door. He's sitting cross-legged on his bed, a textbook open in front of him. Blue flannel pants and a blue T-shirt, bare feet, damp hair.

"Zachary, I need to talk to you."

He watches me, his expression even. Waits for me to say something else.

"What, Mom?" he finally says.

"What do you think?" I hear the sarcasm in my voice. I'm so worried and scared I can't think.

Another pause. He's eyeing me carefully. Suspiciously, almost.

He has his father's eyes.

The thought feels like a slap. It has every time it's crossed my mind, ever since he was a baby. Because he's *mine*. I raised him.

In my mind I see him again as a child, his face lighting when he saw me walk into his daycare room. Running over, wrapping his little arms tight around my neck, giving me sloppy kisses. I see him picking me a sticky bouquet of dandelions from the patch of grass in our backyard. Presenting his Mother's Day card, a crumpled sheet of construction paper with crayon-scribbled hearts.

That's my Zachary. That sweet boy.

He wouldn't have a gun.

But there's a gun in his closet.

"You're hiding something from me, Zachary." The investigator in me says the words, even as the mother in me doubts them. What if he's not? What if there's some other explanation?

What if it's not his?

His eyes don't leave mine. He starts to towel his hair.

"And I know what it is." It's the investigator talking again. The mother in me is waiting for the confusion, the blurted denial.

Because of course that gun's not his. It can't be.

The color drains from his face. He looks away.

No.

When he glances back at me, there's guilt all over his face.

Shit.

The investigator in me feels satisfied, justified. The mother in me, devastated.

I stare at my son.

Zachary, what have you done?

Chapter 5

I flinch as the guilt in his eyes hardens into defiance. "I don't know what you're talking about, Mom."

Don't lie to me. "Yes, you do."

Silence. He holds my gaze, says nothing. His expression looks bland. His face looks like his father's.

I reach out a hand to the doorframe, steady myself. "Tell me why you need it."

His brow furrows. "What?"

"The gun."

He blinks. "What are you talking about?"

"Why do you need a gun, Zachary?"

"I don't know what you're talking about."

"Bullshit." Still, uncertainty unmoors me. He looks perplexed now, genuinely so. But in my mind I see his smirk at the dinner table. *I'm a good actor.*

"Are you afraid of someone?" I ask.

"No!" His brow furrows deeper. He pulls his eyes away from me, looks around the room. In a helpless way, almost, like he's searching for an answer, a way to respond. Like he's truly confused.

And his eyes never reach the closet. Wouldn't they, if he knew the gun was there? Wouldn't that be reflexive? A natural instinct?

I'm a good actor. "Just tell me *why*," I insist.

"Why don't you believe me?" He drops the towel, shuts his textbook, hard. Gives me a look that's even harder.

The question stings. The betrayal on his face stings. I'm his mother; of course I should believe him.

But he's hiding *something*. I saw the guilt on his face.

"Zachary, just tell me the truth."

He shakes his head. "I really don't know what you're talking about." He looks genuine. He sounds genuine.

But he said himself he's a good actor. He had time to recover from the initial accusation, prepare himself for the next questions. I've questioned proficient liars; I know how convincing they can sound.

The fact of the matter is, there was a weapon in Zachary's closet. And if it's his, if he's planning to hurt someone, I need to go to the police. I need to stop him.

But what if it's not his?

What if he really, truly doesn't know the gun was there?

What if someone else left it there? I don't know who his friends are anymore. I don't even know who he's had over.

What if *that's* what he's hiding? The fact that he's associating with people he shouldn't. That he's brought them into our home.

"Mom?" he says.

We stare at each other. I wish I knew the thoughts running through his head right now. *I wish I knew him better.*

"Why do you think I want a gun?"

Want a gun. Not *have* a gun. The word choice isn't lost on me. It's that sort of mistake that tends to trip people up, that helps make the distinction between the guilty and the innocent. I'm trained to spot those mistakes.

"You're not leaving this house, Zachary, until you tell me why you have a gun."

"I don't have a gun!" He says it with an incredulous laugh, like I've gone mad. His eyes don't leave mine, and his pupils don't change.

I believe him.

My instinct, my training, tell me that he's being honest, that he doesn't know there was a weapon in his closet.

He's hiding *something*. And he lied to me about it. But the gun? He seems truly confused.

Prints. I'll bring the Glock into the office, dust it. Figure out who's—

Three knocks at the front door make me freeze. I've always tensed when someone approaches my home. It's my profession, maybe. Or my past. Enemies exist; I know that all too well. And no place is truly safe.

An image flashes through my mind, just for an instant. I'm in that wood-paneled office, and those hands are on my arms, fingers digging into my flesh.

And then, just as fast, another memory takes its place. I'm in the car, speeding down the barren stretch of highway, eyes on the rear-view mirror, hands tight on the wheel. I hear Zachary's small voice from the backseat. *Are we safe, Mommy?*

Three more knocks downstairs, louder this time, more insistent. I'm not expecting anyone. I don't think Zachary is, either. He gives a petulant shrug.

"Stay here. We're not done."

I slip out of his room and head for the safe in my closet. Unlock it, pull out my Glock, check to make sure it's loaded. Walk downstairs with it at my side. Paranoia, maybe. I'm certainly jumpier than usual tonight.

A third image materializes. The hand, resting on the small of the woman's back, guiding her away like she belonged to him, everything bathed in flashes of red and blue.

I peer through the peephole, and it's a face I recognize. *Scott.* I exhale, fear draining from my body, replaced with a different kind of tension. Scott's an agent I once dated, once believed I loved, back when Zachary was in elementary school. It lasted a couple of years, the longest relationship I've ever had, the only one I wish hadn't ended. He married a schoolteacher a year after we broke up, has three beautiful kids now. And he's a damned good agent.

I press the yellow button on the security panel, unlock the door, open it. "Scott," I say. His hair, once jet black, is now salt and pepper, and it makes me wistful. I offer him a smile.

He doesn't smile back.

He has that uncomfortable look I recognize, that one I've worn myself, all those times I showed up at someone's door with terrible news. About to start a conversation they didn't want to have, one that would change their lives. My mind darts to Zachary, a jolt of panic racing through me. He's upstairs; he's safe. But the gun. The *gun.*

"Steph," Scott says with a nod. He shifts his weight from one foot to the other, and I see the discomfort in his eyes. Whatever this is, I'm not going to want to hear it.

"What is it?" I ask. And my mind works to place his current position. Washington Field Office. Domestic terrorism squad.

"Steph—it's about Zachary."

Chapter 6

It's about Zachary.

I process the words, try to make sense of them.

The gun. Scott knows about the gun.

He peers around me, and I lean into the space between the door and its frame, narrowing his view into my home. It's instinct, really. Scott's gaze settles back on me, and this time I see more than just discomfort. I see judgment.

I know that look. I know the feeling behind it. Before I moved to internal affairs, back when I worked crime. When I'd stand in front of someone's parent, and I'd remind myself that no matter my failings, no matter what I'd done wrong in my life, at least I hadn't raised a lowlife.

I see that look on Scott's face now: *At least my kids are decent. At least I've raised them better.*

My hand tightens on the edge of the door. I listen for sounds behind me, but it's quiet. Zachary's still in his room. *Please stay there.*

"What about Zachary?" I ask Scott.

His eyes shift back to the sliver of space beside me, the opening into my home. "Is he here?"

I'm intensely aware that he could bound down the stairs any second. "Yes."

"Steph—can I come in, so we can talk?"

How can I say no to that? *Why* would I say no to that, if Zachary's done nothing wrong?

I open the door wider, even though the move feels dangerous. The cold air sends a chill through me. Scott steps inside. Catches sight of the gun at my side, gives it a long look, then shifts his eyes to my face.

I hold his gaze. He knows my past; some of it, anyway. I don't need to explain, and he's not going to ask.

He hesitates, then walks past me, into the living room, like he knows the place. He *does* know the place.

I can smell his cologne as he passes. It's not the one he used to wear when we were together. Something his wife picked out for him, probably.

I follow him into the living room. Place my gun on the end table, sit down on the couch.

"How've you been, Steph?" He sinks down opposite me without removing his coat.

"Fine."

I should offer him something to drink. An IPA—that was always his drink of choice, too. I wish I wasn't in my workout clothes. Wish I could think of something to say. *Wish I could stop thinking about that gun in my son's closet.*

"What do you want to talk about?" I fight to keep my voice measured. Fight to keep my eyes from drifting to the end table, to my own Glock. It has to be the gun. Why else would he be here?

"Look, I want to keep this informal, Steph. And private, for now. That's why I came alone."

"What do you want?" It comes out more combative than I mean it to, and I see his face harden, just the slightest bit, and I know that look, too. The realization that these people aren't going to cooperate. That they have something to hide.

"Scott," I say, "this is *Zachary* we're talking about." But my voice betrays my fear. I believe my son, but there was a weapon in his closet. And now the FBI is at my door.

"You know him," I add. I remember Zachary perched atop his shoulders to get a better look at the Fourth of July parade, the two of them striding side by side into Camden Yards in matching Orioles jerseys. I used to believe Zachary was one of the reasons our relationship would last.

"Why are you here?" I ask. I want to hear the answer, *need* to hear the answer, but I'm terrified. I can't lie to Scott. I *won't* lie to Scott. But at the same time, I can't get that look on Zachary's face out of my mind. That genuine confusion when I brought up the gun. The stunned laugh in response to my accusation. My son didn't know that gun was there.

"Look, Steph, we're friends. . . ." Scott clears his throat, and I just want him to spit it out. I grit my teeth to stay silent. "Zachary's a good kid." The words ring hollow, like he knows they're what I need to hear. Like he doesn't believe them, not at all. "But he made a mistake, Steph. A very serious mistake."

A mistake. Yes. Every kid makes mistakes. Lord knows I did.

Scott works domestic terrorism. Domestic *terrorism*.

"What kind of mistake?" I ask.

Scott looks away. Over to the chess set. Studies it.

"You need to tell me what's going on." My voice has a nasty edge now, and I don't care.

He faces me again, gives me an even look, and I'm sure he's weighing the consequences of what he knows. I hold his gaze, and I feel like the fog in my mind starts to lift. He's here alone. He doesn't have a warrant. If he's bending protocol for me, this can't be as serious as I'm fearing.

"What do you know about the Freedom Solidarity Movement?" he asks.

Freedom Solidarity Movement. That wasn't what I was expecting to hear, not in the least. And the way he's looking at me, I have the unsettling sense that I'm the one being interrogated. *Better me than Zachary.*

"Not much." I replay the answer in my head and wonder if it was the right one. Shouldn't it be, if it's the truth? I decide to clarify my answer. "Just what everyone at the Bureau knows, I think."

I've heard of the group, sure. An even more extreme offshoot of the Sovereign Citizens, those people scattered across the country who believe they're not subject to our laws. The Freedom Solidarity Movement's been on the Bureau's radar for several years now, ever since a confidential source reported that it planned to target government officials: the sort of plot that, if proven, would elevate the network from anarchist group to *terrorist* group. A critical difference, in my line of work. Because anarchists are protected; freedom of speech and all. Terrorists aren't. But that plot's still uncorroborated. And it's still in sensitive channels; FSM's a relative unknown outside the Bureau.

"So you know it's an extremist group."

"Yeah." And now I know what he's getting at. But Zachary's not part of that. He can't be.

He gives me a pointed look. "And if our intel is right, one that's plotting attacks."

I keep my face impassive, because I know that how I act here matters just as much as what I say. "What does this have to do with Zachary?" The moment the words are out of my mouth, I want to take them back.

"Zach's wrapped up in it, Steph."

"That's impossible." And it is impossible. But my brain is working furiously. Because I know Scott wouldn't be here without some sort of evidence. "Zachary's an honor student. He's not 'wrapped up' in an extremist group. He's president of the Computer Club, for God's sake."

I hear what I just said and almost flinch. He's not president of that club. Not anymore. I search Scott's face for some sign that he knows the truth. Has he been to Zachary's school? The thought makes my heart start to race. I can't read his face; I'm not sure.

Anyway, it doesn't matter. Zachary quitting his extracurriculars was a bad decision. It's not like it means he's an anarchist, a *terrorist*. This is a mistake.

There's a dull pounding in my ears, the blood coursing through my veins. He got caught up in the wrong crowd. That has to be what it is. Wrong crowd, wrong friends, and that explains the gun in his closet. One of these anarchists put it there.

"Tell me what you have," I say.

"You know I can't do that."

That scene in the car flashes through my mind again. The engine humming as we drove down that highway. My eyes in the rearview mirror, watching the road, making sure we were alone. The small voice from the backseat. *Are we safe, Mommy?*

"He's my son. If he were involved with that group, I'd *know*."

Scott's wearing that judgmental look again, the one he had when I first opened the front door. *At least my kids are decent.* "He's a teen-ager, Steph. How well do you really know him?"

I've asked myself that very question, time and time again, more often with each passing year. But it's one thing to ask myself; it's another for someone else to cast doubt on the bond I have with my son. I'm instantly defensive. "You have the wrong kid, Scott."

"Steph—"

"Wrong kid," I snap.

There's sympathy now in Scott's expression, and not a trace of surprise. But of course there's not. I've been in his shoes. I've confronted mothers about their sons. The response was always the same. *He didn't do it. He wasn't involved. My son's a good person. You're wrong.*

"I'm sorry," Scott says, and I shake my head, because I don't need his apology. I need him to believe me.

"He wouldn't be involved in that."

"Look, Steph, I know how you investigate cases," he says, as if switching to a new approach, a new tactic to win me over.

You don't know the first thing about how I investigate, I think, *or who I've investigated.*

"If something's not right, you'll pursue it, even if there isn't enough to bring charges," he says.

Awkward silence follows. He's waiting for me to respond. But I just stare at him, and gradually his expression starts to harden.

"You're his mother," he reminds me, "but you're also a federal agent."

The fury slams into me like a wave. "I'm not covering for him, Scott. Honest to God, he's not wrapped up in this. He's certainly not *violent.*"

But even as I say it, I picture that boy again, the one Zachary pummeled in sixth grade. The look on my son's face in the principal's office, stone cold. The flash of his father I sometimes glimpse in his eyes, the ruthlessness that shakes me to the core.

Scott gives a curt nod. It's one of acknowledgment, an admission that he won't get to talk to Zachary right now. That I won't allow it. "We'll continue this conversation another time."

I say nothing, and he takes that as his cue to stand up. He walks to my front door, and I follow. He opens it, and I try not to flinch at that blast of frigid air. "I know you see the best in him, Steph," he says. "But, please be careful."

Chapter 7

The windowless office is nearly colorless, as well. Off-white walls, drab gray carpet, black computer screen. Even the single framed photograph—four grinning kids on a windswept beach—is black-and-white. A crayon drawing tacked to corkboard provides the only pop of color. Six smiling stick figures in front of a boxy house.

The woman perches on a rolling chair, stares intently at the screen, at a blinking cursor. Text will appear any moment now. They've hacked into this messaging channel, an incredibly sensitive one. So sensitive, in fact, that it's rarely used. Only in exceptional cases.

It was used today. And they've just managed to break the encryption. She'll be the first at headquarters to read the messages. One of the few permitted to access it.

Software is translating the messages into text she can read. She can hear the processor running, a low whir. Her pulse is racing. The first words appear on her screen, one by one.

Operation initiated. Power will be ours, in ways we have only dreamed.

A shiver runs through her. She watches the blinking cursor, now on a new line.

The obstacle?

The cursor jumps to the next line. She holds her breath, waits for the response.

Soon to be neutralized. Her son is ours.

The words disappear. The screen is black again. Message complete, conversation over.

She exhales, blinks at the dark screen. Then her gaze shifts to the crayon drawing. A terrifying sense of déjà vu settles over her. And an overwhelming fear for this woman, this *obstacle.*

Who is she? What are they doing to her?

And what are they doing to her son?

Chapter 8

I close and lock the door behind Scott, then walk into the kitchen, sag against the counter, take a ragged breath.

Scott thinks Zachary's involved in a violent anarchist group. One that's planning *attacks*.

And then in my mind, I'm nineteen. In that office, at my computer, working, trying to perfect a report, to make it shine. The Senate was in recess, and the office had already cleared out for the night. Everyone was gone but the senator himself.

I was nearly done with the final page when the door to his personal office opened. There was Halliday, shirtsleeves rolled up to his elbows, tie loosened. He was young for a senator, looked even younger. Single, though the tabloids regularly linked him to one actress or another.

"You're still here, Steph?" he asked, flashing his megawatt grin, that famous one. *Swoon-worthy*, one of the other interns called it. And swoon she did. I learned, my first week on the job, that at least three of the other interns had applied to the office because of Halliday's looks, his charm, his proximity to fame. I'd applied because his politics matched mine, and because he was *going places*.

I barely saw the grin; I was focused on his words. *Steph.* He knew my name. For an intern, that was quite the compliment. And it meant I was succeeding, that all this hard work was paying off. I'd already been given more responsibilities than the other interns combined, but I wanted more. And I wanted my work to be flawless.

"Almost done, Senator."

He waited a beat, studying me, then spoke. "Where's home for you, Steph?"

"St. Louis."

"Gateway to the West." There was that smile again. His teeth were blindingly white, perfectly straight.

"The one and only."

"And you're a . . . freshman in college? Sophomore?"

"Sophomore."

"And after college?" He leaned against the doorframe, hands jingling the change in his pockets.

"Law school."

"Ah . . . another future lawyer. Just what the world needs." He winked.

"I'm guessing that wasn't a popular opinion at Yale Law," I said, with a smile.

He tilted his head back, laughed. "Surely not. I hid my true feelings well."

I was having a conversation with Senator Halliday. A *good* conversation. The senator was still leaning against the doorframe, watching me, a smile on his face. I worked up the courage to press on. "About law school—I'm starting to research schools, and I'm wondering—"

"If I'll write you a recommendation letter?"

"If I could ask for your advice on the application process." I laughed. "But if you're offering . . ." I said it lightheartedly, but inside I was holding my breath. This guy was a rising star in the party. In the *country*, no less. If Senator Halliday wrote me a letter of recommendation, I had the feeling I could get into any law school I wanted.

"Give me ten minutes to finish up paperwork." He flashed me that famous grin again. "Then come into my office. We'll chat."

I look down and realize my hands are balled into fists, nails digging into my palms. I unclench them, can see indentions from the nails, a row of little half circles. The skin is broken in two places, blood pricking the surface. I hadn't felt a thing.

I focus on my surroundings. My kitchen. My home. That's in the past, long in the past.

I take a breath, in and out. The conversation with Scott comes flooding back.

Zachary.

I head upstairs, pause outside Zachary's room, listen through the door. Music reverberates inside—if you can call it that. Deep, thudding bass; a barked string of angry lyrics. Expletives about the police. *Can't count on the Man. Justice comes at our own hands.* I hate that he listens to this crap.

I raise my fist to knock, then reconsider. When I went in there earlier, it was an impulsive move. I didn't have ammunition to catch him lying, if that's what he was doing. Or to prove that he was telling me the truth. Better to be patient this time. Better to gather the facts, and *then* interrogate my son.

I let my arm fall to my side, then head for my own bedroom. Change my clothes quickly, pack up my work bag. Downstairs, I grab my Glock, slip it into my holster. Scrawl a note to Zachary on the notepad in the kitchen. *Heading to the office. Be back soon.* On the off chance he comes looking for me, he'll see it. It's as much contact as I want to have with him right now. Then I let myself out the front door, lock it behind me.

The front stoop is well lit, even in the darkness. Security lights, ones I installed myself the day Zachary and I moved in. The neighborhood's safe, but my job isn't.

I get into my work car—an unmarked sedan—and start off heading east, slowly. We live on a quiet, tree-lined street near Dupont Circle, brownstones on both sides, all tastefully maintained. It used to drive me crazy when people would speed down our street. There aren't young kids here anymore, but I still drive well under the speed limit. Old habits die hard, I guess.

At the end of the street, I take a left, press down harder on the gas. There's a sound coming from the passenger seat; my cellphone, vibrating. I reach into my bag and pull it out, glance at the screen. *Mom.*

I send the call to voicemail, drop the phone back onto the seat. I can't do it right now. I know she'd hear the stress in my voice. I don't want to deal with the questions.

I need to make sense of what's happening.

Zachary made a mistake, sure. Fell in with the wrong crowd. That's what he was hiding from me.

The gun isn't his. He told me so and I believe him.

My hands tighten on the steering wheel.

The FBI headquarters building is a giant boxlike structure, with rows of evenly spaced windows set deep into the concrete frame, almost like miniature prison cells.

The parking garage is mostly deserted. A few cars here and there, rows of empty spaces, columns casting long shadows, a flickering light at the far end of the concrete expanse.

I park close to the entrance, hurry into the building, bag slung over my shoulder. It feels heavy; heavier than it should. I'm intensely aware of what's buried deep inside.

I make my way into the lobby. The Bureau's seal is on the wall, flanked by American flags. And two framed pictures of men in suits, headshots I pass every morning, every afternoon. Director J. J. Lee, green-eyed and solemn; Deputy Director Omar Jackson, a bright white smile.

I take the elevator up to the fourth floor, head down the hallway to the secure spaces. My agents work in a closed-off section of the floor, one with restricted access. Our files are full of information on other Bureau employees; it's really the only way we can operate.

I badge through two heavy vault doors and quickly make my way through a darkened sea of empty cubicles to my office. I unlock the door and step inside, turn on the lights.

It's a large office. There's a desk in the center, and floor-to-ceiling bookcases on one wall, filled with legal tomes. A row of lockable filing cabinets along another, which doubles as a table for my coffee-maker. A television mounted to the opposite wall. A wide window in front of me overlooks the cubicle bullpen where my agents work.

When the computer boots up, I double-click the online case file system. The whole time, my mind's working. Searching for files on a relative is prohibited, a serious offense. But I know this system. I know the loopholes. I know there've been agents who've exploited them, found what they wanted to find, and never technically broke any rules. We could never prove they'd done anything wrong, seen anything they shouldn't.

Freedom Solidarity Movement, I type into the search bar. It's all about using a circuitous route, and there's nothing prohibiting me from researching the group.

After a few clicks at the top, I access the tagging system and run an entities search. *People,* I click, and the screen returns a long list of names, everyone who's mentioned in a case dealing with FSM. I sort alphabetically, and scroll down to the *M*'s. *Zachary Maddox.* There it is. Case file 3-7659.

I move the cursor back to the navigation bar and run a different entities search, this one on subjects. I scroll down to 3-7659. I read the list of words there, tags for the case file. *Email. Internet. Radicalization. Recruitment.*

"Okay," I murmur to myself. I try to marshal my thoughts. There's no open investigation on Zachary himself. He's one of a long list of names that popped up in another case. This could definitely be worse. But *something* brought Scott to my door. What does he have on my son?

I reread the tags for the case file. God, I wish I could see the file, see what's in there. My gaze hovers on the search bar. It would be easy to do.

But I can't. I pull my eyes away and reread the tags. *Email. Internet. Radicalization. Recruitment.* It fits with what I thought, doesn't it? Zachary got mixed up with the wrong crowd.

Someone put that gun in his room.

And I need to figure out who it was.

I reach into my bottom desk drawer and pull out a forensic kit, the one I have stashed there, and a pair of gloves. I put on the gloves, then reach into my work bag, remove the gun, still wrapped in the paper bag. Gingerly, I open the paper bag and take out the Glock, lay it down on the desk in front of me. I start dusting the grip.

As I do, my mind's racing. If Zachary's prints are on this gun, if he lied to me, then it's over. I'm telling the local police what I found, letting them take it from here. There's no good reason for my son to have a gun. None at all.

I move the brush to the slide, start dusting there.

But my gut feeling is that I won't find his prints. That Zachary wasn't lying, that it isn't his gun.

I finish dusting the gun, the exterior at least. I hold it up gingerly in a gloved hand, turn it this way and that, examine the surface.

There's not a single print. It's wiped clean.

Stomach in a knot now, I lower the weapon, pull out the magazine. It's fully loaded, and there's an extra round in the chamber. One in the chamber—just like *I'd* load a gun, like any law enforcement officer would. The guys on the street, the ones who sleep with guns under their pillows, they don't.

I dust the magazine, then the bullets, all eleven of them. The places where we always find the hidden prints, the ones that few people think to erase. But hardened criminals know. Professionals know.

I hold the magazine up to the light, just to be sure.

Nothing. No prints.

A chill runs through me. Whoever put this gun in my home knows *exactly* how to cover his tracks.

Chapter 9

It's late by the time I get home. I stand in the entryway and listen for sounds, as usual. All I hear is the soft whir of the washing machine in the basement. I head straight into the living room, glance at the chessboard out of habit; no movement. Then my eyes land on the end table. Zachary's tablet is there, in its indestructible black case. I pause for a moment, listen again for any sound from upstairs, but it's still quiet.

I reach for the tablet, bring the screen to life. Then I enter his passcode: 1-4-7-8-9-6, my finger tapping a counterclockwise circle around the screen. I've watched him do the same out of the corner of my eye, more habit than anything, the drive to investigate. I've never used his passcode. Never needed to.

But the fact of the matter is, Scott—the FBI—has some sort of proof that Zachary's involved with this extremist group. Scott wouldn't have come to my home otherwise. If he comes back, it'll be with a warrant. He'll comb through everything in our house. I need to do the same.

If there's anything to find, I need to find it first.

I keep an ear on the stairs and scan the apps. Social media, news sites, games. I open his email app and navigate to sent messages. Open the recent ones and read them, feeling guilty as I do. But this is necessary, and the messages are innocuous, anyway. Few and far between. If he's communicating with people online, it's through social media.

I open Facebook. I scan incoming and outgoing messages, public posts, friends' activity. Some terrible language, some inappropriate comments, the cringeworthy kind. Turns out my quiet, reserved boy is someone else entirely when he's in front of a screen.

Instagram next. Some shots of him at school, with friends I don't recognize. At a Capitals game with his arm around a very pretty dark-haired girl—is that a *date*? She's in the next picture, too, planting a kiss on his cheek. *Me and my girl Lila,* the caption reads. *Lila.* Is this a girlfriend? I've never heard a word about her.

Another picture, at a bar with three teenage boys I don't recognize. Zachary's grinning, holding an amber bottle that's been mostly cropped out of the picture.

He's *seventeen,* for God's sake. That sick feeling settles into my stomach. I haven't been paying enough attention, have I?

I open the Internet browser, the search history. *Busty girls,* he'd typed. I can feel color rising to my cheeks as I scan his other search terms, the raunchy sites he's visited. But he's a teenage boy. This is normal, right? I return the tablet to the end table, aligning the edges so it's just the way I found it.

The tags for the case file run through my brain. *Email. Internet. Radicalization. Recruitment.*

There's nothing suspicious on the tablet. Part of me feels relieved. But part of me feels increasingly anxious. Because Scott must have *something.* What about Zachary's cellphone? His laptop? His backpack? All of that's upstairs. In his room, with him.

I need to look.

What do you think you'll find? challenges the psychiatrist's voice in my head. I can picture her sitting in her chair, watching me with a smug little smile. And I don't know how to answer her.

Scott's words echo in my head. *Please be careful.*

How well do you really know him?

In that Senate office, all those years ago, I waited ten minutes, exactly. Spent it replaying that conversation with Halliday. Trying to think of questions I could ask him, the kind that would make me seem inquisitive, insightful. Trying to figure out how best to highlight the work I'd been doing, the responsibilities I'd been given, so that he'd write me a truly glowing letter of recommendation. Then I shut down my computer, knocked on his open door.

"Come on in," he called.

I stepped inside. The senator was behind his desk. Offered up that grin again. "Why don't you shut the door," he said.

I hesitated, but shut the door anyway. He probably didn't realize the outer office was empty, just wanted to make sure our conversation was private. It was probably habit.

I sat in the chair across from his desk. "Did you finish up the paperwork?"

"I did, indeed." He leaned back in his chair, clasped his hands behind his head. "So. Law school."

"Law school." There was a glass on his desk, half full of something dark. Bourbon? Brandy?

"And you'd like some advice."

"I would. Schools you'd suggest I look into . . ."

"Well, that really depends on what type of law you'd like to practice. Have you decided?"

"I haven't." Criminal, family, corporate—I wanted to learn the merits of each. I still had all these doors open to me. It was the idea of *the law* that I loved. Rules that everyone had to follow. Consequences for breaking them. The law was black-and-white. It was fair.

"You've got plenty of time, Steph," he said with a smile and a shrug. Then, "So what do you like to do in your free time?"

"Um . . . read, I guess?" It was a question I hated, always had. I didn't have any real hobbies to speak of. Didn't feel like I had that much free time, to be honest. There was always schoolwork to do.

"You're what, eighteen? Nineteen?"

"Nineteen."

"Surely you like to go out? Party?" He drained his glass. Swiveled toward the cabinet behind him, pulled out a bottle and another glass. "Want some?"

Want some? I'd just told him I was nineteen. "No thanks."

He shrugged, refilled his own glass.

"So about the application process . . ." I tried to shift the conversation back on track. His recommendation would open so many doors for me.

"This feels so impersonal," he said. "Like teacher and student. It doesn't need to be like that."

Alarm bells were starting to ring in my brain. But he was a senator, for God's sake. My boss.

He stood up. "Let's go sit over there." He nodded toward the couch behind us. I hesitated, but he was already around his desk, already beside me.

I stood, confused. And the way he was looking at me—it made the alarm bells ring even louder.

"You know, I think I should be going," I said. My heart was hammering.

"Oh, come on, Steph." There was that smile again.

"I'm going to head out."

"After all of this?" The smile was frozen in place.

All of what?

"What about your letter?"

I couldn't care less about the letter. Not in that moment. I just wanted to get out of that office. "I have to go." I turned and started walking toward the door.

And then a hand on my arm stopped me. A hand, closing tight, pulling me back, away from the door, closer to him.

And I knew my instinct to leave had been correct.

"Why don't you stay?" The smile was back. The voice was friendly, teasing.

"I'm *leaving*." I shook my arm, tried to shake off the hand. It didn't loosen in the slightest. Tightened, in fact. The smile vanished. Panic flared in my chest.

"Not so fast." His other hand came up, gripped my arm. Two hands now, both closed around my upper arms, squeezing hard. I could smell the sourness of the booze. He pulled me close to him, and then his lips were on mine.

"Stop," I yelped, trying to pull away. This wasn't happening. It couldn't be happening.

His grip on my arms tightened. His fingers were biting into my skin.

"Stop," I said again. But I knew he wouldn't stop. And then my legs were against the couch, and I was losing my balance, falling.

"No!" I tried, but it only made him more aggressive. A hand came over my mouth and nose, smothered them. I couldn't breathe.

The other one came up under my skirt. I tried to fight back, tried to get away, but he was stronger. He was pinning me down with his body, with his weight. I had nowhere to go. No way to fight back.

I was trapped, and I was powerless.

· · ·

Just past midnight, I finally climb the stairs. I stop at Zachary's door and listen. No sound. I open it slowly. Moonlight streams through the slats in his blinds, throws stripes of light over the room. I see him in his bed, asleep, twisted under the navy-blue comforter, the one I used to tuck him under when he was still young enough to demand a good-night kiss.

He's breathing deeply. He always was a sound sleeper. I step inside. Same pale blue walls he's had since we moved in, same old Orioles pendant on the wall. There are a handful of signed baseballs in plastic cases on the oak dresser, a couple of old trophies on top of the bookcase, from his ball-playing days, before high school. I scan the books on the shelves. Nonfiction, mostly. Baseball, science, coding. I don't see anything radical in here. Should I have paid more attention to what he reads?

Why would I need to? He's a good kid. My good kid.

I shouldn't be doing this, I say to the psychiatrist, from the couch in my mind.

Shouldn't be doing it? she tosses back. *Or scared of what you might find?*

His backpack's lying against the wall. I unzip it quietly, pull out the laptop. I open it up, and the screen casts an eerie blue light in the darkness. I look through his documents. Everything seems benign.

I open the Internet browser next, quickly scanning his searches, the sites he's visited. College websites, admissions calendars. Blogs about coding, website design. ESPN, baseball stats. A Google search for prom proposal ideas, then a name—Lila Winter. *Lila*—like the Instagram pictures. He's planning to ask her to the prom, isn't he? And another search: *DC private investigators*. Why is my son looking up private—

Zachary moans and flops over on his side. I freeze, heart pounding. I close the laptop again, holding my body so rigid it aches. If he really was doing anything illegal, he'd hide it, wouldn't he? Encryption, something like that. Zachary knows all about that stuff. If he was communicating with an extremist group, with anyone he shouldn't be, he'd hide it, wouldn't he?

Probably. But I don't know how to access that sort of thing, aside from bringing a device down to the Bureau's lab for exploitation, and it's not like I can do that. Zachary's the computer whiz in the house. He's the one I've always gone to with questions, who's always troubleshot our devices at home. He's always had a knack for that kind of thing.

I rifle through the rest of the backpack. Notebooks. A textbook. A phone charger. I dig deeper, hear the crinkle of a bag. Potato chips. My hand moves on, closes around something at the bottom of the backpack. A videogame. Punishment Hunt—that one that's been in the news lately. Graphic killings, apparently—shootings, explosions, poisonings. I've always absolutely forbidden those violent games, ever since Zachary was old enough to take an interest. Unease creeps through me. But it's just a game. And it's *popular*. It's mainstream.

His phone's plugged in, charging. As quietly as I can, I unplug it and walk a few steps away. I enter his passcode, 1-2-3-6-9-8, a clockwise circle this time, the one I've seen him type, and start skimming through texts. A long string with Lila, mostly small talk. An expletive-laden group chat with four boys whose names he's never mentioned. Most of the ire seems directed at their teachers, from what I can gather. Complaints about homework assignments. A lot of boasting. Gossip about a girl in calculus class, the kind that makes me glad I'm well beyond high school.

I keep scrolling through different threads, keep reading, and then I stop.

John Doe, reads the contact name. I can feel the hairs on the back of my neck start to tingle.

Local number. Cryptic texts, for the most part. Things like *4:30 Wednesday?* and *I'll be there.* No small talk whatsoever. Whatever conversations these two are having, they're doing it in person.

I scroll to the beginning of the chat. Two months ago, give or take. *Here's my number,* reads the first text. From Zachary to John Doe. And a reply: *Nice to meet you today!*

I keep scrolling. It looks like they've met once every week or two since.

The hairs on my neck are fully at attention now. Zachary's hiding something, and I'd bet money it has something to do with John Doe.

I'm at the end of the exchange. Sent today, by John Doe. *3:30 tomorrow?* it reads.

Zachary replied, *I'll be there.*

"So will I," I murmur.

Chapter 10

I hear Zachary's alarm at six, a faint persistent beep. Sleep eluded me last night, and I've been waiting for the sound for hours. Eleven minutes later I hear him on the stairs. He notices me when he already has one hand on the refrigerator door, and he goes still.

"Hey," he says carelessly.

"Morning," I reply.

I watch him pull out a container of orange juice, pour himself a tall glass. He gulps juice, the refrigerator door still open, his eyes finding mine over the glass. They look angry. When it's empty, he puts it down on the counter.

"Zachary," I begin.

He ignores me. Shuts the fridge door, heads into the pantry. I watch him take a handful of protein bars from the shelf, shove them into the back pocket of his jeans.

"Zachary," I say again.

He comes out of the pantry. "What?"

"Tell me about the Freedom Solidarity Movement."

"The what?" And I'm stunned by the resentment in his eyes.

But there wasn't the slightest glimmer of recognition. I'm sure there wasn't; I'd be able to detect it. He's never heard that name before. I try another question. "Zachary, are you involved in an anarchist group?"

His eyes widen, the slightest bit, and his eyebrows arch. *"What?"*

I say nothing, though a million questions race through my mind. I need to see the whole reaction here. His recovery, what he says next, everything.

He gives his head a small shake, like he's trying to rid himself of something unpleasant, like he's completely confused. "Jesus, Mom! Are you serious?"

I nod. His chin droops, his mouth opening into a little circle. "First you think I want a gun, and now *this*? You've gotta be shitting me." His jaw sets into a stubborn line.

I fight the urge to correct his language. "If you made a mistake, let me help you fix it."

He just glares at me, incredulous.

"Or if you've gotten mixed up with the wrong people—"

"I haven't. How many times do I have to tell you?"

And before I can reply, he makes a decision. He storms out of the room.

I hear him in the hall, grabbing his backpack. I hear the door open, then slam.

I think about following him, but instead, I stare down at my mug. The remnants of the coffee are undrinkable, long since cold. There's a faint swirl of white on the top, the cream separating.

Confusion washes over me. Because I know when someone's lying. It's my job to know that. I've been trained to detect deceit.

And I'm convinced that Zachary wasn't lying.

Chapter 11

The phone is on the counter, arm's length from the woman, when it buzzes. Incoming text.

She's spreading grape jam on bread, four brightly colored lunch-boxes open in front of her. The kids are at the breakfast table, arguing, and her husband's refereeing, talking over them in a calm, measured tone. It's his phone, but he didn't hear it.

A week ago, she'd have ignored it. Allowed him his privacy. But today, she can't help but lean over and steal a glance at the screen.

From a contact labeled "O."

Game time. It's all led to this.

"Honey?"

She jerks her head up, heart racing. Her husband's watching her.

She scoops up the phone and hands it to him. He slides it into his back pocket without looking at it. Her cheeks flush.

"Anything interesting?" He says it with the hint of a smile.

Caught, red-handed. "'O' says it's game time."

"Wizards are playing tonight. Big game," he says without the slightest hesitation.

"Right." She picks up another slice of bread, dips the knife into the jam. Starts spreading, and tries to think of a single time in the twelve years they've been married that he's *ever* mentioned the Wizards.

Chapter 12

The bullpen's dark when I get to the office; I'm the first to arrive, as usual. I make my way into my personal office, turn on the lights, sit down at the computer, switch it on.

I check my email, respond to the urgent messages, flag others to return to later. Check my queue of reports, skim over the new ones, jot off a few notes to my agents. And all the while, my mind's racing, trying to make sense of the situation, struggling to understand it.

I glance out into the darkened sea of cubicles. Then I turn back to the computer, double-click the icon for the virtual file system. I move the cursor into the search box, type in the file number. *3-7659.* I hesitate, the cursor hovering over the search button.

I can't do this. Can I?

I let go of the mouse and swivel toward the table behind me, turn on the coffeemaker, feeling numb. Then I turn back to my desk, stare at the computer screen. *3-7659.*

Can I?

I leave the file number in the search bar and open up a new screen, navigate to the Bureau's internal encyclopedia and search for the Freedom Solidarity Movement. It brings back an article, a long one.

More than I'd find online; this one includes information from FBI case files.

I start skimming. FSM, a shadowy network of radical anarchists, established five years ago. Members dispersed throughout the country, connected through online forums, some on the dark web. Leadership structure unclear; those running the group have used encryption to maintain their anonymity online. A single confidential source reported that the group's leaders aspire to conduct attacks against government targets, but there's been no evidence to substantiate that claim, and very little specifics. It's enough to make sure the Bureau's monitoring the group, and it's enough to get the courts to let agents access certain email accounts and telephone records, but it's not enough to charge anyone.

I navigate to the intelligence report about the plot. It's brief, barely any text, barely any detail. And if there *were* any detail, it would be included. The source was no doubt peppered with questions. Everything he knows is in that report. And there isn't much.

The Bureau doesn't have anything that suggests there's a specific plot, that it's moved beyond the aspirational phase. No indication targets have been selected. The source that reported the threat is a new one, with questionable credibility. Analysts assess the threat from FSM to be low. I can feel some of my tension begin to loosen.

I'm just starting a piece on recruitment when light floods the bullpen. I look up, startled, to see Wayne arriving, ambling toward his desk. He joined the division long before I took over, shunted to internal affairs when he could no longer pass the Bureau's fitness test. He looks up at me through the window, waves hello. I raise my hand in greeting, force a half smile, and turn my attention back to the article.

Most FSM members seek out the group online, and on their own. They initiate contact after finding the recruitment email address—one that changes each week—on extremist forums. If FSM recruiters choose to respond, which happens about half the time, they direct the prospective recruit to an encrypted forum for further discussion. At that point, the Bureau loses access to the communications.

And recruitment is growing. I reread the numbers on my screen. A year ago, the Bureau estimated FSM had around two hundred members. Six months ago, three hundred. Now, over five hundred.

Email. Internet. Radicalization. Recruitment.

I look back at the other open window on my screen. *3-7659.*

It wouldn't be *that* bad, would it? It's not like I'm impeding an investigation, or trying to view something above my security clearance level, or something like that. This is just viewing a file. Trying to determine what they have on my son.

I move the cursor to the search button.

It'd be a disciplinary report, at worst. I'll accept the consequences. It's worth it if I can figure out what's going on, why that gun was in Zachary's room.

I click, hold my breath.

Access denied.

The words are red and bold, and they're all my brain can register. I've seen the screen before, when I've come too close to a particularly sensitive case, one with ties to the CIA, to foreign adversaries. But this is *domestic* terrorism; Scott must have gone in and manually removed my access. He must have known I'd try to look.

Shit.

I look up and see that Parker's arrived. The youngest on my squad, bright-eyed and eager. Garcia, too—the only fifty-year-old I know who still sports a nose ring, and the attitude to match. They're at their computers, logging on, joking about last night's basketball game. The three of them are almost always the first to arrive. In about five minutes, as soon as Garcia's skimmed her email, she and

Wayne will leave on a coffee run. Then it'll just be Parker until they get back.

I close the search window. I stare at the screen. *Access denied.*

I bolted from Halliday's office as soon as I could, shaking with terror, face wet with tears. Halliday had been calm when I left; too calm. "If you breathe a word of this, little girl," was all he said. His tone was a warning, his *look* was a threat. Then he took a step closer, pressed a hand against the small of my back. His touch sent a torrent of fear rippling through me. I flinched, certain he was going to hurt me again.

But he merely leaned in close to my ear. "*No one* would believe you," he whispered, and his voice turned the blood in my veins to ice.

I stumbled through the halls of the Senate office building, needing to bolt, to get as far away as possible from him. My footsteps echoed from the high ceilings; his jeer echoed in my brain. *Was he right?* This was *Senator Halliday* we were talking about. He had no shortage of women in his life. Beautiful ones, powerful ones. The truth would sound crazy.

No one would believe you. I could feel that hand on my back, the confusion and terror that ran through me at his touch.

The officer on duty that night was Ronnie, a familiar face, friendly guy. My first week on the job, I caught him watching *Jeopardy!* on the portable television at the guard post. *I love that show,* I'd told him. *You're too young, kiddo. This here's an old folks' show,* he'd said with a grin, and he teased me about it from there on out. He was at the exit that night, in his usual folding chair, beside the metal detector. He smiled as I approached.

"I need to report something," I said, coming to a stop in front of him, swiping my cheeks with the backs of my hands, willing the rest of the tears to stay put. "I was . . . ," I fumbled. The word stuck in my brain, not reaching my lips. I couldn't stop trembling. *No one would believe you.*

"You okay?" His kind eyes were instantly full of concern.

"I'm—" And then I heard footsteps. Men's footsteps. I turned, and there was Halliday, approaching.

He didn't slow, didn't even hesitate as he approached. Flashed his trademark grin. "Night, Ronnie. Night, Steph." His voice was light, utterly untroubled.

Like nothing had even happened. Stunned, I watched him push the door open, disappear outside. He never even looked back.

"Sweetheart?"

I choked back a sob, turned to Ronnie. He watched me with concern.

I needed to do this. I needed to tell the truth, ugly as it was.

"I was raped."

Ronnie blinked, like that wasn't what he was expecting to hear, not in the least. He glanced up at the corridor behind me, instinctively, like he was looking for the predator. Then he reached for his radio transceiver.

Tell him, Steph.

". . . by Senator Halliday."

The hand reaching for the radio stilled. Ronnie turned to glance at the door, the one Halliday had just pushed through. When he faced me again, something had changed in his eyes. Concern had morphed into suspicion. "Halliday." It was a statement, not a question.

"Yes."

There was something else in his eyes now. Judgment, for sure. Maybe even a hint of sympathy.

"*Senator* Halliday." His hand dropped back into his lap. His voice was brimming with skepticism.

"Yes." I was battling tears; once they started again, I knew I wouldn't be able to stop them. I had to get through this, telling the truth. Later I could curl up and cry.

He looked me up and down, ever so briefly. Somewhere down the hall, a door slammed shut. "I don't know what happened up there. Maybe the . . . *situation* . . . spun out of control. But if I were you, kiddo, I would *not* make an accusation like that."

He didn't believe me.

"Ronnie, I—"

He held up a hand, stopping me. "Let it *go*."

Fresh tears stung my eyes. I thought I could trust him. I thought he would *help* me.

But Halliday was right.

No one will believe me.

Finally I see Garcia lean back in her chair, say something to Wayne. He nods. They both stand, Garcia stretches, laughing, and they head for the door. Then it's just Parker, alone.

Now's my chance. I walk over, and he rolls his chair back as I approach. "Morning, Chief," he says. Parker's about my age, but most of my agents have at least a decade on me. That's internal affairs; one of those sleepy, ride-out-the-clock assignments. But Parker's an anomaly, always eager to help. And that makes me feel even guiltier for what I'm about to do.

"Morning, Parker." I hesitate, and then I say it. "I'm having computer issues this morning. Mind printing a file for me?"

I see the briefest flash of uncertainty, one that passes quickly. We all learned at Quantico not to do this. *You can never assume anyone else is authorized access.* But I'm his boss. Of course I'd have access to everything he does, and more. And our computer systems are notoriously frustrating, so it's not exactly unusual that I'd be having trouble. "Sure thing, Chief."

I read him the case file number and hold my breath as he runs the search. There's always the chance they've denied access to my whole squad. If that's the case, Parker's going to get suspicious.

I see the file open on his screen and exhale softly. He navigates up to the print button and double-clicks. "There you go," he says cheerfully.

"Thanks." I try to keep my voice measured, my expression disinterested. Then I head to the bank of printers at the rear of the room.

I listen to the hum of the machine and try not to think about what I just did. But I'll make sure Parker doesn't get in any trouble. I'll take full responsibility, and I'll accept whatever disciplinary measures they see fit. What matters right now is finding out the truth.

The printer goes silent. I gather the stack of paper in the bin and head back to my office. Then I close the door and start reading.

The language is technical, and it's dense. It takes me a few minutes to get through the jargon. By the third page, it's becoming clear.

Our home IP address was used to send a message to FSM's recruitment email address. Fifteen days ago, on a Wednesday.

From an email address I've never seen before, one that includes my son's full name. *ZacharyMaddox345.*

I flip to the next page, heart pounding. There's a screenshot of the message itself.

I'd like to join, it reads. *I have access to targets.*

Signed *Zachary.*

Chapter 13

I *have access to targets.*

I reread that line. Stare at it until my eyes blur, like it'll somehow make sense. But it doesn't. None at all. I can't for the life of me picture my son typing that message. No more than I can see him holding a gun.

This isn't Zachary.

Stomach in a knot, I struggle to focus, put myself in investigator mode, detach myself. I continue skimming the file. There was no response to the email. Nothing further.

Okay. I need to think about this rationally. The email, on its own, isn't enough to charge anyone with a crime. It's free speech. It's a request to join a political group, one with no history of violence. And a sentence that could be interpreted in different ways, at least by a good defense attorney. Access, targets—that could mean anything, really. It's not an explicit threat.

It's not like Zachary was threatening violence.

My eyes drift back to those words. *I have access to targets.* It's certainly enough to warrant an investigation. No wonder Scott came to my house.

My mind flashes back to last night. To finding the gun in Zachary's closet.

Three swift raps on my office door startle me. Instinctively I turn the page over, hide what I'm reading. "Come in," I call.

The door opens just enough for me to see Parker standing there. "Sorry to disturb you, Chief." His cheeks are flushed.

"No problem, Parker. What is it?" I say, even though I already know what it is. *Who* it is. Scott. He must have placed an alert on the file. Shouldn't I have anticipated this? It's what I would have done.

"There's an agent on the phone. Scott Clark, Washington Field Office. He wants to know why I accessed that file, the one I printed for you."

"What'd you tell him?"

"I put him on hold."

"Transfer the call in. I'll talk to him."

Parker just stands there, wringing his hands.

"It's okay, Parker." I give him a tight smile, one I hope is reassuring. "You're not going to get in any trouble. I promise."

He backs away, and as soon as the door shuts, I flip the page back over and continue reading, more urgently now. The IP address resolves to our home; no surprise there. There was some activity that morning; Zachary and I each checked our respective email accounts, our social media accounts, news sites. Then nothing all day, until 4:34 P.M., when the new email account was created. At 4:36 P.M., the message was sent. *I have access to targets.* Nothing else until 5:21 P.M., when Zachary checked his normal email account, his social media accounts.

My phone rings, a shrill blast. I ignore it and keep skimming, faster.

The email account, the new one. There was one outgoing message. No incoming messages. Only one log-in.

Why would Zachary send a message like that and then not check for a response? Why would he send a message like that, *period*?

Another ring. I glance out the window to see Parker staring at me, wide-eyed, no doubt wondering why I haven't answered. I reach for the receiver, hold it to my ear. "This is Maddox."

"It's Scott. You want to explain to me why you ordered a subordinate to access a file to which you were denied access? Or would you rather wait and explain it to the disciplinary board?"

His fury catches me off guard. "I want to explain it to you," I shoot back, even though I have no idea what I could possibly say. No way to make sense of what's happening. "I'll be there in an hour."

"Be here in twenty." The phone goes dead.

Mom hated that I wouldn't tell her who had gotten me pregnant. *It doesn't matter,* I told her. *He's not going to be part of the baby's life.* At first, I was afraid *she* wouldn't believe me, either. Then I was afraid she *would*. She was already looking at me with disappointment. How would she look at me if she knew the truth? Like it was somehow my fault? Like I was as damaged as I felt? I didn't want to find out. It was better to stay quiet, even if it built up a wall between us.

I'd fantasized, repeatedly, about going to the police, trying again. But I couldn't get Ronnie's reaction out of my head. Halliday was right, wasn't he? It would be my word against his about what happened in his office. He was a senator; I was an intern. The more time that passed, the less likely anyone would believe me. And so I didn't tell a soul.

But late one night, when Zachary was just a few weeks old, the truth slipped—part of it, anyway. I was sitting in front of the television, Zachary in my arms. The news was on. It was Halliday, giving some fiery speech about some topic I couldn't focus on. Hearing his voice brought me back to that night, the one I'd been trying so hard to block out. But the terror still felt fresh; a familiar wave of nausea crept over me. In my mind I was back in that office, reliving that terrible night.

"It was him, wasn't it?" Mom said softly, like she could read my mind. And my eyes filled with tears. She knew. I could finally say something, share this burden with someone, share the truth.

I nodded.

"And the relationship . . . it's definitely over?"

Relationship?

Shit, she didn't know. Of course she didn't know. She thought it was a relationship, an inappropriate affair. I nodded again.

"Does he know about Zachary? Does he know he's the father?"

Father. The word made me ill.

"No," I said. I looked down at Zachary. This tiny person who I unexpectedly loved more than anything, and had since the moment I first laid eyes on him.

I'd considered abortion, when I first learned I was pregnant. Made an appointment at the clinic and everything. But part of me wondered if I'd regret it for the rest of my life. And if Halliday forced me into a lifelong regret, wouldn't it almost be like a second assault? Like he was winning, again?

Keeping the baby, in my mind, had been my own small way of standing up to him. Of showing him he couldn't hurt me again.

Zachary squirmed in my arms, opened his little mouth in a yawn. I watched his lips curl into a sleepy smile, and I had the overwhelming certainty that I'd do anything for this baby. *My* baby.

I'd heard stories in the news, about men like Halliday who somehow managed to gain parental rights. There was no way I'd ever let that monster be part of my son's life.

And I couldn't ever let Zachary know the whole truth, either. What would it make him think about himself, and the sort of DNA that ran through him? Wouldn't it make him question my love for him? I couldn't do that. I *wouldn't*.

I stood, tucked Zachary's blanket snug around him, and turned off the television. Halliday disappeared. "And I *never* want him to know. I never want *anyone* to know."

I'd thought, when I decided to keep the baby, that I was standing up to Halliday. That I was fighting back, that I had won.

It wasn't until that moment that I wondered if I'd handed Halliday another victory. Because even if someone *might* believe me, even if I decided that I had an obligation to tell the truth about what he'd done, I couldn't. I couldn't let him know about Zachary.

I knew in that moment, holding my son in my arms, that I would stay quiet forever.

The FBI's Washington Field Office sits inside its own city block, a bleak, grim building that Zachary once aptly compared to a giant Lego. It's a mile from headquarters, the sort of distance that'd be quicker to walk than to drive through the congested D.C. streets, if we didn't always need our cars at the ready.

I make it to the building in just under the allotted twenty minutes and find my way to the counterterrorism wing, then to Scott's cubicle. It's in the back beside the windows, a corner spot. He's in his chair, at his computer. When he sees me, he stands.

"Conference room," he says curtly. He brushes past me and I follow him to a windowless room down the hall. He closes the door behind us and sits at the head of the table. I take a seat diagonally across from him.

"Okay." There's not a hint of friendliness on his face. "Explain."

It's stifling in here. I shrug off my jacket and lay it on the seat beside me. Scott watches me, unblinking. I search for what to say, what I *can* say, and come up empty.

"You know how serious a violation it was to access that file," Scott says.

"I had no choice."

"Why?"

I take a measured breath. "You come to my door. You make this accusation, and you won't tell me a thing. I need to understand what's happening."

"Well, now you know."

He leans back in his chair, eyes me coldly. "*Access to targets.* What does he mean by that, do you think?"

"It could mean any number of things." I hold his gaze.

"Dammit, this isn't a game! This is serious, Steph."

"I get that."

"He said access to *targets*."

"I read the email," I retort, my tone more combative than I intended.

He scowls. "Do you have *any* reason to believe that Zachary could be plotting an attack?"

In my mind, I see the gun, wrapped in paper, concealed in his closet. I see the email, in the case file: *I have access to targets.* I see Zachary shoving that little girl on the playground, staring stonily at the classmate whose face he'd just battered.

Then I see him as a little boy, that exultant smile on his face. Hugging me with all his might, when he barely reached my waist. Whispering a sleepy *I love you* as I tucked him in at night. I see the confusion on his face when I brought up the extremist group. His incredulous denial when I accused him of having a gun.

"No," I tell Scott. I don't believe it. I can't.

"If you have any reason to suspect it—"

"He's a good kid."

"It's an anti-government group, Steph. A bunch of frustrated people who hate the government. Who hate jobs like the ones we have." Is he playing me, softening me up, so that I make a mistake? It's what I'd do. "Don't you think Zachary might have reason to hold a grudge?"

Chapter 14

Zachary was five when I got the long-awaited offer of employment from the FBI. The letter came in the mail, and I ripped it open outside, right next to the mailbox. Saw the embossed letterhead, the *Dear Stephanie,* the *Congratulations.* And a huge smile spread across my face. I'd waited years for this day, and it was finally here.

As I continued reading, as my eyes landed on the date in the letter, my smile disappeared. Quantico would be months in a dorm, no families allowed; I knew that. What I didn't count on was the start date.

"There's got to be something we can do," I insisted, minutes later, phone held to my ear. "Maybe I could start in a later class?"

"It's this or nothing," answered the voice on the other end.

That afternoon I brought Zachary over to my mom's house. He darted out to the backyard and I stayed in the kitchen with her. Sat on a barstool, watched her chop vegetables on the kitchen island, kept an eye on Zachary through the window. He picked up a stick, waved it in the air like a sword.

"I got a job offer," I said.

She looked up, a smile lighting up her face. "That's wonderful, Stephanie."

"I'm going to be an FBI agent."

The smile faded. The knife in her hand went still. "An FBI agent? Seriously?"

"Yes." I hadn't told her it was my goal. Hadn't told anyone. How could I, without telling them *why*?

"You went to law school. You could have a great career. A stable one."

"This is what I want to do."

Her eyebrows knitted together in confusion. I looked away, at Zachary racing across the lawn. My choice didn't make sense to her; I knew that.

She didn't know the whole truth about Halliday; no one did. And she didn't know that midway through law school, I made another decision: that I wanted a career where I could stop people like him, people who abused their power, who preyed upon and victimized others. I would fight for the victims, and I would *believe* them.

I knew from that night that it was wrong to stay silent, to let Halliday stay in a position of power, risk exposing others to what he had done to me. And if it hadn't been for Zachary, I told myself, I'd have done something. Come clean, finally told the truth. Taken my chances that no one would believe me, that he'd smear my reputation, that I'd become tabloid fodder.

But I couldn't do it to Zachary. Couldn't bring that man into our lives, couldn't ever let my son know the ugly truth about his father.

Mom set the knife down carefully on the cutting board. "Think about Zachary. What if something happens to you?"

Her question cut through me. I *was* thinking of Zachary. I was *always* thinking of Zachary. But this is what I had to do. It was the path I'd chosen, the one I knew in my heart was right. I focused my attention on an errant sliver of carrot that had slipped off the cutting board.

"Training starts in two weeks." I crumpled the sliver between my fingers. "I can't bring him. Can you watch him for me?"

"For how long?"

"Four months."

"Oh, Stephanie. You can't be serious!"

"I know it's a long time—"

"He starts kindergarten next month!"

"I know." Of course I knew. Zachary and I had been talking about it endlessly. He'd made me promise him I'd be there at the bus stop on his first morning, cross my heart that he could look out and wave to me the second he found his seat. I'd be there waiting when the bus returned, I said, and we'd go get ice cream and he could tell me everything about his day. "I tried to switch the start date, but I can't. It's this or nothing."

Mom frowned, about to say something. Then she picked up the knife again, turned back to the vegetables. "I'll watch him. I'll be there for him. And for *you*." She resumed chopping, and her eyes flickered to mine, full of reproach. "Because that's what mothers do."

The words stung. I watched Zachary out the window. He put the stick down in the grass and pulled himself up onto one of the swings, wiggling until he was fully in the seat. "It's just four months."

"*Just* four months?" She shook her head. "And then it'll be a career full of long nights. Of putting yourself in harm's way. Honestly, Stephanie. I raised you to make better decisions than this."

I blinked back tears. "This is the right decision."

"For Zachary? Or for *you*?"

Anger and hurt churned inside me. What was I supposed to say?

I couldn't afford a fight, not now. Not when I needed her help. Without another word, I let myself out into the yard.

Zachary was pumping his legs, struggling to gain some momentum on the swing. He gave me a radiant grin when he saw me step outside, and it sent a torrent of emotions running through me. "Look at me, Mom!"

I smiled at him, a smile that I hoped didn't look as heartbroken as I felt. Was my mom right? Was this a terrible mistake? How could I leave him for four endless months?

I sat down on the swing beside him, pushed forward with my feet, let myself drift. I watched him straining to lift himself into the air, legs pumping. After a few moments, he relaxed his legs and just coasted. Shot me a satisfied smile.

"Zachary, there's something I need to tell you," I began. "You know how you want to be a firefighter when you grow up?"

"Yeah."

"Well, I've wanted to be an FBI agent, for a really long time now."

"What's a gent?"

"An agent is someone who helps people. Keeps them safe. Kind of like a police officer." He looked serious, like he was taking it all in. "I'm going to get to do that, Zachary."

He smiled at me, and I felt my heart break.

"But I need to go to school to learn how to be an agent. I need to go stay at the school for a little while."

The smile wobbled on his face. I had to force out the next words. "And while I do that, you're going to stay here with Grandma."

His eyes grew round. There was a solemnness to his face that made him look older than his years. But I had to say the rest. I had to get it all out there. "And, honey? My school starts just before yours does. Grandma will be the one to wave goodbye to the bus on your first day, okay?" It was painful to say the words. I fought back an overwhelming urge to cry.

"But you promised, Mommy." He said it so softly I almost didn't hear him.

"I know," I whispered back. "I'm so sorry."

He looked away. I watched him blink back tears. Then he started pumping his legs again, this time furiously, straining even harder, getting himself higher into the air than I'd ever seen him go. He didn't look at me again.

My heart hurting, I watched him soar. And I pledged that if I ever again made him a promise, I would never, ever break it.

I give my head a shake, send the memory tumbling away. Scott's words ring in my head.

Don't you think Zachary might have reason to hold a grudge?

"Wouldn't your kids have reason to hold a grudge, too?" I say. I'm not going to let Scott blame me for this. I'm not going to play defense any longer. I'm going on offense.

"Steph—"

I lean forward. "Would that make them join a terrorist group?"

"He said he has access to targets," he persists. "I'm sorry, Steph. You know I need to open a formal investigation."

The threat sends a chill through me. I repress a shudder. A formal investigation. A criminal case opened on my son. "Scott—you can't do that."

"I don't have a choice."

"Just give me a little time. Let me figure out what's going on."

He gives me an unflinching look, and my heart sinks. Something else is coming, something bad. I've done this in interviews myself—waited until just the right moment to reveal some critical piece of information, some damning evidence.

"All those days he skipped class," Scott says evenly. "What was he doing?"

Skipping class? What's he talking about? I try to keep my expression blank, but I'm sure I must be failing.

He picks up a pen, drops it. "You look like you don't know about this, Steph."

I say nothing.

"Six absences in the last two months. So many that he was given a warning."

Is that true? Did Scott get a copy of Zachary's school record? Is that really what it says?

"Did you know?" he presses.

"No," I answer, because it's the truth, because I'm sure Scott can read it on my face.

"That's interesting. Because a copy of the disciplinary report went home for parental acknowledgment. And your signature is on it."

Zachary skipped class, forged my signature. Lied. I don't know what to say, what to think.

"You don't know him as well as you think you do, do you, Steph?"

Chapter 15

Zachary's high school is like a miniature college campus, a beautiful place with brick buildings and rolling lawns shaded by tall trees. After the incidents in middle school—all those squabbles and fights—I thought a fresh start might help. Separation from the kids he'd been associating with. So private school it was. And it has always seemed like the right decision: the arguments and fights stopped, and his interest in school grew. But had he gotten mixed up with the wrong crowd all over again?

I've found an empty spot facing his car—the battered old Ford Taurus that used to be mine—and I'm sitting in my car, waiting. The sunshade is up on the dash, bent back enough on one side to let me peer through the windshield without being seen. There's no sun to block; the sky is gray, and wind howls through the sprawling parking lot. The air outside is frigid, and the campus is quiet. The kids are all in class, sheltered from the cold.

I came straight from Scott's office. His words shook me, because I know they're true. I *don't* know Zachary as well as I thought I did. If the last two days have made anything clear, it's that. I don't know what my son does with his time. Or who he's spending it with.

But maybe it's about to become clear. In my mind I picture those texts, the ones with John Doe.

3:30 tomorrow?

I'll be there.

I can't stop thinking about that gun, now locked away in my office safe. About Zachary's response when I brought it up. Genuine confusion. The same look he had when I brought up FSM, the extremist group.

But what if he *is* just a good actor? A superb liar?

I still think the natural reaction would have been to check to see if the gun was still there. To glance in the direction of the closet, at the very least. He's not *that* good, is he? He's a kid, for God's sake. A good kid.

Isn't he?

The fact of the matter is, he's hiding *something*. That much I know. And this John Doe—I have a feeling he's somehow involved.

I raise my fingers to my temples, try to rub away the beginnings of a headache. Scott's face comes into my mind, and his voice, unbidden.

Don't you think Zachary might have reason to hold a grudge?

I drew Chicago as my first post. *Chicago.* Halliday's hometown. It was like the universe was playing some sort of cruel joke.

I thought about saying no. Getting out. My mom was right; I could still get a job at a law firm. Settle down in St. Louis. Stay out of Halliday's world, once and for all.

But then he'd win. I'd be giving up, giving in, once again. Letting Halliday win.

So Zachary and I picked up and moved. My mom kept reminding me it was a mistake, leaving midway through kindergarten. That Zachary would suffer. But this was something I had to do.

We had no family in Chicago. No support system. I found a day-care center, the one with the longest hours in the area. A few baby-sitters I could call on, too. One was a woman, Patty, a few streets away who'd let me drop Zachary off when I got called out in the middle of the night. When we first arrived in the city, I thought it'd be a rare occurrence. It quickly became routine.

I was assigned to organized crime, investigating the Chicago Mafia. To me, it felt like the perfect assignment—potentially high profile, potentially meaningful. A chance to get some genuinely bad guys off the streets. My first week on the job, I realized it was the universe's cruel joke number two.

"Mob runs this town," said my training agent, Nicholson. "And there's not much we can do about it."

"Come on," I protested. It seemed like the opposite of everything I'd learned at Quantico, everything I believed to be true.

He shook his head. "Damned crooked politicians. Mob pays 'em off. That senator, Halliday—he's the worst."

It felt like time stopped. I wasn't expecting to hear that name, not here, not now. "Halliday?"

"Have you ever seen how much cash that guy raises?"

Anger started to run through my veins, like ice. "So why haven't we done something about it?"

"It's laundered well."

"Come on, Nicholson. If you know what's happening . . ."

"Like I said, they run this town."

"So do something about it."

He shot me a crooked grin. "You're on it now, Maddox. *You* do something about it."

I didn't have to, of course. Could have bided my time, like Nicholson, like the others. Worked my nine-to-five, laid low, waited to be transferred to something else.

But I wasn't about to let Halliday win, not again.

Nine-to-five became seven-to-eight. Longer, when I had to. Lord knows there was plenty of work piled up. Plenty to do, for someone willing to do it. And I was. I was *determined* to do it.

After months of working nearly 24/7, I'd developed a few leads into the underworld. Didn't seem like much, considering the time I'd devoted to it, but it was more than the division had had in years.

I ran each one down thoroughly, monitoring communications, building a solid case. Took over a wall in the field office, tacked up headshots of all my targets. Ran masking tape between them, tracking their connections. Before long, the wall was full.

By the time I'd been in Chicago a year, I had the biggest case in the division, one that was being closely tracked even at headquarters. Conspiracy, corruption, the works.

I was considered a rising star in the Bureau, someone with an incredibly bright future. And I barely saw Zachary anymore. An hour a day, maybe two. I wanted desperately to spend more time with him, but every agent in the division was working shifts around the clock to support this case. *My* case. It's not like I could take a break when everyone else was working so hard.

Zachary spent most of his evenings at daycare, many of his nights at Patty's. Sometimes, if I had to be at work before dawn, I'd carry him to the car in the middle of the night, pajama-clad and asleep, and drive him to Patty's, deposit him, dozing, in her arms. I hated it, but what else was I supposed to do?

I almost got myself out. Considered it, once. I was getting close to the leader of the branch of the mob I was investigating. Torrino. We had a shot at turning his right-hand man, or at least we thought we did. I interviewed him, tried to convince him to flip. Promised him immunity in exchange for testifying against Torrino. Thought he might do it, too. And then, in the interview room, when he was about to give me his answer, he leaned across the table toward me. His shirtsleeves were rolled up at the cuffs, and when he stretched forward I could see a tattoo underneath, on his forearm. Two crossed knives, forming an X.

Let it go, he said, slowly and carefully, with a look that made fear rush through me.

I thought about letting it go. Making up some excuse, getting myself off the case. It seemed like the safer thing to do. But I couldn't let these criminals win. And I couldn't leave the case to someone else. It was my responsibility. I needed to get them off the streets.

Three months later it was takedown time. We'd flown in agents from around the region to assist. We had a fifteen-count indictment on Torrino. Federal racketeering, extortion, money laundering. Plans to arrest nineteen of his associates. Warrants issued for a total of thirty-two residences and businesses. It was set to be one of the biggest cases in recent history.

I went home the evening before the operation to steal a couple of hours with Zachary. We ate pasta and ice cream and worked on a puzzle until I could see his eyes droop. He got into pajamas while I packed his overnight bag, and then we got into the car, both of us silent.

He was asleep by the time we got to Patty's. I lifted him out of his booster seat, and without fully waking, he wrapped his arms around my neck, curled his legs around my waist. He was heavy; he was getting so big. I carried him up to the front door.

Maybe it was the cold air, or the movement, or something, but whatever it was, it woke him. "I don't want to go," he whimpered, his cheek buried against my shoulder. It was the first time he'd ever resisted, ever complained.

"I know, sweetheart."

He wrapped his arms tighter around me, like he wasn't going to let go, like I'd have to pry him off of me. "Please, Mommy?"

"Honey, this case is really, really important," I said, and the moment the words were out of my mouth I knew I shouldn't have said them.

"What about *me*?" he asked in a whisper.

At three, I hear a bell ring. In the car, I sit up straighter. Moments later, kids start streaming from the buildings. I watch, hidden behind the sunshade, as they make their way to the parking lot.

Finally I see him. Walking with someone, a slender dark-haired girl. Lila, I think. He's in jeans and a gray hoodie, black bomber jacket over top, a backpack slung over one shoulder, smiling, chatting. The two of them stop beside a white Jeep, hug briefly. She climbs into the driver's seat, and he walks straight for his own car, head bowed slightly. Unlocks the door, slides inside. Hasn't even looked up, hasn't noticed me.

The taillights come to life and the car pulls forward out of the spot. I turn the key in my own ignition, carefully remove the sunshade, and pull out a few car lengths behind. I follow him out of the parking lot and onto the street, careful to keep several cars in between.

3:30 tomorrow?

I'll be there.

I'd traced the number, come up empty. It's someone who wants to stay anonymous. *John Doe.* Someone whose identity Zachary wants to protect.

The farther we go, the more surreal this seems. I'm tailing my own car, surveilling the child I raised, trying to learn more about the person I should know better than anyone in the world. It seems somehow immoral.

He misses the turnoff for D.C., stays in Maryland, driving deeper into the suburbs. I keep my distance as the traffic thins.

The Ford makes its way into a neighborhood, one with winding roads and long drives and homes barely visible from the street.

A sick feeling is forming in the pit of my stomach. Because I've been here. I've been to this neighborhood. I know who lives here. I've driven by, sat outside, surveilled the house. Never logged it, of course. But couldn't resist, not when he was this close. Not when I knew there was a criminal out there, on the street.

Zachary slows, taking turn after turn. I slow, too, and keep my distance. We pass a woman pushing a stroller. An older man walking a fat white dog.

Nothing feels real right now. Because I know where he's heading. I know who he's meeting with.

He turns into a driveway blocked by wrought-iron gates. I hang back, pull off to the side of the street, idle there, some trees as cover. Then I reach into the backseat, pull a duffel bag up to the front seat. My surveillance bag. I unzip it, rummage around, come up with a pair of binoculars. Aim them at Zachary.

He rolls down his window, leans out, says something into the speaker. A moment later, the gates begin to part, and when they're fully open, Zachary drives through. The gates close behind him, and then the car disappears up the drive, out of my sight.

From here, I can't even see the house. Shaking with rage, I slam the binoculars down on the seat beside me.

This is Halliday's house.

Zachary's meeting with Halliday.

Chapter 16

There's a strange ringing in my ears.

Zachary knows Halliday's his father.

He must. There's no other reason he'd be meeting with him.

Does he know the whole truth?

A shudder runs through me.

No. There's no way he'd know that. It's not like Halliday would admit it.

But what would Halliday say?

And *how* did Zachary find him? I've never breathed a word. It's been a sore point between us, a constant source of tension. He's always asked about his father, for as long as I can remember. The older he got, the more it drove a wedge between us. *I deserve to know,* he's always insisted.

And I've always refused. Always stuck to some variation of *It was a relationship I had in college, one that ended abruptly.* He stood to gain nothing by knowing the truth. The truth would only hurt him, make him question everything. I wasn't going to do that to him.

There's only one person who knows about Halliday, even if she doesn't know the whole truth.

Anger is churning inside me. I reach for my phone, find her number on speed dial, hold it to my ear. My hand is shaking.

"Hi, Stephanie," she answers almost immediately, cheery. I hear the radio playing softly in the background, a song from the sixties.

"Why did you tell Zachary?"

"What?"

"Why?"

"Tell him what? You're not making sense, Stephanie."

"Cut the crap, Mom. About Halliday. You told him. Why?"

"Halliday? He found that out on his own, honey."

On his *own*? "That's not possible."

"He used one of those DNA tests. You know, the ones where you mail off your saliva?"

How does she know this? How does *she* know this, and I don't?

"He didn't find his *father's* name, but some other relatives. He figured it out from there. He's a smart boy, that Zachary—"

"He told you all this?"

"Yes. I think he wanted to share it with someone—"

"And what did you say?"

"I told him he was right, honey."

Shock gives way to betrayal, slowly at first, then morphs into anger in a crushing, overpowering wave. "How could you do that?" I can hear the tremor in my voice. "And why didn't you tell me?"

"He asked me not to! I assumed he'd tell you on his own. This was *ages* ago. He never did?"

The words feel like a dig. Like she's highlighting just how distant my son is from me. "How long ago?" It's the investigator in me talking. I need details.

"I don't know. A year?"

A *year* ago? Zachary has known about Halliday for a *year*? But that doesn't square with the texts I read. He's only been meeting with Halliday for a couple of months. None of this makes sense. "It was *not* your place to tell him. Or to keep this from me."

"Stephanie, it's fine—"

"It's *not* fine! You have no idea what you've done."

"I probably shouldn't have—"

"You think?" I jeer.

"Stephanie—" Her voice trembles. I see a car pulling down the drive. Zachary's car. I watch it, heart hammering.

"Look, honey, I'm truly sorry. Really I—"

I press the red button, end the call mid-sentence. Drop the phone on the passenger seat. I don't want to hear her apology. It's not enough; it'll never be enough.

The gates swing open, and the Taurus noses out onto the street. I can see Zachary in the driver's seat, but he doesn't look my way, doesn't see me.

The phone vibrates on the seat beside me. I reach over and press the red button, reject the call.

Halliday knows about Zachary. He's meeting with my son. Talking with him. Influencing him.

I watch the road. Wait another couple of seconds, then pull out a safe distance behind him.

I tail him out of the neighborhood and onto the main roads. He gets on the highway and heads toward D.C. I continue to follow, blindly, my thoughts a jumbled mess. And a short time later, he's winding his way through the northwest part of the city, toward our home.

He pulls alongside the curb in front of the house, and I park behind him. He climbs out of the car, gives me a wave.

I slam the door shut and start walking up the brick path to the front door, my breath crystalizing in icy puffs. He falls into step behind me. Out of the corner of my eye, I see him glancing over at me, a worried expression on his face.

We step inside the house, peel off our jackets. He shuts and locks the door behind us while I punch in the code to silence the alarm.

"Sit," I say, walking into the living room. He follows, sits down on the love seat.

"Tell me what's going on," I say.

"You followed me?" The color has drained from his face.

"Tell me, Zachary."

Embarrassment flickers in his eyes, like he knows he's done something wrong. But the expression quickly shifts, becomes defiance. "I wanted to know him."

It takes all my strength to speak calmly. "He is not someone worth getting to know."

"That's my decision to make, isn't it?"

"How did he react? When you met him?" I'm treading carefully here. It feels like my life is studded with landmines.

"He was surprised."

"He didn't know about you."

"Right."

Silence. I try to think of how best to phrase the next question. "But he remembered me?"

"Yeah."

"What did he say?"

"Why do you want to know?" he tosses back at me.

I shrug, helplessly.

"That you had a relationship. That it ended," my son says bluntly.

He's watching me intently, *too* intently. I dare not look away. "It's in the past, Zachary." With all my heart, I wish I knew what was going through his head right now. I wish I knew what he was thinking.

I wish I knew what *I* was thinking. My thoughts are a mess.

Halliday knows about Zachary.

Halliday's back in our lives.

I stare at the chessboard. And the seed of an idea lodges in the far reaches of my mind, so far that I don't know what it is, what it's going to become. But I can feel it there, like a shard of glass in my shoe, an irritant, something that doesn't belong.

"Tell me about skipping class."

Zachary blinks, like he's surprised by the abrupt change in questioning. Or maybe just surprised that I know about the absences? "It was just English class. Last period."

"How often?"

"A bunch. Five, six times."

He sounds sheepish now. He's telling the truth; at least I think he is. But he's also telling me what I already know, what's no doubt in his school record. "Why?"

"Fridays are 'reading days.' We're just supposed to sit at our desks and do our reading assignments. It's a waste of time."

There was no hesitation in the response. Still, I watch him carefully. "So you left."

He nods.

"What'd you do instead?"

"Went to the gym. Lifted weights. Then got on a bike, did my reading while I was working out."

The explanation makes sense. It sounds like Zachary. It sounds like something I'd be tempted to do, myself. "Shouldn't the school have notified me?"

He blinked. "They did. I signed the paper for you."

"You mean you forged my signature."

He says nothing. A typical reaction during interrogations: an unwillingness to look at me, to admit the truth. But at least he's not lying.

"Why?"

He shrugs. "Seemed easier that way."

I consider my response, try to keep the anger out of it. "You made a mistake."

He finally glances up at me. "Yeah."

"And instead of coming clean, letting me help, you made another."

"I guess."

The seed is starting to take root, burrowing into my brain. I try to ignore it, try to deny it space to grow. Because I know it's the sort of idea that's going to overtake everything, make it impossible to consider any other possibility. And right now I need to be sure.

He glances at the clock, but I'm not ready to be done with this conversation, not yet.

"Zachary, did you ever send an email requesting to join an anarchist group?"

"An anarchist group? Why are you asking me that? Jeez, Mom—first it's a gun, and now you're talking about some nutcase terrorists? Are you crazy?"

"If you made a mistake—"

"I *didn't!*"

I stare at the chessboard, touch the miter on the bishop's head, struggling to process my thoughts. Zachary was meeting with Halliday. That's all he was hiding from me. That's why he looked so guilty when I first confronted him. Sadness creeps through me, that my son would keep such a secret, that Halliday's *still* poisoning our lives all these years later.

"I gotta go to work," Zachary says.

I nod, eyes still on the chess pieces. I hear him grab his keys, the front door banging shut.

The seed of an idea is an ugly weed now, taking over, remorselessly digging its way into every crevice of my brain.

That gun wasn't Zachary's. That *email* wasn't Zachary's. My son's not involved in this.

But who is trying to make it look like he is?

Chapter 17

The man walks from the direction of the Capitol, hands shoved into the pockets of his down jacket, head bowed against the cold. He has a cap pulled low on his brow, mirrored shades beneath. No one gives him a second glance.

A black messenger bag is slung diagonally across his body, shoulder to hip. He walks at a brisk pace up the incline to the Washington Monument, his breath escaping in little white bursts.

At the top, a frigid gust of wind whips through. Dozens of flags unfurl, stars and stripes vivid against the gray sky. He watches them flap, almost violently, then heads off to the right, sits on the end of a low bench, his back to the monument.

A single occupant sits on the other side of the bench. An older man in a long wool coat, collar turned up. There's a fur-lined trapper hat on his head, flaps covering his ears, the sides of his face. He doesn't turn to the newcomer, doesn't move, just stares straight ahead.

The younger man pulls off the messenger bag, sets it down on the bench between them. There's another bag already there, a black one, nearly identical. The two bags lean against each other, touching.

"Getting colder," says the younger man.

"Indeed."

A family walks by. Mother, father, two young children waddling in puffy coats. The men watch them until they're out of earshot, on their way down the hill toward the war memorial.

"How long are you here?" asks the younger man.

"Long as I need to be."

There's a low growl in the distance, one that's quickly escalating. A helicopter thunders by overhead, low and fast. Military green. Marine One, maybe. The older man watches with a look of quiet contempt.

The sound fades away. In the distance, a dog barks.

"There's a problem," the younger man says, still staring straight ahead.

At this, the older man finally turns. His pale blue eyes are full of reproach. "I'm aware."

Silence settles around the two. Another burst of wind lashes through, with a howl, sends the flags flapping. Dark clouds are gathering on the horizon. The monument grounds are slowly emptying.

The older man gets laboriously to his feet, reaches for a bag, the one that's farther from him. He casts a glance at the other bag, still on the bench. "What you need is here."

The younger man lays a hand on it, pulls it close. His hand is trembling, just a little.

The older man turns and leaves without another word. He never looks back.

Chapter 18

I get into my car and start driving, in a daze. It feels like a weight has been lifted from my shoulders. Yet another, heavier one has taken its place. My son didn't make any sort of terrible mistake. He's not involved in any criminal activity.

He's being framed.

I let the words echo in my mind. I hear how they sound. Crazy. Paranoid.

But I know what I saw. Zachary had never heard of FSM. He never sent that email, has no involvement with an anarchist group.

What other explanation is there?

Maybe you're seeing what you want to see, suggests the sly voice in my head. The psychiatrist.

I shake my head. No. I know my son.

She gives me a wry smile, one that reminds me of Zachary's during our dinnertime conversation. *Maybe he's a good actor.*

A chill runs through me.

I force her from my mind, and in her place comes a vision of myself, back when I was a new agent. Standing on doorsteps, telling mothers what crimes their sons had committed. The denials would come first, swift and insistent. We'd talk, and I'd start to see the flicker of truth reflected in their eyes.

Then the defenses would go up.

And more often than not, a very specific claim would come first. A counteraccusation, really. *It's a setup. He's being set up.*

Who's setting him up? I'd always ask. *And why?*

Two questions they could never answer, not convincingly.

Who's doing this? mocks the voice in my head. The psychiatrist is back. I squeeze the steering wheel even more tightly, but that does nothing to dispel the jeer in her tone.

Halliday. It has to be Halliday. He knows about Zachary. He knows there's proof—

The blast of a car horn pulls my attention back to the road. I focus just in time to see headlights, the hood of a car, rapidly approaching, head on. I'd drifted into oncoming traffic. I yank the wheel to the right and swerve back into my lane, just in time. The car whizzes past.

I stop on the shoulder of the road. I sit shaking, terrified.

Halliday knows there's proof of what he did, all those years ago. *Zachary* is proof.

Halliday's warning me to keep silent.

"Can I help you?" bleats an indistinct voice. A woman's.

I hold my credentials up to the camera. Frigid air is rushing in through my lowered window. "Steph Maddox, FBI." I glare into the little glass circle, imagine he's staring right back at me.

I hear the wind lashing at my car. The first icy pellets strike the windshield.

"Come on in," I hear through a crackle of static. The gates purr open and I drive through.

It's a long drive, winding and treed. I press too hard on the gas. Slam on the brakes at the top, almost a mini parking lot, several luxury cars in a row. Pull in, askew, behind them, blocking them. Get out, head to the door. I knock on it, hard, anger traveling from fist to door.

A woman answers. His wife; I know that from keeping an eye on the news, everything about him. From sitting outside his house, watching. She's twenty-something years his junior. Married five years now. She's in skintight workout clothes, her blond hair blown out and her face fully made up. Surprise flickers in her eyes.

Before she says anything, Halliday rounds the corner behind her.

All these years, hearing his name on the news, catching glimpses of his speeches—each time I'd been transported back to that horrible night, forced to relive it in my mind. I'd always thought, especially in those early days, that if I saw him again in person, I'd be terrified. But now here he is in front of me, tanned and fit and infuriatingly *smug,* and I'm not afraid. I'm *angry.*

He lays a hand on his wife's shoulder, speaks to her, keeping his eyes on me. "I've got this, honey."

She flinches at his touch, the smallest bit, scarcely perceptible. But she and I both know I notice it. She holds my gaze a moment longer than she needs to, then drifts away, wrapping her arms around her slender body.

"Come inside," he tells me.

"We can do this right here, right now." It's freezing on the doorstep, but somehow I don't feel it. "What the hell are you doing with my son?"

He doesn't even blink. "He came to see me."

"What do you want from us?"

His brow furrows. "He came to see me. He sought *me* out—"

"You're setting him up."

"What the devil are you talking about?"

But I know what a good liar he is. "You know *exactly* what I'm talking about."

He stares at me. Then he gives his head a confused shake. "Honest to God, I don't."

I take a step forward, point a finger in his face. I can smell his aftershave, the same scent he wore that night so long ago. It makes me dizzy with rage. "You know about Zachary now. And you're scared. But if you think you can blackmail me into silence, you're dead wrong."

He doesn't back away, not in the slightest. In fact, he smiles. "I've *known* about Zachary. For years."

The words shock me into silence. I have this vision of him sitting outside my home, peering through the windows with binoculars. I feel violated once again.

"I've followed your career, Steph."

It's the first time he's spoken my name. I want to vomit.

"If I'd wanted to blackmail you, why would I wait until now?"

He knew. He knew about Zachary all along.

But I was silent. Maybe he believed I wasn't going to tell anyone. That I wasn't a threat.

Had that changed when Zachary showed up at his doorstep?

"I'm not worried, Steph, because *no one would believe you.*"

"DNA would prove it. Paternity tests."

"We had a relationship. It ended." He says it evenly, without a trace of deception. His tone sends a chill through me.

"Sure, you were an intern." He shrugs. "But you were an adult. It was mutual. I was single. And you quit the internship and left town. Without telling me about the pregnancy."

"You and I both know what you did!"

"Did you tell anyone that, Steph? Or are you just now remembering it, eighteen years later?" He shoots me a skeptical look, the same kind I know he'd give the cameras.

My blood's boiling now. It would be my word against his.

No one will believe you.

"If you want to come forward with this lie, this slander, you're digging your own grave," he warns.

"You're not going to win."

He cocks his head. "You say someone's framing Zachary? Really? For what?"

I just glare at him.

He smirks. "You sure the kid's as good as you think he is? As blameless?"

"Go to hell."

That smile flickers on his lips again. "Well, it's not me, Steph. I swear to you."

"Bullshit," I rasp. But doubt's beginning to creep through me.

"Maybe it's someone you've investigated. Ever think about that?"

I think of sitting in the bar beside Hanson yesterday. *I have a wife, kids. A mortgage.*

How many people have lost everything important to them, because of *me*?

"Or maybe you were *too* successful in Chicago." He doesn't even bother to lower his voice. "Maybe you pissed off the wrong people."

The operation happened in the predawn hours, when the neighborhood was hushed and quiet. We took up our positions under cover of darkness, all around the house. I stood, heart pounding and breathing shallow, my hands tight on my gun, and waited for the command post to give us the all clear.

When it came, SWAT agents hit the front door with the ram,

broke it open after the second smack. More SWAT agents swarmed in, ready to clear the place. I was right behind them. This was my guy, my case. With the charges against him, Torrino was going away for decades—that much was a guarantee. And I wanted to be the one to slap on the cuffs, to see his face when it happened. It had become *personal.*

There was commotion by the time I made it through the door, something happening in the living room, which wasn't right. Torrino and his wife were the only ones home; we'd had surveillance on the house for days. And it was the middle of the night; they were supposed to be upstairs in their bedroom.

Torrino sat in a chair, facing the unlit fireplace. Two agents kept their guns trained on him. His wife sat weeping on the sofa, dressed in a flannel nightgown and wearing slippers.

I took a step closer. He was dressed in a collared shirt and pressed pants. Sitting unmoving, placidly observing what was going on all around him. Observing me. It looked like he was expecting us.

I walked briskly over. Informed him he was under arrest. Read him his Miranda rights. He didn't move, his expression inscrutable. "Do you understand?" I pressed, when I finished Mirandizing him.

He tilted his head, narrowing his pale eyes at me. "Maddox, right?" he said, and hearing my name come out of his lips sent a chill through me. "You should have listened, Miss Agent Maddox. You should have *let it go.*" There was the ugly shadow of a smile on his lips.

"You're going to pay for this," he promised.

Chapter 19

Work has always been a place where I've felt like I'm on offense. I've been the one pounding down the field, heading straight for the goal, locking away the criminals. Now, I have the constant, unsettling feeling that I'm on defense. Fighting to stand my ground, to protect what's most important to me.

I pull into the parking garage and into my assigned spot, start walking to the building. The bag on my shoulder feels lighter today, and I can't help but think of the Glock, the one I brought to work yesterday, the one that's locked in my office safe.

I walk through the lobby, catch sight of the pictures on the wall: Director Lee, Deputy Director Jackson. My pace slows, my eyes drawn to them. In my mind I see that image, just for an instant. The hand on her back, bathed in flashing red and blue. I turn away and continue walking.

The cubicle bullpen is emptying out by the time I get there. A few agents say hello as I walk toward my office; I greet them back. It's as if everything's normal, when that couldn't be further from the truth.

I thought, when I showed up at Halliday's door, I had it all figured out. That he was to blame. Now I don't know what to think.

My brain tells me it's him. It's too much of a coincidence, otherwise. Zachary had found him. He has everything to lose if the truth comes out. His career, his marriage, his reputation, *everything*.

But deep down I'm not sure. Zachary doesn't know the whole truth; Halliday must have seen that. And if the gun hidden in my son's room was intended to warn us that we needed to stay silent, why isn't Halliday ordering me to stay quiet? Why bother denying it?

Besides, if he knew about Zachary all along, he's had plenty of time to do this already. He seems genuinely convinced no one would believe me, that his lies would shield him, that his career would withstand the blow of a firestorm of gossip about an unwise affair with a foolish young intern.

And it probably would.

What if it's Torrino? Is it the payback he promised? He's in prison, but he still has reach. But why now, after all these years? *Why now?*

Or it could be someone else.

Maybe it's someone you've investigated.

I sit down at my desk, eye the filing cabinet below. In my mind I can see that file in the back, the unlabeled one. . . .

Maybe you pissed off the wrong people.

My phone rings, jolting me back to the present. I look down at the screen. *Mom.*

My finger hovers over the green button, lands on the red. She told Zachary about Halliday. An apology won't cut it. Not this time.

The ringing stops. I stare at the phone in my hand, half expecting her to call back. But the phone is silent.

Focus, Steph.

I take a loud breath, turn my thoughts back to Zachary, the situation at hand.

I need to talk to Scott. I need him to know that Zachary's not part of this.

I push Mom out of my mind and dial.

"He admitted to skipping class," I say when I hear the call connect.

"Steph—"

"Immediately," I interrupt. "No hesitation. And he wasn't doing anything nefarious. He was at the gym." The visit to Halliday's house crosses my mind, but I shake off the image.

"Steph," Scott says again, and this time I let him continue. "Admitting to that isn't in the same *realm* as admitting to what's in that email. You know that. That doesn't prove anything."

"It doesn't make sense! None of it makes sense. Sending the email, never checking it again . . ."

"So what are you saying?" he demands.

The answer runs through my mind but doesn't reach my lips. I hesitate, because I know the reaction it'll elicit. But what choice do I have?

"He's being framed."

"Framed," he repeats. It's a statement, not a question.

"Set up." I need him to understand that I'm serious. That this is the truth.

"So you're saying *someone else* sent that email?"

"Yes."

"Someone's trying to make it look like Zachary wants to join a terrorist group."

"Yes."

"Someone came into your house, created an email account in Zachary's name, and sent the email?" Now his voice drips with skepticism.

Not just *someone,* I think. A powerful someone who has every reason to want to silence me. Us. But I can't say that, not yet, not until I'm ready to come clean about everything, change our lives forever.

And not until I know for sure it's him. No matter what he's done in the past—I need to know that he did *this*.

"Yes."

"Do you know how crazy that sounds?"

"Of course."

"Steph, dammit, think about it rationally. Put yourself in my shoes. It *just doesn't make sense*. If someone wanted to hurt Zachary—or you—there are easier ways to do it."

"Put yourself in *my* shoes, Scott. What if someone accused one of your kids of something like this?"

"It's completely different."

"Why?"

For the first time, he hesitates, and I know what he's thinking. *Because my kids are good. My kids wouldn't do something like this.*

"I know Zachary. You know Zachary. He didn't send that email."

Scott exhales heavily. "You can't be objective, Steph. You're way too close."

I picture the conversation with Zachary. The blank look on his face when I brought up the Freedom Solidarity Movement. He'd never heard of FSM. I'm certain he hadn't. This isn't about objectivity. It's about the facts. I know my son.

I need Scott to know the truth. And I need to stop playing defense. "So what *you're* saying is that Zachary came home from school, created a new email account, sent an email requesting to join FSM, and *then never checked that email account again*. Does *that* make sense, Scott? And how did he know where to send his email, anyway? There's no indication he ever visited any extremist forum."

"Not from that IP address," Scott points out.

It's what I would've said if it were my investigation, but I'm not going to be deterred. "FSM's email addresses change weekly."

Scott's quiet. I sense I'm winning. He's starting to realize the truth. I feel a rush of confidence.

"It makes no sense, Scott. Admit it. Zachary would have checked for a response."

"Unless he realized he made a mistake."

I shake my head, even though deep down I know he has a point. The activity would be consistent with someone who sent an impulsive message, changed his mind, didn't care about receiving a response. Regretted the email, probably.

"Kids make mistakes, Steph. They all do."

"Not like this. Not Zachary. You know him, Scott."

He sighs. "Steph, it's just that I know *you*."

That wasn't what I was expecting, not at all. "What's *that* supposed to mean?"

"Maybe you're imagining the Zachary he was when he was a kid. Maybe you're thinking of people who've hurt you in the past, imagining they're coming after you again. But, Steph—those people have moved on. I'm sure they have. I think you're the only one who hasn't."

The accusation pushes me from unsettled to angry, because he has no idea. No *idea* who might be coming after me, what they have to lose.

I squeeze my eyes shut and take a soft breath. "Just give me a little longer," I bargain. "I'll find proof, and I'll tell you everything."

"Find it soon." There's an icy pause. "I'll talk to you later, Steph," Scott says, and ends the call.

But the line doesn't disconnect immediately, almost like someone else is on it. Like someone else is listening.

And then the line goes dead.

Chapter 20

I'm pacing the house, unable to settle. Someone was there, on the other end of the line; someone was listening. Finally I race upstairs and change into running clothes. Grab a windbreaker and my running belt, tuck my keys inside. I unlock the front door, pull it open, and—

Mom's on my doorstep. Bundled in her heavy plaid parka, the one she's had forever.

"What are you doing here?" I snap. I hate it when she shows up unannounced, and she knows it. Yet she's been doing it for years, ever since she moved to Virginia.

"You wouldn't take my call."

"What do you want?"

"Are you going to invite me in? Or do you want all your neighbors to know our business?"

I glare at her, but reluctantly open the door wider. She brushes past me in a wave of perfume, removes her parka, holds it out to me.

"Stephanie, honey, I'm sorry."

"You're *sorry*?" I don't think I've ever been this furious with her. She had no right to meddle in my life, expose my secrets.

"It wasn't my place."

"Damn right it wasn't." She's still holding out her parka. I make no move to take it. I'm not going to give her permission to stay. I'm not going to make her feel welcome.

She sighs, pulls the parka to her chest, hugs it. "I didn't want to betray his trust. He needs *someone* he can turn to."

"What's *that* supposed to mean?"

"Things between you and Zachary . . . The boy is drifting away, Stephanie."

"That *boy* is *my* son, and this is *my* life."

"Of course. But you don't know him the way you should. You're not around—"

"*This* again? *Now?* Are you kidding me?"

"Time is precious, Stephanie. And time is slipping away. You—"

"Just stop, Mom."

"Zachary needs to be your first priority, honey. A child—"

"Don't do this."

"A child should *always* be a mother's first priority."

Fury is spreading through me like wildfire. "How *dare* you say that? Zachary is my *life*—"

"Your *work* is your life. Zachary comes second. He always has."

"You need to leave. *Now.*"

"Honey, I just want to help you fix things. Before it's too late. Before you don't have any relationship at all with your *child*."

"Because you have such a great one with *yours*?"

"I have *always* put you first."

"Then I guess there's more to being a good mother than just that."

Pain flares in her eyes, but I have no intention of stopping. I want to hurt her right now, the same way she hurt me.

"You think you and I have a great relationship? You think *you're* one to be dispensing advice?"

"We used to be close. Before—"

"Yeah? Did we?" I taunt, even though I know it's true. Even though I know the rest of her thought: *Before you got pregnant. Before you decided your career was more important than my grandson.*

"I *know* you, Stephanie. When it comes to you and Zachary—"

"You don't know me," I slash back.

"Of course I do, honey. Even when you've been reluctant to tell me something, I've *known*. Like your relationship with that senator. You didn't tell me. I *knew*."

The patronizing look on her face makes me unable to hold back the ugly words tumbling toward my lips. "It wasn't a relationship, Mom. It was *rape*."

She recoils, like I've struck her. Her face pales.

"And if you really knew me, you'd know that. You'd understand *why* my career is so important to me." I brush past her to the door. Open it, wait for her to leave my home.

"Oh, honey . . . Why did you never tell me that?" Tears cloud her eyes.

A lump is rising in my throat. In my mind I'm nineteen again, irrationally terrified that she'd think less of me if she knew the truth, that it would hurt her, destroy our relationship. Certain, in my stubborn teenage way, that I knew best. That I could salvage our relationship with secrets and lies.

She'd wrap me in a hug right now, if I'd let her. But I won't. What she did—exposing this truth to Zachary—wasn't right. The things she said to me were too hurtful. I go in for one last dig, one I know will wound: "I guess we weren't as close as you think, Mom, were we?"

It's freezing again tonight. Dark, too; the moon is a cold sliver in the sky. Everything's quiet at this hour; the streets are almost deserted. I start off at a jog, heading west. At the end of the street, I take a left and pick up my pace.

The conversation with Mom replays itself in my head. *It was rape.* The words that have been at the forefront of my mind for eighteen years now, held back by an invisible dam, one that cracked the moment I saw Zachary with Halliday.

The hurtful things we said to each other: *Zachary comes second. He always has.*

I guess there's more to being a good mother . . .

I run harder, try to stop this endless loop in my brain. Focus on my breath, the white puffs in front of me. My knee, aching in the cold.

Through the heart of Dupont Circle. O'Neill's is up ahead. Inside, there's a warm orange glow. I can see the bar as I pass, rows of bottles stacked high, a bartender with a shaker in his hand. I look for Marta, even though I know she's not there. I heard she'd stopped going. In a way, though, that makes things easier. Even if I hadn't tried to do the right thing, those days would be done.

We met at this bar, Marta and me, ages ago. We were both attending a conference at the hotel across the street, one sponsored by the Department of Defense, open to agencies around the federal government. Intended for women working in male-dominated environments. And somehow, inexplicably, each of the presenters was a man.

I snuck out as one particularly dry Army captain droned on about workplace attire. Made my way to O'Neill's. Slid onto a stool, scanned the menu of bar snacks, ordered a ginger ale. Would have liked something harder, but I was on the clock, and I was armed.

There was a woman two stools away, a short glass of something clear in front of her. She wore a conference nametag. *Marta M.* No agency listed beneath her name. The only people I'd encountered that day without an agency listed were either FBI or CIA—the ones trying to hide where they worked.

She glanced over, caught me watching her. Her gaze traveled down to my own nametag. Her lips quirked. "You escaped, too?"

"If I hear one more *man* talk about what it's like to be a *woman* . . ." I smiled at her.

"Yes!" She grinned. Then she stood, reached for her drink, and slid onto the stool beside me. "I'm Marta."

"Steph."

She nodded toward my nametag. "Agency or Bureau?"

"Bureau. You?"

"Agency." The bartender placed a tall glass of soda in front of me. I thanked him, turned back to Marta. "What brought you here?"

"I'm between field assignments. It was either sit at headquarters and twiddle my thumbs or fill the time with crap like this."

"You may have made the wrong call."

She threw back her head and laughed. "What about you?"

"The bosses recommended it." I could have stopped there, but her honesty encouraged me to continue. "And I have an eight-year-old. Barely ever get home in time to see his Little League games. . . . These things always end early, you know?"

"Thank God! Not sure how much more of this anyone could handle." She took a sip from her glass, pursed her lips like it was sour.

"How's it been for you, working in a 'male-dominated' world?" I used air quotes as I said it.

"Agency's not so bad. Worse in the field than at headquarters. Some of those station chiefs . . ." She shrugged.

The television caught my eye. Halliday, on the Senate floor. My throat tightened in that all-too-familiar way. I focused on my drink, the beads of condensation on the glass.

"*Steph?*" Marta was giving me a quizzical look. She had obviously just said something, but I hadn't heard it.

"Sorry, what was that?"

"What about you? Any experience working for a terrible boss?"

I looked back at the television screen. Halliday was still there. I nodded toward the screen. "I worked for that guy right there. *Nine* years ago."

Marta followed my gaze. She was quiet.

Why did I just say that? I looked back down at my drink. My cheeks felt hot. I hadn't come this close to telling the truth about Halliday since that night with my mom, when Zachary was an infant. And here I was saying it to a perfect stranger.

I glanced back at Marta. She was still watching Halliday on the screen. *What was she thinking?* Finally, she turned to me. Offered me a smile, and I had the strangest sense that she could somehow see the truth, and that she didn't think it was crazy. "I always did think that guy was a bastard."

A peal of laughter draws my attention back to the present. I see three girls on the sidewalk, practically teenagers by the looks of them, with arms linked, heading toward me, toward the door to O'Neill's. Smiling, not a care in the world. I was one of those girls, once. It seems more than a lifetime ago.

I pick up my speed. My route is familiar. Fourteen miles, a loop that runs seven into Maryland, seven back. I've been running it for almost two years now, ever since I learned that woman's identity, found out where she lived.

The one from the crime scene. I see her now, in my mind. Walking away from me, heading for the door. That hand on her back, washed in flashing red and blue . . .

The National Cathedral's up ahead, its towering Gothic spires glowing against the dark sky.

There are no cars around; my feet hitting the pavement is the only sound. I pass a woman under an overpass, bundled thick in reeking layers, a worn duffel bag at her side, a makeshift tent behind her. She doesn't even look up as I run by.

I head up Wisconsin Ave, north into Maryland. There's a sign on my right: WELCOME TO FRIENDSHIP HEIGHTS. Marta's part of town. I could use her now more than ever. But I ruined the friendship we'd built. All because of that woman, because I didn't let it go.

Faster now. I focus on the pavement in front of me. The road up ahead. And I try to keep my mind clear. But questions keep forcing their way in.

Who's doing this? Who's trying to manipulate the facts to make my son look treasonous? Halliday's the most obvious answer, the most logical answer. But what if it's someone else?

I can't imagine anyone wanting to hurt *Zachary*. I can't picture him making someone angry enough that they'd do this.

But that means it's someone who wants to hurt *me*. And that thought is sickening. Not just because it would mean it's my fault, that I'm the one who dragged my son into this, but because of the people who might be doing it. Halliday. Torrino. Someone like Hanson, any number of others I've investigated, whose careers I've destroyed.

The image flashes in my mind again. The hand on her back, the blinking lights. And then another: my filing cabinet at work, that file tucked in the back, unlabeled.

My lungs are burning, filling with air so cold it feels like fire. I'm in the neighborhood now, the one I've visited many times the past couple of years. I wind my way down the familiar streets. I see her house up ahead. Small, boxlike, the front porch addition that looks vaguely out of place.

I slow my pace as I approach. The house is dark, vacant, as always. The bushes out front are brown, in need of pruning. Grass has frozen in the cracks of the sidewalk.

I come to a stop in front of it. Bend down, hands on my knees, wheezing. Then I look up, at the house, into the uncurtained windows, pitch black inside. I picture her, the only time I saw her. Shell-shocked, scared.

I try to imagine her inside the house. Happy. Safe. But all I see is blackness, nothingness.

A porch light flares on next door, and I take that as my cue to move on. I start walking.

Wherever she is, I hope she's safe. I hope she's happy.

I give the house one last look, then break into a jog. I wish I could get her out of my mind, but I can't.

What happened to her?

Zachary's alarm goes off at six on the dot. Four minutes later, the shower turns on.

I carry my third mug of coffee into the living room, aim the remote at the television and find the morning news, the anchors who look far too cheery for the early hour. They're laughing about something. I stare at the screen and listen to the water upstairs.

Traffic report. Weather. Then on to politics. More Foreign Relations Committee hearings; Russia, as usual. *"How can we call Moscow an ally when the Russians are making every effort to interfere in our elections?"* comes a question from offscreen. Jackson's testifying again; I don't listen for his answer. I look away, down at the chess pieces, focus on them.

Minutes later I hear Zachary thunder down the stairs. His hair's still damp, and his T-shirt has little water spots, like he pulled it on before his skin was fully dry. He notices me when he already has one hand on the refrigerator door, and he immediately goes still.

"Hey," he says.

I stand up, face him. "I need to talk to you. Who's been in our house recently?"

"Huh?"

"Which of your friends?"

"No one. Not since I broke up with Kelly."

That was months ago. "I won't be angry, Zachary. You won't get in trouble. I just need you to tell me."

"Mom, I swear." The confusion in his eyes deepens. He doesn't look the slightest bit like he's lying.

And the truth is, I believe it. He's never been one for having friends over. When he was younger, he'd always prefer to go to other kids' houses. And since he turned thirteen, got his own phone, he stopped doing even that. All the kids did. They just sit on their phones all the time, or they go out somewhere. There's no hanging out at a friend's house. It's not like it was when I was his age.

"Any other girls?"

"No."

"What about Lila?" The moment the name slips from my mouth, I wish I could yank it back.

"Lila?"

"Has she been here?"

"How do you know about Lila?"

"Does it matter?"

"Have you been going through my *stuff*?" His eyes are stormy. I feel like I'm looking at a stranger. No, not a stranger. *Halliday*.

I could say yes. I could tell him he's living in *my* house, and I have every right to do that. But the anger on his face reproves me, and I settle for a half-truth. "You put pictures *online*, Zachary. What about Halliday? Has he been here?"

"No."

"Never?"

"Never!"

"Or anyone else?"

"Just Grandma!"

"I'm not talking about Grandma. Someone claiming to be a re-pairman, anyone like that?"

"No." The fury fades, and relief washes over me. *Was I just afraid of my own son?* He holds my gaze for a long moment, then opens the fridge, pulls out the juice carton, moves over to the counter to pour himself a glass. I wait until he's finished. I suddenly realize how tall he's become, how much he resembles his father. I feel sick.

"Zachary, is there anyone who might want to hurt you?"

"Mom, jeez, what is it? What's going on?"

"Or get back at you for anything?"

"I told you—no. Why are you asking these questions? Why won't you tell me what's wrong?"

Someone came into our house, sent that email. Planted that Glock. Halliday, maybe. Or someone else? So much isn't clear. *Who, what, where, when—*

I know *when*, don't I?

When the email was sent, at least. When the gun was planted, too?

I think back to the report, try to recall the date. Wednesday, a little more than two weeks ago. Then another thought hits me, snaps together with the previous one in a perfect fit. I set the mug down and reach for my phone, navigate to my texts. I find the chain with Zachary and scroll until I find the exchange I'm looking for. There it is. I check the date stamp. Wednesday. It's a match.

Zachary, 5:16 P.M.: *Did u forget to set alarm?*

Me, 5:16 P.M.: *No, why?*

Zachary, 5:19 P.M.: *Just got home, it was off.*

I remember that day, those texts. Looking at them at work, dis-tracted by the allegations about Hanson, only half trying to remem-ber if I was the last to leave or Zachary was, trying to think of what was happening that morning that could have made me forget to set it. Feeling the slightest twinge of unease, one I pushed from my mind, because there was no reason to think anyone would be trying to get into our house, trying to get close to us. Not now, anyway. Maybe once, but not now. Life was good; we were safe. It was paranoia to think otherwise.

"What is it, Mom?" comes Zachary's voice.

What if it wasn't paranoia after all? Someone broke into our home, sent that message. Didn't trip our alarm, turned it off. Someone with the skill—or the power—to do that.

"Mom? What's going on? You're scaring me!"

I see faces in my mind, almost like a lineup. Men from my past, all of whom had—or have—something to lose. Scott thinks they've moved on. But what if one of them *didn't* move on?

Who? I hear the psychiatrist's jeer in my head again. *And why?*

"Mom, what's the matter? What's wrong?"

How am I supposed to answer that? "It's just a work thing."

"Maybe I could help. If you just tell me—"

"It's work-related, Zachary. I don't want you involved."

"'Cause *that's* never happened, right, Mom?" he says bitterly.

A week after the takedown in Chicago, my boss called me down to his office. I assumed it was going to be another commendation. More praise for the operation. There'd already been plenty, reaching from as high up as the director himself, and it wasn't letting up. But when I walked into his office, I could tell from the look on his face that this was something else. Something very different.

"Have a seat, Steph," he said, and I sat down in one of the chairs opposite his desk. Waited for what I somehow already knew was going to be bad news.

He clasped his hands and set them carefully on the desk in front of him. Took a noisy breath, sighed, then spoke. "You've been greenlighted."

Greenlighted. They put a hit out on me. The mob did. *Torrino* did. He wanted me dead.

I said nothing, because I didn't know what to say.

"How we proceed here is up to you."

I knew what he meant. I could stand my ground, brush off the threat, be more aware, and hope for the best. Or I could leave. Take a transfer, get out of town. Let them settle me at a desk somewhere where I'd be invisible, out of their reach.

I knew the right answer. The one he was looking for. "I'm staying," I said. I was strong; I could fight.

He smiled. "Attagirl." Then his face grew more serious again. "I'll put a couple of agents on your house at night, at least for the next week or so. Have them follow your son to school, if you want."

Your son. Zachary's face filled my mind. The way he looked clambering onto the bus in the morning, so small, so determined and vulnerable. Holding tight to his plastic dinosaur, the one he was bringing for show-and-tell. "Okay," I said quietly. Some of the fight had suddenly drained out of me, and uncertainty had filled the spot where it had been.

"And I'd recommend making sure your affairs are in order. Just to be on the safe side. I know you're a single parent and all . . ."

The uncertainty was expanding, pushing out the remaining defiance. What would happen to Zachary if they got to me?

What if they came after me when he was around? And what if he was caught in the crossfire? Or if he was the one who found my body?

"Okay," I said, more softly.

He cocked his head to the side, studied me. I felt like he could see through me, like he knew the fears running through my head. "I talked to headquarters already. We can get you a position in D.C. Internal affairs."

Internal affairs. I'd be out of Chicago, away from Torrino and his men. In what would essentially amount to a desk job. It would be the end of my ambitions, a dead-end job.

"Out of sight, out of mind," he added, and I knew what he meant. If I quit investigating the mob, Torrino would leave me alone. Change the green light to red.

But I'd be giving up. Letting him win. Sacrificing a promising career, everything that I'd worked so hard for.

"I don't know," I said.

He nodded. Waited for me to say something else, but I didn't. I couldn't; I didn't know what else to say. I didn't know what the right decision was.

"Tell you what," he said, leaning forward. "How about six weeks in D.C.? A short rotation. We'll let things cool down here, see where we stand."

I reluctantly agreed, and when I spoke to Mom on the phone later that morning, I told her the plan.

"Washington, D.C.?" She sounded incredulous. "You're picking up and moving *again*? When?"

"Now. Today."

"Today? You've got to be kidding me, Stephanie."

"I'm not."

"You're telling me you're picking up *in the middle of the school year* and moving to another city for *six weeks*? What about Zachary?"

"What *about* Zachary?"

"He's in *school*."

"There are schools in D.C., Mom, believe it or not."

"This is serious, Stephanie. For once, you need to think of your son."

"I *am* thinking of my son," I exploded. I couldn't win. I thought I *was* doing what was best for Zachary. *Was I wrong?*

"I don't see how that's possible."

"I don't have a choice, Mom."

"You always have a choice."

"I don't!"

"So leave this damned job! Find something stable. Something safe. For pity's sake, what's wrong with you? Put Zachary *first* for once, Stephanie."

Tears of frustration stung my eyes. I couldn't leave the job. I couldn't give up, let Torrino win. I couldn't let *Halliday* win. This was my purpose. If I didn't have this job, I was nothing but a victim.

I could do what was best for Zachary *and* make something of my life.

That afternoon, with unmarked government cars dotting my street and armed colleagues guarding my house, I packed our suitcases. Clothes, shoes, books, and toys, what we'd need for six weeks, at least. In the back of my mind, I wondered if we'd return at all.

I quickly loaded everything I could into our car. Picked up Zachary from school, saw his face light up with happiness when he saw me standing there. The grin stayed on his face even as I strapped him into his booster seat. And then I said the words I'd been dreading. "Honey, we have to leave here."

I watched his face crumple, happiness giving way to confusion. "We're coming back, right?"

Were we? "I don't know," I answered honestly. I watched the confusion morph into disbelief. Saw the truth slowly dawn. His eyes filled and his chin quivered, but my wonderful, brave kid was using every ounce of his strength to keep the tears from spilling.

"I'm sorry, honey," I said, and the apology seemed so inadequate. I wished I knew what to say. I wished I knew what to do.

We got on the highway, with one black Suburban in front and one behind, a caravan driving much too fast. The escort lasted until we reached the county line. The SUVs peeled off, and then it was just us. I watched in the rearview mirror as they did U-turns across the median of the highway. Then they were gone, and we were on our own, just the two of us.

I continued speeding down the highway, my eyes searching the road around us, committing each car to memory, keeping a list in my head. I wanted to be sure we weren't being followed.

I was watching a set of headlights in the rearview mirror when I heard his small voice from the backseat. "Are we safe, Mommy?"

I shifted my gaze over to him, saw his face white with worry. My heart was breaking. And in that moment, I knew. This move was permanent. The realization filled me with a confounding sadness, a sense of longing for what could have been that was as stunning as a blow.

"We're safe, sweetie," I answered, my throat tightening.

I watched in the mirror as the fear faded from his face. He twisted in the booster seat and looked out the window, and didn't ask any more questions.

Eventually his blinks became slower, the lids taking longer to rise again with each flutter shut.

By the time he was asleep, there was not a doubt in my mind, and the wave of sadness had ebbed, replaced with a sense of peace. We were going to stay in D.C. I was going to work in internal affairs. We'd never go back to Chicago. And Zachary and I would no longer be in danger. My job wouldn't put him in jeopardy, ever again.

"I'll always keep you safe," I vowed, as much to myself as to him. "I promise."

Chapter 21

The man walks through the airport terminal. Washington National this time. Third flight in as many days, all under different names.

He's in dark jeans and a dark gray sweater, a black leather overnight bag on his arm. Has dirty blond hair, closely cropped. Nondescript features, a forgettable face.

He bypasses baggage claim, walks straight outside to the curb. There's a car there, a massive black SUV, darkly tinted windows. He opens the back door, slides inside.

A partition, also tinted, separates front seat from back. It stays closed. The car pulls away from the curb.

There's a black messenger bag sitting on the backseat. He reaches for it. Opens the flap, unzips it. Rifles through. Finally pulls out a manila folder, opens it up.

There's a photograph on top. Five-by-seven, black-and-white. A surveillance shot. The man focuses his attention on it. Stares at it, intently.

It's a boy. Backpack slung over one shoulder. The camera caught him just as he was turning his head. A shock of hair falls across his forehead. He's looking off to the left, completely unaware that anyone was there, that anyone was photographing him.

The man closes the folder. Then he turns and looks out the window. They're crossing over the Potomac now. The Jefferson Memorial's just up ahead. Beyond that, the Washington Monument.

The rest of the city is mapped in his head. The Capitol dome. The White House. FBI headquarters.

A smile creeps to his lips.

The game has begun.

Chapter 22

I'm the first of my team to arrive in the morning, like usual. I make my way through the darkened bullpen to my office, turn on the lights. Start up the computer. Swivel toward the coffeemaker on the file cabinets, start that up, too. My gaze settles on the stack of folders on the corner of my desk. The to-do pile, reports from my agents that I need to review, investigative actions that I need to approve. Usually there are two or three items awaiting my attention. There must be a dozen folders in that pile right now. I can't force myself to concentrate.

Someone sent that email, tried to make it look like it was Zachary. Someone's using him to get to me.

And someone put that gun in Zachary's closet.

Which means someone got past the alarm. Someone broke into our home, the place I've always felt safest.

Who?

Who's doing this to us?

The faces appear again in my mind, that lineup of men from my past.

Halliday. He has so much to lose. Senior United States senator.

Chair of the Foreign Relations Committee. In line for a leadership post. Chatter, even, about more than that.

But it doesn't make sense. Halliday thinks if I come clean about my past, he'd easily cast me as a liar. A disgruntled employee. That no one would believe me. And when I brought up the gun, he seemed genuinely confused.

Just like Zachary.

But he also showed no signs of deception when he suggested he'd claim we'd had a relationship. He's clearly a superb liar.

Like Zachary?

Torrino. He swore he'd make me pay. But now? The timing doesn't make sense. It's been too many years. *Now,* at the same time Halliday's back in my life?

What if it's someone else? What if it's *him*? In my mind I see that hand, on her back, the swirling red and blue lights. . . . Why can't I let that go?

There's a rap on my glass door and I spin my chair toward the sound. Then I force myself to take a deep breath. I rise and open the door.

"You look like hell, Steph," Scott says, brushing past me.

"I'm living there," I answer honestly.

We sit, me behind the desk and Scott on the other side.

"What is it, Scott?" All of my nerves shriek. I don't know what's coming. I'm not the one in charge of this situation and it scares me.

"It's odd that Zachary would send that email and then never check for a response. You're right about that."

I feel a surge of hope. "It shows—"

He shoots me a hard look and gives his head the briefest of shakes, like I don't get to ask questions. "Unless he was contacted offline. Unless they met in person."

He watches me closely. I wonder how my face looks. As bewil-

dered as I feel? Because he has something; obviously he has something. Maybe there's more tying Zachary to this plot than just the
email, the weapon in his closet. *What if there's more?*

"I did some digging into the other email accounts that contacted
FSM," he goes on. "Looked for a similar case—an account that sent
a message, wasn't checked again."

"Did you find one?" What if the answer's *yes*? What would that
mean?

"I did. One case."

"And?" I press. I need to hear the answer and at the same time I'm
terrified.

"The email address was created just before the message was sent.
No future log-ins. Long lulls in Internet usage on either side of that
particular activity."

It's just like Zachary's case. But why? What does it mean?

There's more. I know Scott so well: I can see it on his face. He
clears his throat. "The user's IP address. It's in this area. And his
message was sent just before Zachary's. His name's Dylan Taylor."

I stare at him in stunned silence. I search his face for some explanation, but I find none. He's uncertain, too. He doesn't understand,
either.

Dylan Taylor is twenty-one. He lives in Arlington, Virginia, in a
rough section of town. Dilapidated houses, plastic lawn chairs on
crumbling front porches. Overflowing trash cans, littered beer bottles, and a cloying shadow of despair.

There's a loose board on the steps to Taylor's house; we step over
it. A calico cat's watching us from the corner of the porch, green
eyes glowing intently.

Scott knocks. Moments later, a young man swings it open. He's tall and bony, with stringy blond hair that falls to his shoulders. T-shirt and shorts, bare feet, even though it's forty degrees out. "Yeah?" He eyes us warily.

"Dylan Taylor?"

"Yeah?"

"Special Agent Scott Clark, FBI." He flashes his credentials. "And this is my colleague." He doesn't introduce me by name, and Taylor doesn't seem to notice, or care. His bleary gray eyes strain to focus on Scott's credentials, then land back on Scott's face. He looks nervous, but that's normal. He doesn't look panicked.

"We just have a few questions for you," Scott says.

"Okay." Taylor doesn't invite us in, doesn't step outside, just waits, his hand on the door. A pulse has started to jump in his cheek.

"Can you tell us what you know about the Freedom Solidarity Movement?"

"The what?" he asks. There's not a spark of recognition in his face. His voice is reedy, like a teenager's.

"Freedom Solidarity Movement. FSM."

"Never heard of it."

"It's an anti-government group."

A half smile comes to Taylor's face. I'd swear he looked relieved. "Sorry, man. Think you've got the wrong guy."

"You're not a member of any anarchist group?"

"No. Don't even know what *anarchist* means." He says it with a snigger.

"Never sought to join one?"

The smile fades. "No, man. Hey, I'm telling you, you got the wrong guy."

"Can you tell me where you were on the afternoon of the twelfth? Around four-thirty?"

Taylor's expression shifts. "What day of the week was that?"

"A Wednesday."

"At four?"

"Four-thirty."

"On my way to work, I guess. I work Wednesdays and Thursdays. Usually leave around that time, or a little before." His hair falls across one eye in a way that reminds me of Zachary's. He swipes it away.

"How do you get to work?"

"Drive."

"Alone?"

"Yeah."

Alone in his car. Same alibi as Zachary.

"Do I, like, need a lawyer?" He's finally realized this is serious. His anxiety has become palpable.

Scott's about to respond; he's going to shut this down, I know. And I can't blame him. It's what I'd do. Taylor mentioned lawyering up; safest thing is to stop talking. But I'm not ready for the conversation to be over. It's obvious to both of us he didn't send that email, that he's never heard of FSM. What isn't clear, in the least, is how he's connected to this. To my son.

"Do you know a Zach Maddox?" I ask. "Zachary Maddox?"

"Okay, okay," interjects Scott. Out of the corner of my eye, I see him shoot me a warning look.

I ignore it. "Do you?"

Taylor looks from me to Scott and back again. He blinks. "No. I don't." He shuffles his feet. "Hey, guys, it's freezing out here," he whines.

"Thanks for your time, Mr. Taylor." Scott says it firmly, then gives me a pointed look. He's done with this, cutting off any further questioning on my part. "We'll be in touch."

He turns to walk away, and I know I'm supposed to follow. But I don't want to leave, not without figuring out how he fits into this.

"Am I, like, in trouble?" Taylor asks me, and in his voice I hear my son's. The same helplessness, the same confusion.

"I don't know," I answer honestly. Then I turn and follow Scott, and I don't look back.

"He'd never heard of the group," I insist as we drive away. "You could see that."

He doesn't respond, but I see his jawline tense.

"Zachary had the same reaction, Scott. He'd never heard of FSM, either."

"I don't know that, Steph," he snaps. "You wouldn't let me talk to him."

I should let him do it. Talk to Zachary. I know that's what he wants. It's standard procedure. But at this point it seems dangerous. He'd be skeptical of anything he hears. He'd assume Zachary had been briefed on the situation. Coached. And the truth is, Zachary doesn't know about any of this.

It's just too much of a risk to let the *FBI* interview my *son*.

I watch the sun glint off the Potomac as we cross the bridge back into D.C.

"Are you saying someone's setting them *both* up for a fall?" Scott finally asks. "I don't understand."

"I don't know," I reply bleakly. I don't have the faintest idea how Dylan Taylor fits in. God, I wish I did. It would make everything so much easier. Right now, though, it doesn't matter. What matters is proving to Scott that Zachary isn't involved, and this helps make that case. "But we both know Taylor didn't send that email. And neither did Zachary."

"Who's doing this, Steph?" he asks quietly. And for the first time, I feel a surge of hope.

Halliday. Torrino. I want to say their names, want to spill everything, the whole story, but I can't. He doesn't even know Halliday is Zachary's father. My refusal to share that truth was one of the reasons our relationship failed. I can still hear the hurt in his voice: *You're never going to trust me enough to tell me, are you?* But I couldn't risk opening a door that might let that monster into our lives. Couldn't risk that Scott—this man I trusted more than I'd ever trusted anyone—might not believe me.

And what proof do I have? If I tell him everything, if I tell him about that gun in Zachary's closet, and he doesn't believe me, then all I've done is give him reason to arrest my son. And whoever's doing this—whoever's trying to keep me quiet, or get back at me, or whatever—what will he do if I come clean?

I close my eyes and take a breath. But what I see isn't Torrino. It isn't Halliday, either. It's that hand again, pressing hard against that woman's back, bathed in spiraling lights. I'm watching him walk to the door with her. Watching him bend to whisper in her ear. I know he's about to turn, about to make contact with me, and I open my eyes, send the memory tumbling away. But I feel like I'm gasping for breath.

As I continued to drive down that highway all those years ago, I couldn't stop shifting my gaze between the rearview mirror and the road, still watching for a tail. If there wasn't one by now, my brain told me there wouldn't be, that I could relax. My heart told me not to, that I should never relax, not when my son was involved.

I looked at Zachary in the mirror. His eyes were closed, his head tilted sideways. Fast asleep, so peaceful and quiet. And it made me hope that maybe our life could go on as normal. Maybe everything would be okay.

The farther I drove, the more I told myself I'd made the right decision. I still had a good reputation. I'd work hard in the new position. It was internal affairs—that wasn't all bad. Surely there were people in the Bureau like Halliday, abusing their power. Maybe there were even some like the one I once was—vulnerable, afraid. Maybe I could find a way to make a difference.

It wasn't until we were halfway to D.C. that the thought occurred to me. If, in this new job, anyone *did* retaliate, it would be someone with the best training, with access to formidable resources. Someone who'd lost—or who stood to lose—everything. Someone, potentially, with power.

If there was another threat, it would be by someone on the inside. Getting out of town might not be enough.

It could make my life much, much worse.

Chapter 23

Zachary grabs another slice of pepperoni pizza from the box, his third one. It seems like just yesterday I was cutting his food for him, promising dessert in exchange for finishing his dinner. Where did that little boy go? Where did the *time* go?

He catches me watching him. "You okay, Mom?"

I set down the slice I'm holding. Of course I'm not. If he had any idea what's going on . . . "Yeah."

He keeps his eyes on me as he chews.

Is *he* okay? It occurs to me that I haven't spoken with him about his visit to Halliday, not really. The fact that he's finally met his father. I don't know what to say, really. But I should say something. Surely that should have been my first concern.

"About Halliday," I begin.

He pauses his chewing. His expression grows guarded.

"About the past . . ."

He finishes chewing the bite, watching me the whole time. Doesn't take another, just waits for me to go on.

What am I supposed to say? The mother in me is at a loss for words; the investigator takes over. *Start with what you know. Lead up to what you don't.* "You took that DNA test. Grandma said a year ago?"

"Something like that."

"And then you got in touch with Halliday. Couple of months ago?"

"I guess."

"You waited a long time to contact him." It's a leading statement, the kind that should make him say *something*.

He reaches for a napkin. "I wasn't sure what I wanted to do." He wipes a smudge of sauce off his fingers. "I spent some time looking into him. Online. And—"

My phone vibrates against the table. I glance at the screen. *Fairfax County Police.*

A jolt of panic runs through me. Not now. The police can't be involved now. Not until I figure this out, until I can unmask whoever has set up this trap.

The phone's still vibrating, dancing ever so slightly on the table. Zachary's still watching me, waiting for me to answer it. I force myself to reach for it, press the green button. "Hello?"

"Stephanie Maddox?"

Not now. Not yet. "Yes?"

"Ms. Maddox, this is Officer Diaz with the Fairfax County Police Department. I'm afraid I have some bad news."

"Yes?" My voice sounds foreign, like it doesn't belong to me.

"There's been an accident."

An accident. No. No, Zachary's here; Zachary's safe.

"It's your mother. Joan Maddox."

Mom. "Is she okay?" Now my voice sounds distant, like I'm speaking from very far away.

"Ma'am, I'm sorry to say she's in critical condition."

· · ·

"Ma'am?"

In my mind I see my mom, her smiling face. I hear her laugh. And then I remember the ugly words we said to each other last night.

"Ms. Maddox?"

The tears in her eyes, the pain in her whisper. *Oh, honey . . . why did you never tell me that?* The way I went in for one final, hurtful, unnecessary dig.

"Mom?" Zachary's voice. "What's wrong?"

"What happened, Officer Diaz?" I say into the phone.

"Looks like she took a fall—a bad one. Down a flight of stairs. In one of the stairwells of her condo building."

Oh God. I'm staring at the chessboard, all these black and white squares, all these pieces waiting to be moved. *Time is precious, Stephanie. And time is slipping away.* My panic is fierce. I bite my lip, hard, to keep from crying. What if we never find the time to finish the game?

"What hospital?"

"Fairfax," he says, but I'm already reaching for my coat, motioning for Zachary to do the same.

Mom's hooked up to a tangle of tubes and machines, unconscious, bandaged. The ER doctor told me her prognosis is uncertain, that the next few hours are critical.

She's got multiple fractures, but that's not what has the doctors most concerned. It's the head injury. Cerebral edema. Swelling in her brain.

I sit by her bedside and hold her hand. And I try, with all my heart, not to focus on the painful charges she leveled at me. *Your work is your life. Zachary comes second. He always has.*

There's been a steady stream of doctors and nurses flowing

through the room. I've asked each of them for updates, frantic for any shred of information. They've all been noncommittal, impossible to read.

Zachary was here, too, but when his restless toe-tapping made me want to shriek at him, I suggested he grab a bite to eat from the cafeteria. At the moment it's just Mom and me. And I can't stop thinking of the terrible things I said to her. Awful things I didn't even mean, that I said only to hurt her.

There's more to being a good mother. . . .

We weren't as close as you think, Mom. . . .

"We *were* close," I whisper, even though there's no sign she can hear me. Will she *ever* be able to hear me? I need to set things right.

Time is precious, Stephanie. And time is slipping away.

I watch her chest rise and fall. I listen to the relentless beep of the machines. And I let the tears come, streaming down my face, clouding my vision until everything is a blur.

Chapter 24

By the next morning, Mom's prognosis is less grim. She made it through those first critical hours. The doctors seem slightly more optimistic.

I let HR know about the accident, requested a day off. *Take all the time you need,* the chief said. *Let us know if you need anything, Steph.*

I've continued to press for any scraps of information about her condition. Spent far too much time Googling medical terms. And I haven't been able to shut off the loop in my brain, the one that's replaying our awful last conversation.

What if those are the final words she hears me say? *Why* did I say them?

Alone, when it's just Mom and me, it's so quiet. I can't stop thinking of the way she reacted when I told her the truth about my past. The pain in her eyes, in her voice. *Why did you never tell me that?*

"How's she doing?" Zachary asks when he stops by the hospital after school. He's in jeans and that faded maroon hoodie he wears way too often, the one with the hole in the side seam. He drops his backpack on the floor, then sinks into the empty chair.

"About the same. But it's a very good sign she made it through the night."

"She doesn't look like herself."

"It was a bad fall. Her injuries . . ."

I'm still searching for the right words when he speaks again. "Mom . . . is she going to be okay?"

I squeeze her hand in mine. It feels so terribly frail. "I hope so, honey." God, I hope so.

My cellphone chirps, an incoming text. I reach for it and check the screen. It's Scott. *I heard about your mom. You doing ok?* I blink at the words, try to think of how to answer that, in a *text*. If only he were here, in person, I wouldn't feel so alone—

"Mom? What's going on?" Zachary nods at the phone in my hand.

"Nothing."

"Nothing? You won't take your eyes off the screen."

"It's Scott."

"Scott? What does *he* want?"

"He heard about Grandma."

His frown deepens, and a terrible thought strikes me. What if Scott found a way to confront Zachary, without my permission?

"You haven't talked with him recently, have you?" My voice betrays my panic.

"Not in years."

Thank God. "What, then? Why the attitude?"

"I don't have an attitude," he mutters.

"*Zachary.*"

"It's just . . . I don't like him talking to you."

"What? Why?"

"He's hurt you before. After you broke up . . . I remember how hurt you were."

My phone chirps again, but this time I don't look. I can't tear my eyes away from Zachary, like if I stare at him long enough, maybe this incredibly odd conversation will start to make sense. "Zachary, our relationship ended. It's nobody's fault. It happens."

He gives his head a frustrated shake. "I just want to make sure he's not hurting you again."

I send Zachary home and remain at Mom's bedside throughout the night. I watch her, silently implore her to wake up, to stay with me. There's no change in her condition, at least none that I can see.

That strange conversation with Zachary has continued to run through my mind. *You don't need to protect me,* I'd told him. He'd only shrugged, cheeks reddening. Mumbled something about needing to do homework, grabbed his backpack and left.

And yet when he was gone, when it was back to just Mom and me, I felt less alone than I had just a short time before. We might have our differences, Zachary and me. And there's certainly distance between us. But deep down, he *cares.*

The doctor that's examining her now is a young woman, surely younger than me. I've continued to pester each doctor and nurse for updates, for their opinions. The investigator in me is frustrated. I want *facts.* I need to know when she's going to be well.

"Her injuries are severe," she says. And then she hesitates, casts me a sidelong glance.

"What?"

"It's just . . . Was your mom ever unsteady on her feet?"

"I'm sorry?"

"Has she fallen before?"

"No." I search her tired face, trying to understand where this is going. "Why?"

She shrugs. "Nothing. I mean, falls can happen to anyone. It's just . . ."

"What?"

"Well, the extent of the injuries, the severity of the fall . . ." She straightens from the bed, frowns at me. "It's the kind of trauma we'd expect to see if someone had been *pushed* down the stairs."

Chapter 25

The only sound is the relentless beep of the machines. The young
doctor is gone, off on her rounds. On her way out, she had
tried to dismiss her suspicions, assure me that falls can happen to
anyone, especially at Mom's age, that it was more than likely just an
accident.

Those stairs were steep. Concrete. Hadn't I warned Mom a half
dozen times to be careful on them? To take the elevator? It was only
a matter of time until she tripped and fell, wasn't it?

Pushed.

No. It was surely an accident.

I reach for her hand, avoiding the IV. It was the stairs—those
stairs were dangerous.

I close my eyes, and in my mind I see Halliday's face. She knew
the truth about him, the whole terrible truth. What if . . .

Impossible. It was an accident, a horrible accident.

Wasn't it?

. . .

Midmorning, I need to act. I force myself to leave Mom's bedside, drive to her condo building in Vienna, out in the suburbs. Park in a visitor's spot at the rear of the lot, trek to the entrance, eyeing each individual I pass: an older man who nods politely in my direction; a young woman with earbuds; a middle-aged man in a suit, yammering into his phone.

I'm in the property manager's office now, a small one, barely bigger than a closet, crammed tight with filing cabinets. "How is your mother, Agent Maddox?" he asks, pushing his glasses up on the bridge of his nose with his index finger, his eyes darting this way and that. He clasps his hands on the desk, then unclasps them.

"Improving, slightly."

"I'm glad to hear that." He pushes up his glasses again, even though they hadn't slipped. "What can I do for you?"

"I want to talk about the accident."

"Of course." His fingers start drumming the desk.

"What sort of condition were the stairs in when the fall occurred?"

"Excellent condition, Agent Maddox."

"Not slippery for any reason?"

"Absolutely not."

"A handrail was present?"

"Of course. Everything is up to code." He casts me a nervous smile. "Accidents happen, Agent Maddox."

"Do you have security footage? I noticed a camera in the lobby."

His smile fades. "We do. Lobby and parking lot."

"I'll need footage from two days ago."

"Of course." He swivels around to the computer behind him, begins typing commands. "I'll just make you a copy now."

"Thanks."

Moments later, he hands me a flash drive, fiddles with his glasses once more. "Why do you need the footage, Agent Maddox?"

I tuck the drive into my pocket, stand to leave. "Just want to be thorough."

I sink down in the chair beside Mom's bed. Her eyes are still closed, her skin still terribly pale. The bandages on her head look freshly changed. I listen to the relentless beep of the machines. The chatter of nurses in the hallway. And I breathe in that ugly sterile hospital stench.

I dig the flash drive from my pocket and plug it into my laptop, start reviewing the footage. It's grainy, and black-and-white. I rewind to the beginning of the footage, the lobby camera first, and pore over it.

Zachary stops by, hovers in the doorway. His hair looks shaggier than usual, in need of a comb. He's wearing jeans and a black T-shirt with white lettering: STOP POLICE INJUSTICE. "How is she today?"

My eyes are still on the shirt. "*Really*, Zachary?"

He glances down at his chest. "What, you don't think we should?"

He's trying to get a rise out of me. I'm not going to let him. I tilt my head toward the hospital bed. "The doctors say she's improving."

He stays in the doorway, looking at her. Then, "I'm going to get some food from the cafeteria. Want anything?"

I shake my head.

"You okay, Mom?"

"Hanging in there."

His gaze rests on my laptop. I look at it, too. The video's paused. There's a grainy image, a man frozen, standing in the lobby.

By the time I look back at the doorway, Zachary's gone.

• • •

The latest MRI showed decreased swelling in Mom's brain, and the lacerations on her head are healing. I call HR again the next morning, request another day, get the same reply. *Take all the time you need.* They're probably eyeing my sick leave balance. Over a decade of accumulated leave. I can't even remember the last time I took a sick day.

I move on to the security footage from the parking lot, start running traces on every license plate that's visible to the cameras.

Midmorning, Mom wakes up. She's groggy, disoriented. But she recognizes me. And that leaves me shaky with relief. I can't imagine what it would be like if she didn't know who I was.

"Stephanie," she rasps.

I reach for her hand and squeeze it. "Mom."

I can barely feel the pressure when she squeezes back. Tears sting my eyes. She's always seemed so strong to me, so invincible. But she's smiling.

"How are you feeling?"

"I've been better."

"You had quite a fall."

Her eyes search mine. A cart rumbles down the hallway, the scent of boiled vegetables in its wake.

I should wait to ask, but I can't. "Mom, what happened on those stairs?"

"I fell."

"Is that what you heard the doctors say? Do you actually remember falling?"

She blinks.

My fingers tighten on her hand. "Mom—was anyone else in that stairwell with you?"

"Anyone . . . ?"

"Did someone push you?"

She blinks again. "I fell, Stephanie."

"If there was someone there, if something happened—"

"I tripped, and I fell." I'm scaring her. I know I shouldn't be pressing her on this right now. I know I should be letting her rest.

"Okay, Mom. Get some sleep," I whisper, reluctantly. I can continue this later. "We need you better. *Soon*."

But it hurts to look at her, to see how frail she is, how *broken*.

I turn my attention back to my laptop, switch back to the footage from the lobby camera. I zero in on the time of the accident. I've watched this endless times now. A woman with wild red curls bursts into the lobby from the stairwell, says something to the front desk attendant, who picks up the phone. The woman turns and races back into the stairwell, attracting stares from three other people in the lobby, and moments later the front desk attendant follows her. Six minutes pass before paramedics push into view.

I rewind to the moments before the woman enters into the lobby, before the 911 call was placed. I focus on the face of each and every person who entered that lobby. The young guy in running clothes, wiping sweat from his brow. The woman with grocery bags on each arm. The man in the suit, a briefcase at his side. I pause the footage, zoom in, repeat. Desperate for something, anything.

I hear a knock at the door and look up. It's open a crack, and Scott's hovering in the doorway.

"Can I come in?" he asks.

"Of course." I feel almost dizzy with emotion. Wistfulness, I guess. Like he *should* be here. Like if life had unfolded differently, if I hadn't destroyed things between us, he'd be here by my side, going through this with me, going through *life* with me.

He slumps into the empty chair beside me and frowns when he catches sight of the laptop.

I look down at the screen. It's paused on a grainy close-up of a man's face. The guy in the suit. He has thick dark hair and wide-set eyes. There's nothing remotely familiar about him. "Security footage."

"Of?"

"Mom's condo building."

Scott shakes his head. "How's she doing?"

"Getting better."

"Good." His gaze drifts back to my laptop. "It was a terrible accident," he says. I'd swear he emphasizes the word *accident*.

"It wasn't an accident," I say quietly, impulsively. I'm surprised by how defensive I sound. But I mean it. I know it now, with every fiber of my being. This was intentional.

Scott nods thoughtfully, but I can see that he doesn't believe me. "I'll tell the office you need more time."

And I know him so well, I hear what he really means. *You're unstable. You shouldn't be at work.*

The words make me angry, but they fill me with doubt, too. What if I *am* being crazy? What if it *was* just an accident? Suspicious timing, sure, but an accident nonetheless. Old people lose their balance and fall. What's wrong with me? Why can't I accept that?

Why am I being so paranoid? *What if this is all in my head?*

"I'm fine," I say, as much to myself as to him.

He nods again, but gets to his feet immediately. "I better be going. Just wanted to see how she's doing. And how *you're* doing."

His gaze rests on me. So kind, so concerned. God, I wish he was still in my life.

He lays a hand on my shoulder, leans in close and kisses my cheek. "Remember: I'm here for you, Steph."

His kindness sends a shiver running through me. I can't find the words to respond.

And then he's gone.

I squeeze my eyes shut, fighting tears.

He doesn't believe me, but he doesn't have to. I'm not paranoid. This isn't in my head.

Halliday's behind this. It's too much of a coincidence, otherwise. Mom knew the truth about Halliday. I *told* her the truth. And this is what happened to her. Was it a warning? *Be quiet—or else?* If he's willing to go after my mother, why wouldn't he go after my son?

I swipe my tears away, fast-forward to the moment that woman bursts into the lobby. Then slow it to one-quarter speed.

Three people at the mailboxes, one at the front desk, two near the revolving doors, on their way in. All of them stop and stare at the commotion. A man and a woman at the mailboxes exchange a few words. Over on the left side of the screen, almost off camera, the elevator door opens. A man in a dark cap walks off, head bowed, straight out to the revolving doors. Doesn't look up, doesn't look around, doesn't pay any attention to what's going on at the desk. Just disappears from the screen.

I rewind, watch it again, my eyes only on him this time. I can feel my pulse starting to race.

I close that footage and open up the other, the shot of the parking lot. I wind the tape to the same time stamp. Watch the man in the dark cap exit the lobby, head still bowed. Watch him walk through the lot, to a small car, a hatchback, and slide inside, never looking up, his face never visible. A minute later, the hatchback drives out of view.

I rewind, watch again. I pause the tape just as the hatchback is about to disappear from sight.

It's not white or black, something in between. Virginia plates, but I can't make out the characters.

I stare at the grainy image, commit it to memory.

I need to find this car. And I need to find this man.

. . .

I finally have a lead. I finally have *something*.

I can't see the man's face, but still, it's something. It's proof that I'm not paranoid. It's proof that someone was there when Mom fell. Someone saw her fall. *Someone pushed her.*

I close the laptop, drop it into my bag. Stand up, stretch.

Coffee. I'm going to head down to the cafeteria, grab a cup of coffee.

I stoop and kiss her forehead. "Be back in a minute." She doesn't stir.

I'm nearing the end of the corridor when a man approaches me. Average height, average weight. Dirty blond hair. His gaze is locked on me and suddenly my skin starts to crawl, that sixth sense that something isn't right.

His sleeves are rolled up to his elbows. There's a tattoo there, on his forearm. I see the design, and my heart stutters.

Two knives, crossed in an X.

Chapter 26

My heart is pounding. Did I really just see that?

I stop and turn. He's just stepped into an open elevator. He's facing me, still staring directly at me. The elevator door is starting to close. And just before he's gone from my sight entirely, I'm certain his lips quirk in a smile.

Move, Steph.

I bolt to the elevator, punch the button hard, three times. But it's gone, headed down. I'm too late.

I step back and watch the light. *4. 3. 2.* It stops at two.

I run for the stairwell. Slam open the door, jog down the stairs, two at a time. Third floor, then the second, and I push my way out into the corridor.

I don't see him anywhere.

I check the numbers above the elevator. It's below me, on the first floor now.

Back into the stairwell, down the last flight. Push my way out into the lobby, look around.

I lost him.

"Mom?" Zachary's voice. I spin around. He's there, behind me, frowning. "Mom?"

I try to bring the man's face back into my mind. I'd never seen him before; I'm sure of that. But what did he look like? The placement of his eyes, the shape of his nose, anything.

I can't. All I can picture is that damned tattoo.

I rake my fingers through my hair, frustrated. Was it really the same tattoo, the one on Torrino's man? Or was my mind playing tricks on me?

But that smirk, the one on his face just as the elevator closed. The way he looked at me . . .

"Mom." Zachary's voice, sharper. "What's going on?"

Unless it was in my head. Stress and exhaustion—it's a dangerous combination. *What if I'm losing it?*

I'd been so sure it was Halliday. But that tattoo . . . And if it's the mob, *why now?*

I look at my son, the question in his eyes. *What's going on, Mom?* What am I supposed to tell him? How can I possibly explain it, when I don't understand it myself?

Chapter 27

The penthouse apartment is on the Potomac, with floor-to-ceiling windows that offer sweeping views of the city. It's sleekly furnished, whites and grays, minimalist style. There's a black leather messenger bag hanging on a coat rack by the door. From deep inside it, a rhythmic buzzing.

Wes walks over to the bag. He's lean, with deeply tanned skin, and a thick head of hair that's starting to turn silver in a way that makes him look distinguished. He unzips the front compartment, pulls out a smartphone, holds it to his ear. "Yes."

"It's me."

He walks back into the living room. Sits down on the couch, slowly.

"It's falling apart." There's panic in the voice on the other end of the line.

"It's under control."

"But—"

"It's *under control.*" He looks at the chessboard in front of him, on the coffee table, midway through a game. Of course, the game wasn't actually played *here.* But the board looks exactly the same as the one that *was* played, the one that's paused. He knows they're stuck. He knows they're thinking of their next moves. He likes being able to see what they're considering. He likes being in their heads.

"I don't understand."

Wes leans back in the couch, stretches out his legs, crosses his feet at the ankles, resting on the coffee table. A smile curves his lips. "We're adapting."

"Adapting." It's a statement, not a question.

"We've done it before, and look where we are today."

"But now there's even more at stake—"

Wes pulls his feet down, sits up straight, his face now serious. "And the payoff will be even greater. We're close now. *So* close. And we *will* succeed."

Silence stretches between them.

"What if she finds out the truth?" the caller demands.

The smile creeps back to Wes's face. He relaxes back into the couch. Eyes the board once again. She thinks the boy will move the rook. The boy doesn't want to sacrifice it. Neither one of them sees the best move on the board. "The *truth*, my friend, is extremely complicated."

Chapter 28

I wake up from a sleep so deep and dreamless I could have been drugged, and I have a few blissful moments of peace before everything comes flooding back. Mom. The gun. The man with the tattoo.

I reach over to my bedside table, fumble for my phone. No messages, no missed calls. Nothing happened to Mom overnight. Relieved, I dial the hospital just the same, just to check. She's awake and alert, the nurse assures me. Continuing to improve.

Zachary's already in the kitchen when I come downstairs. He has a box of cereal in his hand, that protein-packed one that tastes like cardboard.

"Morning, honey," I say.

"Morning." He walks over to the fridge, pulls out the jug of milk. Slops some into his cereal bowl, carries it to the table.

When my coffee's done brewing, I take the mug and sit down at the table across from him. He doesn't look up at me. He's more sullen than usual this morning. "What's wrong?"

He shrugs, takes another bite.

"Zachary?"

"Shouldn't I be asking *you* that question?"

"Meaning?"

"Something's going on, Mom. Your mind is elsewhere. And these questions you've been asking me . . . I have a right to know."

I look down at my coffee, fold my hands around the mug. How much should I say? Probably nothing.

"It's an email, isn't it? To that group you mentioned. Freedom whatever." He keeps his eyes on me as he chews.

I answer carefully. "That's part of it."

"From our IP address."

He's trying to piece things together. Using all the questions I've asked him, all the fragments of information. He's doing exactly what an investigator would do.

"Let it go," I say.

A hint of triumph lights his eyes. He knows he's right. "And it's supposed to look like it's from me."

A vague sense of fear settles down around me. I don't want him involved in this. It's too dangerous. If they've hurt Mom, they could hurt him. *"Let it go."*

"But obviously it's not," he persists. "So . . . who's it from?"

"Zachary, this isn't a game."

"I get that."

"This is serious."

"It's about *me,* isn't it? I think I know that."

His tone chills me. But he's right, isn't he? He's almost an adult. And he's involved in this, whether I want him to be or not.

"You asked me about a *gun,* Mom. I have a right to know what's going on."

Does he? I take a ragged breath.

He doesn't. Not if it means dragging him in deeper. I need to keep him out of it, as much as I can. I need to keep him safe.

My silence seems to encourage him. He dumps more cereal into his bowl and says, "I can look into this alone, or we can do it together. It's up to you."

I'm not going to be able to stop him, am I? *Should* I?

I picture Mom, in that hospital bed, the tangle of tubes, the machines beeping. Of course I should stop him. This is dangerous.

But it's dangerous one way or another, isn't it?

And he knows computers. Maybe he'd actually be able to help. Maybe he could figure out who sent the message. Find proof that Torrino's behind this, or Halliday, or whoever it is.

Find proof that Mom's fall wasn't an accident.

Proof that we can use to stop whoever is doing this to us.

I look away, out into the living room. I catch sight of the chessboard, and I feel that familiar, swelling sense of panic growing like a cancer between us. He's almost gone. What if our relationship never improves? *What if I run out of time?*

I look back at my son. His eyes have that round look again, like he's wary, on the verge of being hurt, and in them I can see that trusting little boy I miss so much.

"Together," I say quietly, and I regret the words as soon as I've said them.

Zachary's thrilled to be helpful. He spends the morning in front of his computer screen, visiting encrypted forums, searching the deep web. I'm terrified Scott will find out, that Zachary's digging himself further into a hole—and that I'm the one who handed him a shovel—but he's convinced he's covering his tracks.

I hover nearby, watching, thinking, trying to process everything. Someone broke into our home, sent that email: *I have access to targets.* Planted a gun. Someone who was able to get in without tripping our alarm. Someone who didn't leave behind a single print.

And someone pushed Mom down those stairs.

Who is it?

God, how I wish I had someone on my side right now. A partner to deal with this. In my mind I see Scott. But I can't turn to him. Can't risk what might happen to Zachary if I tell him the truth, if he doesn't believe me. I can figure it out myself. I have to.

This has got to have something to do with Halliday. Zachary just came into his life, after all these years. *Visited* him. It must have turned Halliday's life upside down. He'd have reason to want to threaten me, to warn me into silence. And Mom knew the truth about him, shared some of it with Zachary. Now she's hurt.

But framing Zachary? What sense does that make? If it came out that his biological son was involved in a terrorist plot, it would sink his political career. Not to mention if Halliday's own role in setting up his son ever came to light, or, worse, his involvement in Mom's fall. Why risk it?

Torrino? I'd swear I glimpsed that tattoo at the hospital, the same one I saw on Torrino's man, all those years before. Torrino is still in prison, will be for at least another decade. He has men he can call on for his dirty work, ones who know about breaking and entering, removing prints, carrying out hits. But why come after me now, after all these years?

And right as Halliday's back in our life? Surely it's too much of a coincidence.

Unless . . .

Unless it's *not* a coincidence.

Unless Torrino's involvement has something to do with Halliday.

I flash back to those words my training agent spoke, my first week on the job. *Damned crooked politicians. Mob pays 'em off. That senator, Halliday—he's the worst.*

Could they be somehow linked?

Chicago's cleaner now. They've never tied Halliday to any wrongdoing. But what if it's true? What if the mob still considers Halliday *theirs,* and they're the ones who see us as a threat?

The thought makes sense. Perfect sense, really. Torrino wants Halliday in a position of power. And I'm a threat to that. I'm a threat to Halliday's career, and to his power, and to his ability to protect Torrino.

It feels like all the pieces are falling into place.

And the picture that's appearing is even more frightening than I thought.

Chapter 29

Zachary's focused on the screen in front of him, scowling, concentrating. I watch him. "Any luck?" I finally ask.

He shakes his head, eyes still on the screen. "Nope."

"Progress?"

"A bit." He glances up at me, shrugs. "I'm figuring out these forums. Where they communicate, you know."

"Anything interesting?"

"It's all encrypted." He looks like he's about to say more, but stops.

"And?" I prompt.

"Well, there's a user . . ." A shadow crosses his face. Confusion, I think. Or maybe concern? "He has my name."

"Your name?"

"ZacharyMaddox345."

Same as the email address. "What's he posted?"

"Nothing. His communications are all private. Direct messages, user-to-user. But I'm trying to hack in."

I feel a quiver of trepidation, but I do my best to keep my face a mask. "Okay."

I slip back out of the kitchen, let him concentrate. Pace the house, restless, and finally grab a broom. Sweep the hardwood floors, wash them, vacuum the carpets and rugs. My gaze keeps drifting over to Zachary, watching him work, watching the fierce concentration on his face. *ZacharyMaddox345*. I'm growing increasingly anxious.

Hours later, he's still at it. I call the hospital, speak with Mom. To my relief, she's starting to sound more like herself—her voice less raspy, more upbeat. I ask her again about her fall, if she's sure she was alone in that stairwell. "I'm sure, Stephanie," she answers firmly, annoyed with me. "No one pushed me. You know what a klutz I am!"

I change into workout clothes, get on the treadmill, start running. Three miles, then four. Trying to clear my head.

I stare at the chessboard as I run. He'll move his rook, I'll take it. Then he'll move his queen, even though he'll lose that, too. Protect the king, at all costs. Even if it means sacrificing the queen.

Unless I'm missing something. Unless there's a move I can't see, can't anticipate. Panic flares again in my chest.

Seven miles, eight. At mile eleven, I hear Zachary's voice. "Mom?" he calls. "I think I found something."

I turn off the belt, hop off. Blot sweat from my face with a towel, then sling it over my shoulder as I walk to the table. I come up behind him, look over his shoulder. It's a black screen, green writing, almost like it's from another decade.

"What'd you find?"

"A file. It was sent to that user. ZacharyMaddox345. Haven't opened it yet."

He double-clicks and a file opens up. It looks like a PowerPoint presentation. The first slide is a red image on a black background. Looks almost like a skull, with three letters.

FSM.

Freedom Solidarity Movement. It must be.

He clicks. The next slide is black, too. No image, just a line of text, in the same red color.

The day is near.

He clicks again, and I feel this overpowering urge to tell him to stop, to tell him I don't want to see what's next.

Your assignment: Target #2.

Another click. Photos, five of them, one in the center and four surrounding it. A man, leaving his house, wearing a suit. A shot of him in running clothes, on a tree-lined street. Another of him opening a car door. And a fourth in front of an office building.

Reluctantly, my eyes settle on the center photo. This one is a close-up, the same one that graces the lobby of the building where I work.

I take a sharp breath.

It's J. J. Lee. It's the director of the FBI.

Chapter 30

"Holy shit," Zachary murmurs, and I don't chide him, because the exact same thought is running through my own mind.

These are surveillance photos. Of a *target. Target #2*. In the possession of an extremist group that wants to attack government officials.

This is a plot. A plot to attack—to kill—the director of the FBI.

I feel like I can't think straight, like fury is keeping my brain from working the way it should. "Who sent this?"

He narrows his eyes at the screen. "Username DTaylor."

DTaylor. Dylan Taylor.

"When?"

"Yesterday. Yesterday morning." His voice is thick with fear.

"Who else has seen it? Can you tell?"

"I don't know. It was a private message. Maybe no one?"

"But you found it."

"I hacked in."

Someone else could do that, too. The Bureau could do that, *easily*. Then what?

If the Bureau finds these slides, Zachary will be arrested. There's no way he wouldn't be. Whoever's trying to make it look like he's part of this group, like he's part of a plot, they have more on him.

There's a pounding in my brain, in my ears. I study the computer screen, the four surveillance shots of Director Lee, the headshot. *Target #2.* This would get Zachary sent to jail, no question about it.

"Mom? What do we do?"

It might not be a real threat. If it's fabricated evidence, it could be a fabricated plot. And if not, surely Scott's squad is already on it, running it down.

But what if it's real? A real threat against the director of the FBI? There's no way I can possibly keep this to myself.

I need to warn the Bureau.

But I need to find a way to do it *without* getting my son thrown in prison.

It's a moonless night; clouds fill the sky. I hurry down the front steps toward my car, sidestepping a patch of ice, baseball cap pulled low. I'm in black track pants and a sweatshirt, bundled in a long black jacket. I slide into the driver's seat and close the door behind me. No movement around me except a neighbor's cat, slipping through the shadows.

I start the car and head off toward Northeast D.C., my eyes on the rearview mirror, alert for a tail. I take a roundabout route, double back several times, make a couple of stops: gas, coffee. Squarely in surveillance detection mode. But the streets are quiet. No one's following me.

Twenty-six minutes later, I pull up to the curb in front of a 24/7 convenience store, one that I know from previous investigations doesn't keep records, doesn't have cameras. We can never trace prepaid phones from here, prove who bought them. And that's exactly what I need right now.

I turn off the engine and wait for several minutes, watching. No cars, no people. The street is deserted. No one tracked me here; I'm confident about that. Finally I get out of the car, walk into the store.

It's cramped inside, narrow rows stocked with snacks and drinks. I head to the register, eye the phones behind the counter, a selection of prepaid cells.

"That one, please," I say, pointing to the one on the end of the row. I keep the hat brim low, but the clerk doesn't even give me a glance, doesn't care what sort of illicit business I'm involved with. Just rings up the phone, takes my cash, hands me the phone. And I know from experience that employees here don't trust the cops, don't say much when we come around. This guy won't betray me.

I leave the store, get back into my car. Check the streets again— still quiet. I rip open the packaging and set up the phone, alert for any movement around me.

I dial the Bureau's tip line. After two rings, the recorded message begins, instructs me to leave details after the tone.

When I hear the beep, I lower my voice. Leave all the details I know, as quickly as I can. FSM plot. Director of the FBI. Surveillance conducted, weapons obtained.

I press the end button and realize my hands are sweating. I pull the battery from the phone. Then I get out of the car, wedge both pieces under the front tire. My heart is thudding. There's no actionable intelligence on those slides beyond what I just shared. The Bureau now knows everything about the plot that I know.

When I turn the key in the ignition and press down on the gas, there's a satisfying crunch as the tire crushes any proof that it was me who made the call.

I've gone barely half a block when I see headlights coming toward me. A black Suburban, darkly tinted windows. A government vehicle. Law enforcement, maybe. Or just someone who wants to look that way.

I can't see the driver as the Suburban surges past. And I say a silent prayer that he can't see me.

The parking garage is mostly vacant at this hour, just a scattering of cars here and there. The building, too, is hushed. There's a single security guard at the post. She gives me a disinterested nod as I swipe my keycard and goes back to her iPhone.

I pass the pictures on the lobby wall. Director Lee, Deputy Director Jackson. My pace slows as I approach them, like usual. Today my eyes go straight to Lee. I stare at his picture, the dark green eyes, the thick black hair, and it morphs into the one on Zachary's laptop. In my mind's eye I see the four surveillance shots arrayed around it. Shit.

I continue up to my office, walking quickly through the sea of darkened cubicles. Boot up my computer, eye the growing stack of folders on the corner of my desk. I haven't been here in three days, not since Mom fell. It feels like pressure's mounting, like it's only a matter of time until the investigation deepens, until Scott opens an investigation, until Zachary's under a cloud of suspicion so thick it could smother him.

My agents won't start trickling in for another two hours, at least. I spend the time searching for proof that Zachary's not involved, that someone's spinning an elaborate web around him. I read through everything I can find on FSM. Read through the case file again, the one that's still in my desk drawer, at least for now. As soon as Scott lets someone else know about Zachary, about me accessing the FSM file, I'm sure I won't have access to it anymore. I won't have access to anything at all, probably.

I do some digging, as covertly as I can, on Halliday, and Torrino, even though I've done it before, periodically over the years. Looking for anything suspicious, anything that could tie them to that email, those slides, that gun.

Halliday's made a couple of high-profile trips recently—Iowa, New Hampshire—and he's reached out to a number of political action committees. Laying the groundwork for a national political campaign, no doubt. He purchased a second home last year, a beachfront one in Delaware, where his wife spends most of her time. When she's not at charity events, that is—she's on the boards of several philanthropies, mostly children's ones. Gossip columns regularly report the couple is planning to adopt a child, and neither she nor Halliday shut down the rumors. Maybe it boosts his poll numbers.

Torrino earned another commendation for good behavior in prison. Guards are closely monitoring his outgoing messages; no sign of any concealed communications with the outside world.

I'm feeling increasingly desperate. Nothing proves Zachary's just a pawn in a bigger game. I have nothing that would convince Scott, or anyone else, that he didn't send that email, and didn't do whatever else might be pinned on him.

I turn to the coffeemaker on the filing cabinets, pace as I make a cup. My mind drifts back to that call with Scott, the stretch of silence before the line disconnected. Someone was listening. Someone who'd have the power to be on that line.

My eyes shift down to the file cabinets. To one drawer in particular. Then, impulsively, I unlock and pull it open. I scan the files—agents I've investigated over the years, investigations I've overseen since I've been a supervisor—and my gaze settles on the last one, tucked in the back, no label. A plain file, cryptic notes inside.

The Suburban outside the convenience store. The presence on the phone line. What if . . .

Chapter 31

The next thing I know, there's light flooding into the office from the cubicle bullpen, and I have the vague sense that it had been dark, that the light just went on. I lift my head, peer groggily out the windowed door, and there's Parker in the bullpen, giving me a quizzical look. I sit up straight, smooth my hair, do my best to shrug off the remnants of sleep, try to look presentable.

Zachary. I reach for my cellphone. A couple of missed calls from him, a series of texts, increasingly concerned.

You gonna be home soon?

Is everything ok?

Hello? Mom?

I unlock the phone and type out a hasty reply. *Sorry. Fell asleep at my desk. I'm fine.*

I'm not fine, not by a long shot.

I call the hospital, check on Mom. She's doing well; she tells me happily that her doctor even mentioned the possibility of a discharge soon, with outpatient rehab. I'm just hanging up when I see Scott walking through the bullpen, toward my office. I open the door before he can knock, greet him.

"Talk to me, Steph," he urges. He doesn't sit down.

I can feel his eyes on me, waiting for me to say something. Time's running out and we both know it.

"I wish you'd tell me what's going on." He's annoyed.

I close the door, turn back to him. But not before I see that Parker is watching us from his cubicle. "I can't. Not yet," I tell Scott.

He frowns. "First you say Zachary's being set up. Then you insist your mom's fall wasn't an accident. . . ." He shrugs, helplessly, like he's completely confused. And a little angry, too.

"I'll prove it," I promise softly.

He stares at me a moment, then turns away, looks out the window, out at my agents. I watch him, see the frustration in the way he holds his shoulders. In the bullpen, Garcia and Wayne are getting to their feet, heading out on their coffee run.

"Steph . . . it's going to get worse for Zachary, you know," he finally says.

My heart starts to pound. "Why?"

"The plot. It's real, I think."

He turns toward me, away from the window. I see the unhappiness in his eyes. And I suddenly remember the day we broke up, the hug he gave Zachary before he left our home. *See you later, champ.* "Someone else reported a threat."

"Yeah?" I keep my expression blank. He knows me so well. I can't afford a misstep now.

"Yeah. Didn't believe it, before. Source seemed like the type just looking for a big payday, hoping reporting a threat would earn him one."

I nod, because I don't trust my voice to work.

"Steph—this is enough to get Lee and Jackson involved. They're going to be pushing for open investigations on FSM."

Oh God. What have I done? Trying to do the right thing just

made things a hell of a lot worse for my son. "Just give me some time. Please, Scott."

"Time's running out. Just talk to me, Steph," he urges, but he's moved toward the door, at least. "We can figure this out."

Frustration gives way to anger. An open investigation on Zachary. What will happen then? What else will they uncover? I need Scott out of here.

I think of the presence on the phone line, and the black Suburban. In my mind's eye I see Zachary, in prison. I open the office door.

"You're never going to trust anyone, are you?" he says as he brushes past me.

Around noon, I pick up the phone and dial Scott. I'm going to ask, one last time, for him to delay opening an investigation. I'm going to ask for just a little more time.

He doesn't answer, the call goes to voicemail. I try his cell; still nothing. I repeat the process after an hour, then again after two. Now I'm starting to worry. What if he's already done it? What if he's avoiding my calls? I grab my things and head out.

"Everything okay, boss?" Wayne asks, as I make my way through the bullpen. There's an open bag of Cheetos in front of him. His fingers are stained orange.

"Is it your mom?" Parker chimes in.

"She's doing much better," I tell them.

"That's great," Parker says enthusiastically.

"Are *you* okay?" Garcia wants to know.

"Of course I am," I snap. Flint and McIntosh exchange a concerned glance. Great. Now my agents are worried about me, too, just like Scott. Now they're watching me extra closely. Just what I need.

Fifteen minutes later I'm at the Washington Field Office, walking down the hall toward Scott's cubicle.

I round the corner, and at the sight of his cubicle I freeze. There are cardboard boxes on the desk, on the chair. Fear takes hold.

Scott must have heard me, but he doesn't turn, doesn't stop what he's doing. He reaches for a frame on his desk. It's a picture of his kids, three miniature blond versions of himself. He lifts a stack of folders, places them in a different box.

The television in the corner of his cubicle is on. CNN. A round-table of political analysts, all jockeying to give their opinions. But the sound is muted; their efforts seem futile.

"What's happening?" I manage to force out.

He doesn't turn, doesn't answer. A stapler goes into the box. A pair of scissors. The news commentators disappear from the television screen, and a shot of a political rally takes their place.

"Scott?"

"I'm being transferred."

My brain struggles to make sense of this. There must be an understaffed squad in the field office. One that's in need of a senior agent. Because there's no other reason—

"To Omaha. Effective immediately."

"*What?*" Scott's one of those guys who isn't supposed to go anywhere. Someone who's served his time moving around the country, who's earned the opportunity to stay in one place, who made it clear he intended to do just that. He has a house here. His wife's career is here, his kids are in school. His whole life is here.

He's finally looking at me, that implacable expression on his face. One I remember from that final argument we had, all those years before. *I can't be with someone who won't open up to me, Steph. Who won't trust me.*

"I don't understand," I say, even though deep down, I do.

I can see that he blames me. He knows this is my fault, even if he doesn't understand how, or why.

I glance away. On the TV, the camera's zoomed in. It's Halliday. He's yelling about something, his face pinched, furious.

"We can fight this," I tell Scott quietly. "Together."

He stills, but doesn't turn.

"I'll tell you everything," I bargain.

He shakes his head. "I don't know what you got yourself into. Who's responsible for this. But I have kids to think about, too."

He lifts the box, steps past me, conversation over. On the television screen, Halliday's smiling now. Relaxed, happy. Like a totally different person.

"Get out of here, Steph."

Chapter 32

I make it back to headquarters blindly, by rote. As I walk into the office, the bullpen goes quiet. A few of my agents pretend to be working; Parker glances in my direction and then is suddenly engrossed by something on his computer screen. Others don't hide their curiosity—Garcia leans back in her chair and watches me, unabashedly.

I get to my desk and boot up my computer, and minutes later there's a knock on my door. Garcia opens it before I say a word, steps inside. She's holding a file folder at her side.

"What do you need, Garcia?" I snap.

"It's about this case. . . ."

"Which?" She's working two at the moment. Or is it three?

"Pitowski. You know, the mortgage fraud one?"

"Right. What about it?"

She flops down into the chair across from my desk, and my mind flashes back to Hanson, the day this all started. *I have a family. A wife, kids. A mortgage.*

Then, just as quickly, my thoughts turn to Scott. What's going to happen to *his* mortgage? His house? His family?

"Boss?"

I blink. Garcia's waiting for me to respond. I didn't hear a word she'd said. I have no idea what she asked me.

"So do you think I should talk to the DA?" she repeats, slowly.

"Do it."

She opens her mouth to say something else, but thankfully shuts it again, gets to her feet.

When the door closes behind her, I face my computer screen. *Dylan Taylor.* Taylor is connected to this, somehow.

I run a background check, jot down notes. Dylan's a waiter, employed by a company that provides surge staffing for special events, mostly at hotels. His mother died of throat cancer when he was sixteen; his father two years later, in a skiing accident. He graduated from the best high school in the area, near the bottom of his class; no college. No criminal record. Nothing noteworthy.

I spend the next hour searching for anything I can find on the parents, Bruce and Anne Taylor. They were both physicians, seemed to live a quiet existence. I can't find any red flags. But I'm not willing to give up. I have an address, the home where they used to live, where Dylan grew up. And since that's about all I have, that's where I go.

The house is a two-story colonial in a middle-class neighborhood, on the end of a cul-de-sac, flanked by large bare oak trees. There are blue shutters on all the windows, a long, shaded porch. A minivan sits in the driveway; a new family's living there, one that probably never knew the Taylors. But the neighbors—they might have.

I park on the street and walk up the steps to the front porch of the home next door. There are two white Adirondack chairs on one side of the porch, a swing on the other. Large flowerpots are on either side of the door; the soil is dry, the flowers long wilted. I ring the doorbell, and I hear footsteps a few seconds later. The woman standing there is in her sixties, probably. She's staring at me, frowning, wearing a drab gray dress and a bright red sweater.

"Steph Maddox, FBI." I flash my badge. "I'm hoping I can talk to you about some former neighbors of yours. Bruce and Anne Taylor."

Some sort of emotion passes across her face. Suspicion? Sadness?

"Did you know them?" I press, when she doesn't answer.

"Quite well." She blinks, touches the cross at her throat. "We lived next door to each other for twenty years."

"So you knew their son?"

"Dylan? Of course." Her body tenses. "Is Dylan in trouble?"

I answer her question with another. "What can you tell me about him?"

She stares at me, touching the little silver cross again. After a moment, she says, "He's a good kid. *Was* a good kid, at least, when I knew him, poor thing. I tried to keep up with him after Bruce passed. Anne would have wanted it, you know? But I lost track of him."

"Did you know him to be involved with anything illegal?"

"Dylan? No. He wasn't like that."

"No drugs, anything like that?"

"No."

"Didn't fall in with the wrong crowd?"

"No. Why? Is he in some sort of trouble?"

"Anyone who might have wanted to get back at him for anything?"

Surprise flares in her eyes. "I can't imagine that." She says it firmly, daring me to contradict her.

I nod. I hesitate, because I'm not sure how to ask the next questions, how to get the answers I have to have. "Do you know if the family spent any time in Chicago?"

"Chicago? Not that I'm aware of."

"Any connections to Congress?"

Confusion clouds her features.

"Did Dylan ever work on the Hill, intern there, anything like that?"

"I don't think so. But Anne and Bruce did, back in the day. That's where they met."

"Do you know who they worked for?"

"I have no idea."

Her voice has gone cold. She's shutting down. More questions at this point seem futile. "I appreciate your time, Ms. . . . ."

"O'Connell. Mary O'Connell."

"Ms. O'Connell." I reach for a business card, hand it to her. "Call me if you think of anything else, okay?"

She looks down at the card, then back at me. "He's a good kid, Agent Maddox."

So's my Zachary. "Thanks for your time."

In the car, I thump the steering wheel, frustrated. I didn't learn anything useful. There's no reason to think Dylan has a connection to those men from my past. Or to Zachary. *How does he fit in?*

None of this makes sense. And I don't know what to do next. Maybe it's time to confront Torrino. But is that the right move? Would I risk spooking him into making things even worse for Zachary?

And what if I'm wrong? What if someone else is pulling these strings?

I'm halfway back to the office when my phone trills. I reach for it, look at the screen. *Zachary.* "Hi, honey."

"Mom?" His voice sounds unsteady and my heart quickens.

"What is it, honey?"

"I did some more digging into that forum. The encrypted one."

"And?"

"Mom—we need to talk."

Chapter 33

We meet at a park on the banks of the Potomac, a large expanse of land with a brightly colored playground, a handful of soccer and baseball fields, a popular wooded walking trail. I haven't been here in years, but it's a place I once knew well. I used to bring Zachary to the playground when he was young, back when the equipment was still gray. Soccer after that, and Little League, all those Saturday morning games. Then the games switched to evenings, and my memories of the park taper off.

Today it's nearly empty. There's a toddler on the playground, bundled in a thick red coat. His mother's hovering near, with a younger sibling wrapped in a carrier close to her chest. The fields are deserted, a far cry from the Saturday morning bustle I remember.

The park's an easy place to spot a tail; that's why I picked it, when Zachary said we needed to talk. But no one's followed me here today. No one's listening.

I sit on a bench overlooking the playground and watch the toddler climb the ladder to the slide, very carefully, then struggle to seat himself at the top. He sits, then freezes. His mother moves around to the bottom of the slide, motions for him to let go, slide down.

The crunch of footsteps on dry leaves draws my attention away. Zachary's approaching, hands jammed in his jacket pockets. I'd seen him pull up; the Taurus is the only other car in the lot, besides mine and the minivan that belongs to the family on the slide. There's a look on his face I don't like, one that's stressed, uncertain. He slumps down beside me.

"What'd you find?" I ask.

He stares straight ahead, his jaw working. And a shattering sense of panic runs through me. He was going to look into whether other users had seen the slides. If he's this troubled, that means someone else has seen them.

"Zachary?"

"The users . . . the people on the forum . . ."

"They saw the slides?"

"Yeah, but it's not that."

"What is it, then?"

"The activity . . . the account setups . . ." He trails off again. I've never seen him look so uncomfortable. He's scaring me.

"What, Zachary?"

"I don't think they're real people."

Whatever I expected, it wasn't this.

"I mean, some of them are. But some of them . . . I think they're bots."

"Bots," I repeat. Fake users. My mind is spinning, failing to make sense of this.

"Hundreds of them." He shakes his head. He looks confused, and scared.

And how could he not be?

Bots. *Hundreds of them.*

I blink at the playground, realize the mom and her kids are gone.

Someone created a forum full of fake users. Someone planted evidence there that makes it look like Zachary's part of a terrorist plot.

"Who would do something like that?" I ask urgently. A rhetorical question, really. "And *why?*"

"I've never seen something like that before," Zachary says. "It's like . . ." He gives his head another shake.

I finish the thought, softly. "It's like something the *Russians* would do."

Chapter 34

That day sticks in my mind; everything about it. It was almost two years ago, in May. The morning started as any other. I was in my office at the Washington Field Office, reviewing reports. My agents were in the bullpen, researching and writing.

All of a sudden, the office was buzzing. There was that charge in the air, the one that runs through the office when something's happened, almost like an electrical current. I saw the chatter between my agents, the excitement on their faces. Something had happened. Something big.

I walked out of my office, into the bullpen. The door to our wing was propped open, and there was commotion in the hall, agents on the move, gathering gear.

"What's going on?" I asked. And then I heard pounding footsteps in the hall, looked up to see two agents run past the door, down the hall.

Ginny Meyer, one of my agents at the time, answered. "Won't even sound real if I say it." She sounded dazed.

I heard the crackle of a radio in the hallway, caught just a smattering of words. "*. . . two dead in the residence. One is a CIA officer. . . .*"

"Were our agents involved?" I asked Meyer.

"Oh yeah."

It was all I needed to hear. Something big had happened. Two were dead, including a CIA officer. There'd be a thorough investigation, no doubt about it. My squad would be involved—we had a mandate to investigate any potential criminal wrongdoing by agents in the field office. And as the squad's supervisory special agent, I'd be leading the charge. I wanted to get ahead of this. I had to be sure our agents acted appropriately, that protocols were followed.

I needed to go to the crime scene and see it for myself.

I arrived a short time later at a row house on a tree-lined residential street in Northwest D.C., one that was now teeming with police cars, marked and unmarked, lights flashing. Uniformed police and plainclothes agents were filing into and out of the residence. Curious neighbors were standing on stoops in nervous huddles, casting anxious glances at the house with the blue door.

I pulled on a raid jacket, *FBI* emblazoned on the back, and hung my badge around my neck. Made my way quickly past the crime tape, through the front door. The row house was a small place, with far too many people inside. I stood in the hall and looked around, tried to evaluate the scene, make sense of it. Two bodies covered in white sheets, one on the floor, another in a chair. A dozen or so bullet casings scattered around the carpet.

I'd heard the basics already, on the way to the crime scene. Three of our agents had been surveilling a counterintelligence target, a CIA officer. The agents heard a shot, entered the residence, found one victim, bound to a chair, deceased; a female, who appeared unarmed; and the target, who was armed. After a brief exchange, the armed man had raised his weapon, and our agents had fired.

I walked deeper into the residence. In the kitchen, two of our agents stood talking to a uniformed officer, who was taking notes.

Both had that stricken look, so familiar in crime scenes. I didn't see the third agent. Or the witness, the female.

I saw an agent I recognized, a supervisor who looked like he knew what was going on, like he might have been one of the early responders. He saw me approach, gave me a tense nod. "Maddox," he said.

"Wood." I gestured toward the kitchen. "Those are the responding agents?"

He glanced in that direction. "Two of them, yeah. Daniels and Kidd."

"Where's the third?"

Wood pointed mutely toward the living room. I followed his hand, toward the couch. From where we stood, I could see the backs of two heads; one male, one female, clearly deep in conversation. "That guy right there. Jackson."

I recognized the name. Counterintelligence agent, Washington Field Office. "And the woman? Is she the witness?"

"Yeah. CIA, apparently."

"What's her story? Why was she here?"

"Wish I knew. Jackson won't let anyone else near her."

The back of my neck was starting to tingle, that sixth sense that something was wrong.

Wood shot me a quick glance, then shrugged. "They're old friends. She's understandably shaken up. I'm sure he's getting more out of her than we could."

That tingle kept coursing through me, growing stronger. *Won't let anyone else near her*. Those words echoed in my brain. That behavior wasn't normal, certainly not under circumstances like this. Standard procedure would have been a debrief, one that involved at least two agents.

I was vaguely aware that Wood had moved on, deeper into the apartment. I walked over to the couch, almost like my legs had a mind of their own. I was there before I thought of what to say. Both looked up as I approached. Jackson wore jeans and a raid jacket, stretched tight across his large frame. His expression was cold, unfriendly.

"Could I speak with you for a moment?" I said to the woman.

It was Jackson who answered. "This is under control, Agent . . ."

"Maddox," I supplied, turning to him. "I'm sure it is." I deliberately turned my attention back to the woman. She was tall and fair, with hair that cascaded over her shoulders in loose waves. "But I'd like to ask you a few questions."

She nodded, ever so slightly. Her eyes were a clear, intense blue.

"Alone," I added, giving Jackson a pointed look.

There was a stretch of silence, of stillness, and then he stood abruptly, not bothering to hide his reluctance, and stalked a short distance away, over to the window.

"Are you okay?" I asked the woman. I could feel him watching us.

"No," she replied softly, honestly. She didn't look away, kept her eyes locked on mine.

"What is it?"

Her lips thinned.

"You can tell me."

She gave her head a shake, a small one.

I leaned forward, lowered my voice. "Whatever it is, you can tell me."

"I can't."

"I'll believe you."

She gave me a searching look, and I thought for a moment she might actually say something. Then I watched her gaze shift up, and her expression close down. I could feel a presence behind me.

"We need to be getting you home," came Jackson's voice.

I ignored him, kept my eyes on the woman. "I will," I told her again. *I will believe you.*

"Let's go," Jackson urged.

The woman held my gaze and I shivered involuntarily. I recognized the haunted look in her eyes. Then she stood. I saw Jackson put his hand firmly on her back, guide her, almost pushing her, toward the door. My eyes focused on the hand, bathed in flashing red and blue lights from the cars outside.

I saw him pause, lean down, whisper something in her ear. She went still. They continued on toward the door, and I couldn't tear my eyes away from the hand, the way it rested on the small of her back, like he knew he was completely in control.

And then just as they reached the door, he turned, ever so slightly, and his eyes went straight to mine, like he could feel me watching him, like he knew I was there.

He smiled at me, and something in his expression sent a chill through me. It was as if he could see through me.

And then I was walking.

Forward, toward her, toward him.

The door opened, and she slipped out. It closed behind her.

I was going after her. I was going to talk to her, make sure she was okay. I had just reached for the doorknob when a hand grabbed my arm.

Squeezed tight, fingers biting into my flesh.

I swung around to face him. "Let her go," Jackson said, and the way he said it, the smugness of his voice, made fear shoot through me, an overwhelming conviction that I was right to worry about her.

A conviction, too, that as of that very moment, she wasn't the only one in danger.

I yanked my arm free. Pulled down the handle, pushed open the door, rushed outside.

But it was too late. She was gone.

Chapter 35

*I*t's like something the Russians would do.

I look at the confusion on my son's face, and instantly I'm shaken by regret. I never should have let him poke around into this. I should have kept him out of it, far away from it all. I should have protected him better. *What have I done?*

"Mom? What does it mean?" he wants to know.

"Don't tell anyone what you found."

"What's going on?"

"I don't know," I say. I turn away, back to the slide, the empty playground. I don't know, not yet, not fully. But it's *him*, isn't it?

"Mom?"

I face Zachary again. I hate this look on his young face, this fear. "I need you to stay out of it now."

"It involves *me*."

"Let me handle it."

"Mom, my *name* was on that forum."

I take another look around the park, my eyes raking the naked trees, the shadows across the park. Could anyone have followed us here, and I didn't see it? Didn't hear it?

"Let's go," I say, standing from the bench.

Zachary hesitates, looks like he's about to protest, and I'm relieved when he doesn't. He falls into step beside me, his long legs keeping pace easily with me. I keep forgetting how tall he's grown.

"It's not fair to keep this from me, Mom."

"I'm doing what's best for you."

The minivan's gone now. It's just our two cars, parked a space apart. "I can help," my son says quietly, when we're at our cars.

I tighten my grip on the door handle. Hesitate, then pull it open. "You can help by staying out of it," I snap, and wince at the ice in my command.

The Russians. *Him.* The man from that deadly row house encounter. Is it really him? My brain's spinning uselessly. What about Halliday? What about Torrino? I thought I had it all figured out. Now I'm completely confused.

Nothing's clearer by the time I park at headquarters, walk into the building. My gaze goes straight to those portraits on the wall. Lee. Jackson. I stop in front of them, and I stare. This time, I focus on the one on the right. Jackson.

And this time, the face I'm staring at morphs into that face from the row house. Agent Jackson, then. Deputy Director Jackson, now.

Without thinking, I turn, get in the elevator. My heart is pounding, my brain churning through information. I step out when the doors open, and when they shut behind me, I realize I'm not on my floor. I'm on another floor. *His* floor. I'd gone straight here, without even realizing it.

I'm looking down the hall, toward his office, when there's movement. A door opens. A cluster of agents appears, dark suits and earpieces, the kind that surrounds someone important, someone powerful. It moves at a brisk pace, a little cloud of protection around a central figure, heading my way.

The agents are coming closer, and I'm frozen in place, like my feet are buried in sand, like I can't move, like I can do nothing but watch.

The cluster parts just enough for me to see the man in the center. *Jackson*. His eyes land on me, like he knew I'd be there. They stay on my face. And I don't pull mine away, don't do anything but stare back.

He's almost to me now. The lead agents in the security detail are even with me, passing me, but my eyes are locked on his, just as they were two years ago, in that row house. I see the expression I remember. Determined. Relentless. The same flash of fear sizzles through me, but this time it's trailed by something else.

Fury.

I'd pulled up his file that day when I reached my office. Studied the photograph, the face that sported a grin, so much different from the hostile face I'd just seen, almost like he was two different people. Read the file; it was clean. Jackson was a counterintelligence agent, focused on Russia. Never disciplined, spotless record, superb reputation.

But something wasn't right. The way he rushed that woman out of the row house, prevented me from talking with her. A man confident of his ability to control a woman, to shape events. And I knew what it was like to be trapped by a man in power, to feel helpless, alone. I couldn't let that go.

I waited for the reports from the shooting to start trickling in, but they didn't. Hours passed, then a day. I tried to track them down, learned they were placed in compartmented channels. Codeword restricted; access I didn't have. I asked my boss for access; he didn't have it, either. Went up another level, to the head of the field office. Still no access. My fear for the woman's safety increased. And my suspicions of Jackson did, too. Something wasn't right.

I called Marta, over at CIA. Described the woman, asked her to tell me who it was. Marta worked Russia, and the incident was clearly related to Russia; she should know. I could tell from the way she went silent when I asked that she did know, but she wouldn't say a word.

I debated what to do. I couldn't stop thinking of the woman. And I couldn't stop thinking of the way Jackson held my arm, the pressure of his hand against my skin, gripping it too hard, trying to silence me.

Finally, I picked up the phone. Called the next supervisor in my chain of command, the deputy director, Glen Barker. I never thought I'd do something like that, but there I was. No other options, if I wanted to know what happened, if I wanted to protect that woman. I requested access to the files, requested access to *her*, and Barker agreed to look into it. Told me to come down to his office in the morning.

I didn't sleep that night. The next morning, I went over to headquarters, arrived at his office. Glen ushered me in and shut the door. "I've got some bad news for you, Maddox," he said as he sat down behind his desk. "I can't get you access to those files. I don't have it myself."

I felt like something was pressing down on my chest, forcing out all the air. He was the deputy director. How did he not have access? "I don't understand," I told him.

He ran a hand through his hair, rumpling it. "I don't have access to everything," he conceded. "Apparently it's an extremely sensitive case."

"The woman. She was terrified. I'm worried about her."

"Of course she was terrified. It was an ugly situation. Look, I asked Director Lee about her. And good news: she's fine."

"She is?" I heard the challenge in my voice.

So did he. He frowned. "I received assurances on that point. She's quite safe."

I waited for him to say more, but he didn't. Something was wrong: every instinct I had was screaming that something was wrong. It didn't make sense that everything was so tightly sealed. Two men were dead, one of them one of us. "Where is she?"

Glen folded his hands on the desk in front of him, played with the wide gleaming band of his wedding ring. "I have no idea."

"Who does?"

He blinked at my tone, too challenging. "Apparently only three people."

"Three people?"

"FBI director, CIA director, and one agent, the one who resettled her. Someone by the name of . . ." He glanced down at a legal pad in front of him. But I knew that he was going to say, even before it came out of his mouth.

". . . Jackson."

Once again, I felt his hand grip my arm, hurting me. His face morphed into Halliday's, the same triumphant look, and I once again could feel *that* hand on my arm, all those years before.

I needed to say something, even though it felt like every fiber of my being was warning me not to. "That agent. Jackson. There's something off about him."

"Off?"

"I don't know. He just. . . . I saw him at the crime scene, and something didn't seem right."

He raised his eyebrows. "Meaning?"

"I think he's hiding something."

"Hiding *what*?"

"I don't know." I felt like an idiot. I knew better than to do this. And helpless, like I never should have jumped in without a clear way out.

"What evidence do you have?"

"None, right now." I didn't have a shred of evidence. Maybe I would, if I could talk to the woman. All I had was my gut feeling. How could I explain that? How could I explain that everything in my past had led me to this conclusion?

Barker leaned back in his chair, steepling his fingers. "Jackson's reputation is spotless, Steph."

"I know."

"What are you saying? You think he's dirty?"

"I don't know, maybe. I just know something isn't right—"

He held up a hand. "You know better than that, Steph. You can't make a charge like that without proof." Anger simmered in his voice. "I'm going to let it slide this time. You have a good reputation, and you're lucky you do." He leaned forward again, hands now folded on the legal pad. "But if you keep throwing around spurious charges, you're not going to have a reputation to protect."

My throat was very dry. I forced myself to swallow. "Yes, sir."

"Jackson's going places, Maddox. He's on the fast track." He gave me a piercing look. "If I were you, I'd let it go."

Chapter 36

The cluster passes, and then all I can see is the backs of heads, the backs of suits. Dizzy, I turn, brace myself against the wall. I see a ladies' room and push inside. I make my way to the bank of sinks and lean on one with both hands, stare at my reflection in the mirror. I think I'm going to vomit.

Jackson could have planted that gun. He'd know how to erase prints, how to bypass the alarm system. He's senior management—enough power to get Scott transferred, to listen in on my calls.

But *why*? Why *now*?

And what about the guy with the tattoo? What about the fact that this is all happening just as Halliday's back in our lives? *None of this makes sense.*

I finally force myself to leave the ladies' room. The hallway's clear now; Jackson and his entourage are gone.

I take a ragged breath, and I start walking toward Jackson's office.

• • •

Two days after my conversation with Deputy Director Barker, big news broke. There had been a massive disruption of Russian sleepers. Twenty-five arrested. The story was plastered on the front page of every newspaper, covered relentlessly on the news networks. And it was all anyone in the Bureau could talk about.

More sensitive details spread like wildfire throughout the Bureau. That Jackson had made it happen, that he was the guy who deserved the credit. And within weeks, he was promoted; a huge promotion, at that. He was named Special Agent in Charge of the Baltimore Field Office. Barker was right; Jackson was going places.

I couldn't stop thinking about him. The look he gave me in that row house. The hand on that woman's back. The terror in her eyes. I couldn't stop worrying about her safety.

One night at O'Neill's, Marta had a few too many. Drink had loosened her tongue in the past, like the time she slipped and told me they'd recruited a new asset, someone high up in the Russian government. "Old guy," she'd confided, her words slurred. "Code name Justice Ranger."

This time I tried to use it to my advantage. Described the woman again, said she was CIA, asked for any information. Marta didn't bite. "I'm not allowed to say."

"You have to tell me," I begged. "Please, we're friends." I was desperate, and I knew Marta had the answers I needed.

"Don't do this, Steph," she warned. She looked me straight in the eye. No loose tongue, no slurred words this time.

"It's important."

Silence ensued. I didn't budge, and neither did she.

"Her name's Vivian Miller," she finally said. She dug out her wallet, pulled out a couple of twenties. "She's been temporarily resettled, out of the country. I can't tell you any more than that." Then she plunked the cash down on the bar and left without another word, and without looking back.

She wouldn't take my call the next day. Wouldn't, for months to come. Things between us were never the same.

But at least I had an answer. A name. I tracked down an address for Vivian Miller. Bethesda. I drove by the house. Vacant, the lawn weedy and overgrown, a little red bicycle with training wheels outside in the grass. It looked eerily similar to the one Zachary had once ridden.

I'd been warned to let this go, but I couldn't. I started to drive past the house regularly. Ran by it sometimes, too. Seven miles, fourteen round-trip. I'd pause on the street in front, peer into the darkened windows, wonder what happened to her.

She was a victim of someone more powerful, and I was in a position where I could have helped her, could have protected her, and I failed. I let her walk out that door and disappear. I let Jackson get away with something, and I still didn't know what it was.

So I kept digging. Every morning, I'd run a search on the Russian sleeper case, see if anything turned up on her, or on him. Months passed, and I couldn't find a thing. Nothing about Vivian Miller. Not a shred of evidence that Jackson had done anything wrong. He was making waves in Baltimore, keeping his name in the news. All the talk around headquarters was that they were eyeing him for senior management ranks.

And then one day, Barker called me down to his office. Wordlessly, he slid a large envelope across the desk toward me. Inside was a single photograph.

"That's her," Barker said. "The woman you've been worried about."

It was an odd shot; she was indoors somewhere, but the background was indistinguishable. Could have been a house, could have been a jail cell, for all I could tell. Vivian Miller wore a placid expression, looking straight at the camera. There was a date stamp at the bottom. Two days ago.

"She's fine," Barker told me.

"Thanks," I said, because I wasn't sure what else to say. Confusion swirled inside me, and I couldn't quite pinpoint why. I slipped the picture back into the envelope, held it tightly in my lap. When I looked back up at him, there was an odd expression on his face.

"Maddox, I'm recommending you for promotion. To head up the Internal Investigations Section at headquarters."

The words made me forget about the envelope in my hands. I almost gasped aloud.

"What?" I realized how ridiculous I sounded. But this was the absolute last thing I expected to hear. I'd been at the Washington Field Office for almost a decade now; had worked my way up to Supervisory Special Agent. I'd been doing good work, but nothing flashy, nothing that had garnered attention from headquarters. Nothing like Chicago. It didn't seem like anyone had noticed.

"I'm on my way out," Barker admitted with a shrug. "Soon. And before I go, I want to promote people who deserve it. You're one of them."

I was getting promoted. To head up a division—albeit a small one—at *headquarters*. After Chicago, after all this time, it was actually happening.

"What do you say, Steph?"

For the first time, I actually thought about what it meant. A leadership role—a real one. I'd be in a position of power; I'd be responsible. There'd be no running this time, if things went sour. Even all these years later, Chicago still felt fresh in my mind. But Zachary was in high school now; in a few short years he'd be off to college.

"Thank you, sir. Thank you so much."

He nodded, no smile. It was at that moment I realized how off his demeanor was, that he looked more troubled than pleased.

The next morning Deputy Director Barker resigned, citing health concerns, and the troubled look made sense. It was the stress of the medical diagnosis, no doubt.

That afternoon, his replacement was named.

Jackson.

I was in my office when the news broke. I stared at his picture on my screen again, this one accompanying a press release on the Bureau's website. There was a folder on my desk, a plain one. Inside, a legal pad, cryptic notes I'd jotted to myself. No labels, no subject, because instinct—and my conversation all those months ago with Barker—told me not to write down his name, not to write down my suspicions, to keep it a secret.

And the picture, the one that Barker had given me. Proof, finally, that Vivian Miller was safe. All this time, she was safe. Maybe my instinct about Jackson had been wrong. I still hadn't found a shred of evidence suggesting any wrongdoing on his part. He was a star in the Bureau, universally respected. And now, his promotion meant he was my boss. The second most powerful individual in the Bureau.

It should have been a red flag, the rapid rise to power. I knew that, deep down. But no one else seemed suspicious. There had to be people who knew details of the case. Dozens of them, probably, across the river at the Agency. If no one else had qualms about him, and if I knew Vivian Miller was fine, why was I still concerned? My worries about her were unhealthy, almost obsessive.

I heard Barker's voice in my head. *If I were you, I'd let it go.*

I closed the folder and held it in my hands. I was finally moving up. Finally making something of my career, after all these years. Did I really want to jeopardize it?

Deliberately, I moved the folder over to the burn bag below my desk, the one for sensitive trash. It could soon be nothing but ash. There would be no trace of my suspicions, no record of them. I let the file hover there, and I willed myself to drop it.

Then, slowly, carefully, I placed it back in the drawer, locked it. I wasn't going to let this go.

I couldn't.

The door to the office suite is oversized, and dark wood, a sharp contrast to the sterile feel of the rest of the building. There's a plaque beside it: OFFICE OF THE DEPUTY DIRECTOR. I stand in front and tell myself what I'm planning on doing is insanity. Then I open it and step inside.

The anteroom is richly furnished. There's a heavy, ornate secretary's desk, front and center. Wide windows behind it overlook the city below. Off to the left, there's a waiting area: two stiff red couches opposite each other, a low table in between, a Persian rug underneath. And another door beyond that: the deputy director's private office.

The dark-haired woman behind the desk glances up. "Can I help you?"

"I'm here for a meeting with Deputy Director Jackson."

She frowns, glances down at a calendar in front of her, then back up at me. "Agent Maddox, right?"

"That's right."

"I'm sorry, I don't see you on his schedule."

"Just ran into him in the hall. He told me to come up." The lie tastes bitter. I fight to keep it from reaching my eyes.

The frown deepens. "Well, I'm afraid he was just on his way out. He's not expected back anytime soon. . . ."

"He asked me to wait for him in his office."

She looks uncertain. I smile and start walking to the door to his private office. I wait for her to say something, to stop me. I'll need to turn, act indignant. I'm a senior manager, after all. But she doesn't say a word. I open the door and step inside, close it behind me. And then I exhale a breath I didn't know I was holding. My heart is hammering.

I'm in. I stand still, looking around, taking in my surroundings. It's a huge office, ostentatiously big, a row of windows along one wall, a glorious view. I can see the National Mall, the top of the Capitol dome. There's a large desk in the center of the room, a black leather couch and two chairs opposite it. Tall bookcases flanking one wall, filing cabinets along the other. Framed diplomas and awards cover nearly every inch of available wall space.

I head first for the filing cabinets. I open one drawer, look through the file names, the tabs at the top, searching for anything that might mention Zachary. Nothing. I close that drawer quietly, open another, repeat the process. I'm moving as fast as I can, because I don't know when he'll be back. My ears are straining for any sound from the anteroom. My heart is pounding. I don't know what will happen if he finds me rifling through his files.

Next I go to his desk. I start with the lowest drawer, open it, look through the contents. A raid jacket, an empty holster. Repeat with the second drawer. Files, none related to Zachary. Loose papers, nothing of interest. Then the top one, a small drawer. A stapler, a pair of scissors, a box of business cards. This is a stupid, stupid idea. It's not like he's going to be keeping written records of illicit activity in his office.

Or maybe I'm wrong. Maybe I'm searching through the deputy director's office because what happened to me as an intern permanently scarred my judgment.

There's only one drawer left, the wide one just under the surface of the desk, the kind that's usually cluttered with pens and paper clips and rubber bands.

I pull it open. And just as I do, I hear footsteps. I slam it shut again. Heart thudding, I dart for the chair, slide into it just as the office door opens.

It's the dark-haired assistant. Her expression is wary. Suspicious.

"Yes?" I say, my voice even.

"The deputy director called. I told him you were here waiting."

"And?" I say serenely.

"He said he won't be back anytime soon. That you shouldn't wait."

I nod and stand, because I know there's no way she'll leave me alone in the office this time.

"And he asked me to pass along a message." She crosses her arms in front of her chest. "He said *you should have let it go.*"

Chapter 37

The restaurant is quiet; it's always quiet at this hour. Lunchtime is when it's busiest, politicians hashing out backroom deals, lobbyists wooing congressmen over steaks and booze. The lighting is low, the tables all topped with crisp white cloth. Waiters in white shirts and black ties move soundlessly around, efficient and discreet, materializing only to refill glasses and deliver and clear plates.

Tucked away in a corner booth in the back, set far from wandering eyes and curious ears, Wes sips a glass of bourbon, neat, and waits. He's in a shirt and slacks, no tie. Attracted a few stares on the way in, but he's used to it by now.

He glances at his watch, and moments later Jackson slides into the booth across from him. The newcomer doesn't say a word. Picks up the menu and opens it, focuses his attention on that.

Wes takes another slow sip of bourbon and watches him, waits for him to look up. When it doesn't happen, he speaks. "Did you do it?"

Jackson keeps his eyes on the menu. Finally he closes it, sets it down on the table. Looks at Wes, but says nothing.

The waiter appears out of nowhere. "Can I get you anything, sir?"

"No, thank you," Jackson replies. He shifts his gaze to Wes. "I'm not staying long."

Wes's face remains impassive. The waiter nods and disappears, and the two men at the table continue to watch each other.

"Did you do it?" Wes asks again.

"Yes." Jackson's jaw tightens.

"Any trouble?"

"None."

"Good." Wes nods. He lifts the glass to his lips, tilts it back, doesn't take his eyes off Jackson.

Jackson leans forward, lowers his voice. "She's threatening the whole operation."

Wes slowly places the empty glass back on the table in front of him. "I told you, it's under control."

Jackson's eyes flash. "We should have chosen the other option."

"That would have been a mistake. We needed her."

"It could've been an *accident*."

The two men glare at each other in silence.

"There'd have been an investigation," Wes finally says. "A job like hers? They'd look into everything she was working on."

"We could have sanitized everything."

"What if we missed something? She's done too much digging. Left too much of a trail."

Jackson stares at him, his jaw clenched tight.

"Besides. This way we've got someone on the inside. She's in a good position. We can use her."

The waiter reappears, sets a plate down in front of Wes. Filet mignon, his usual. "Can I get you anything else, sir?"

Wes glances at his food. "Not right now."

The waiter nods and leaves. Wes turns his attention to his plate. Slices into the beef, releasing a pool of red juice. Spears a bite with his fork. "And the boy," he says, lifting the fork toward his mouth. "Two for the price of one."

"The *boy* ruined everything," Jackson mutters.

Wes ignores him. "He's quite good at what he does. Rivals even our own—"

"It's a risk."

"We have leverage." Wes takes another bite, chews slowly, eyes the man across from him. "You know, none of this would be necessary if she hadn't grown suspicious."

Jackson seethes quietly, his nostrils flaring.

Wes keeps his eyes on him as he chews. He swallows, then cuts himself another bite. "Everything was perfect. And then everything was jeopardized. *Because of your mistake.*"

"I didn't make a mistake!" Jackson snaps. Then he takes a measured breath. "We've been through this. I don't know why she suspected me. I went over *everything*. If I made a mistake, I'd admit it. *I didn't make a mistake.*"

Wes says nothing. Lifts another bite to his mouth, chews quietly, his eyes never leaving Jackson's.

Silence crackles between them. Finally Wes sets down his fork, blots the sides of his mouth with the corner of his napkin, glances around. Then he pulls out a flash drive, slides it across the table. "Boss's plan. Do as instructed."

Jackson's hand closes around it, just as he sees Wes's gaze center on something behind him. He senses movement, turns his head, sees someone headed in their direction. His eyes zero in on the man's forearm. There's a tattoo there. Two knives, crossed in an X.

His eyes shift to the stranger's face, but it's too late. He was too focused on the tattoo; the man's even with their booth now, his features obscured. All Jackson sees is a tilt of his head, an almost imperceptible nod, aimed at Wes.

He turns his attention back to Wes, a question in his eyes. But Wes's gaze is still locked on the man with the tattoo. He returns the nod, ever so slightly.

Then he looks at Jackson, and the shadow of a smile comes to his lips. "As I've said, the truth is complicated."

Chapter 38

It's him. Deputy Director Jackson is weaving this net of evidence around my son, trying to make it look like he's plotting a terrorist attack. And it's because of me. Because years ago I decided I needed to know the truth about him, and because I wouldn't let it go.

I feel an overwhelming swell of anger. This is my *son* we're talking about.

But why *now*? What has changed? I've been staying quiet. I haven't said a word about my suspicions, not since that meeting with Barker. And if Jackson knows I'm suspicious, if he's afraid I'll start talking, why not do to me what he did to Scott? Get me transferred. Fired, even.

Why frame Zachary? Why nearly kill my mother?

I ask myself the questions, but I know the answers. Because it wouldn't be enough to just send me away. Because I suspect him. He'd have to assume I'll keep digging away, or worse, sharing my suspicions with someone else. I'd still be a threat to him, even in another office, another city.

And yet: *Why now?*

And why Mom? If he's willing to hurt my mother, *why not just hurt me?*

Confusion is swirling inside me, so powerfully that I fear I'm going to vomit.

Everything made sense when I believed it was Halliday. Now Mom's accident doesn't fit.

Unless it was really, truly an accident.

But the man with the tattoo, *in the hospital* . . .

And the timing—all of this happening right after Zachary found Halliday . . .

I hurry down the hall, to the bank of elevators. I press the down arrow, hear a muted ding as the elevator arrives. The doors open and I step inside, press the button for my floor. My heart is trip-hammering and my mind is racing.

Whatever Jackson is hiding, whatever he's done, this is surely too much just to make sure I stay quiet. Zachary . . . Mom . . . It's too complicated.

It's not just my silence he wants. It's something more.

What?

The elevator stops on the way down, one floor after another. Faceless strangers crowd on.

That look on Barker's face—it wasn't about a medical diagnosis. I don't know if there even *was* a medical diagnosis; I never heard a word about his health again. My promotion wasn't because I deserved it, even if I did. It was about turning my attention elsewhere. Convincing me to drop it, giving me reason to stay silent.

And it worked, sort of, didn't it? I stayed quiet.

The house is in Great Falls, Virginia, in a gated community with rolling hills and freshly paved streets and huge homes on acres of land. I looked up the address on my way here—one of the perks of being able to access any personnel file. I flash my badge at the gate, and I'm waved through.

The wide drive is flanked on either side by evenly spaced dogwood trees, bare, just starting to bud. I park beside a Lexus and follow the paved walkway to the oversized entrance door, painted red. There's a wrought-iron bench near the door. Potted green plants, the hardy kind that can withstand the cold. I ring the bell. It chimes inside.

A moment later I hear footsteps approach, then there's a pause, like someone's looking out the peephole. "Can I help you?" It's a deep voice, one I instantly recognize.

"Special Agent Steph Maddox," I say. I flip open my credentials and hold them close to the peephole. "Internal Investigations Section. I have a couple of questions for you."

There's another pause, and I realize I'm holding my breath. He'd be perfectly justified right now calling headquarters, seeing if I have reason to be here. Or, more likely, just telling me to leave.

There's not a doubt in my mind that he remembers our previous interactions. That I raised my suspicions about Jackson, and he silenced me. Did he know the truth about Jackson then? I'm not sure, but he must know now. And he can rightly assume my reason for being here has something to do with just that.

I hear a latch unlock, and I exhale. Then another, and finally a third. The door swings open, and Glen Barker's standing there in front of me. He's in khaki pants and a collared shirt, tan and fit. He's wearing leather slippers and no socks. No sign of the mystery health issue that prompted his abrupt resignation as deputy director.

"Special Agent Maddox." He doesn't smile. "What can I do for you?"

"Mind if I come in?"

He gives me an appraising look, hard and distrustful, like he's debating. Finally, reluctantly, he opens the door wider.

The room I enter is dark, with heavy brocade drapes, antique-looking chairs. Oversized oil paintings decorate the walls flanking the fireplace. There's a row of pictures on the mantel, in silver frames. His family. A silver-haired wife, grown children, a couple of young grandkids.

"Please, have a seat," he says, his voice cold.

I turn from the mantel and sit in one of the stiff chairs, perched on the edge.

He sits opposite me, crosses his legs. "What can I do for you, Ms. Maddox?" We both know he doesn't want me here.

I don't answer his question. I want to be the one directing the conversation. "It's been a while since we've spoken, Mr. Barker. I imagine you remember our conversations?"

"Indeed." His jaw sets in a firm line.

I hold his gaze. "I'd like to talk about your resignation."

Somewhere deep in the house, classical music is playing.

"You resigned because of health reasons," I persist, when he doesn't answer. "Is that right?"

"What do you want, Maddox?" He asks it bluntly.

"If you don't mind me asking, what was the problem?"

"I do mind. It's none of your damn business."

"You look healthy."

He gives me an even stare, doesn't respond.

"Did you know Jackson was going to take your place when you resigned?"

He rises. "You need to leave. Now."

I stay seated. My heart is thumping in my chest. "What did he do? How did he get to you?"

"I've warned you about spurious charges—"

"Why's he doing this?" I interrupt. "What does he want?" There's a hint of desperation in my voice, one I don't want there.

He turns his back on me, starts toward the door. "Now, Maddox."

"If you tell the truth, you won't be the only one," I insist, standing. "There's two of us; they'll believe us."

He reaches for the door handle.

"Do the right thing," I say.

He stares at the door like he's thinking of something, remembering something. Then, abruptly, he laughs. When he turns to face me, the fear in his eyes makes me shiver.

"Be careful, Maddox. You have no idea what shit you've stepped into."

Chapter 39

An old episode of *Law & Order* is blaring when I step into Mom's hospital room. Mom's propped up on a pillow, watching intently.

"Hi, Mom. How are you feeling?"

"Way better." She aims the remote at the TV, mutes it. "You look tired, sweetheart."

I collapse into the chair beside her bed. I came straight here from Barker's house, and his words won't stop recycling through my brain. *You have no idea what shit you've stepped into.* He laughed when I told him they'd believe us. He actually *laughed.* And I can't get that sound out of my head.

"Nice of Zachary to stop by yesterday."

He stopped by? He never mentioned it. But the last thing I want is to admit to my mom I didn't know. That I really don't know *what* my son does on a daily basis. So I settle for nodding.

"And that friend of his. Lila. Such a sweet girl."

He brought *Lila*? When he won't even *talk* to me about her?

"What's wrong, honey?"

"Nothing," I lie. *Everything's* wrong. Zachary, pulling away, facing a threat he doesn't even know exists. Mom, here in the hospital. And this isn't just Jackson. This is something more powerful, more dangerous. That terrifies me. Even worse, I can't do anything about it. Without some sort of proof, it would sound crazy. *No one would believe me.*

And it would be dangerous. Maybe Mom's fall was an accident, but maybe it wasn't. Maybe Jackson was behind it. And he wouldn't have done it himself, so there is more than one of them. I can't risk that they'd do the same to Zachary, or worse.

"Is it work?" she presses.

I smile. "Yeah." I hope that'll be enough to change the topic. Hope she'll let it go, and I haven't just opened the door to more criticism about my career, about the way I'm dividing my time.

Mercifully, she just nods. I wonder if our last argument is as fresh in her mind as it is in mine. We both watch the silent picture on the television screen. McCoy and Briscoe are deep in a heated conversation. My mind starts to wander.

Jackson's working for the Russians, isn't he? It seems like the most logical explanation. The obvious one. He was a longtime Russia agent. That operation in the row house was clearly connected to Russian intelligence. And then there's that encrypted forum full of bots that Zachary found.

But Jackson was responsible for the biggest ever disruption of Russian sleepers. Why would someone working *for* the Russians help orchestrate the arrest of their own deep-cover agents?

And there's absolutely no proof that he's done a thing to support the Russians. I've looked for it, ever since that day in the row house. By all accounts, he's clean. I haven't found a single thing about our assets in Russia being uncovered. Nothing that suggests our intelligence-gathering efforts have been disrupted. Nothing I'd expect to find if someone in power was really working for a foreign adversary.

I glance over at Mom, realize she's watching me. She offers a sad smile, but doesn't avert her eyes. The air is heavy with unspoken thoughts.

"What is it, Mom?"

"Nothing, honey."

McCoy's in front of a jury now, making his case. Mom's pretending to be absorbed, even though the picture's silent, even though I'm sure she's seen it before. She's pleating the sheet between her fingers, no longer watching me.

"Anything you want to talk about?"

"I don't have the energy for another fight, Stephanie."

There's a row of get-well-soon cards propped up on the table beside her bed. A bear on the front of one, holding balloons. Two pastel cats on another. I realize I have no idea who might have sent them. "We could just *talk*."

"Oh, honey. When was the last time we ever did *that*?"

The words sting. "We were close, once. You said it yourself."

"And *you* told me it was all in my head." She sighs. "Maybe it was. I never knew you had such secrets. Before Zachary . . . we used to talk about *everything*, Stephanie."

"I know," I say quietly. "Things . . . changed."

Pain flares in her eyes. "I thought I knew you."

"You *did*."

"Jesus, Stephanie. What that senator did . . . how could you have kept a terrible thing like that from me?"

How is it that every time I talk to her, *I'm* somehow the one at fault? The one in the wrong, the one who should be apologizing? It's infuriating. "I can't handle this right now, Mom. Another bash-Stephanie session."

"I'm not *bashing* you. I'm simply asking for an explanation."

"And I'm simply telling you this isn't the time." I need to go, I need to escape this room, this conversation.

"Go ahead, Stephanie. Run." She leans back against the pillow. "It's what you do."

I don't sleep that night, again. I can't. Every time I close my eyes, I see someone I don't want to see. Barker. The fear in his eyes. *Be careful, Maddox.*

Mom, that disappointed look. *Go ahead, Stephanie. Run. It's what you do.*

I'm in the kitchen now, coffee noisily streaming into a travel mug.

I called Marta late last night, dialed her cell. It went straight to voicemail. *Can we talk?* I asked. *It's work-related.* I don't know what I'll say to her when we sit down face-to-face. But I need to say something. I need to find out what the Agency knows, if they have any idea the Bureau's been infiltrated.

I watch the last of the coffee drip into the mug, then screw on the lid. I grab my work bag, sling it over my shoulder, and head to the living room, where the TV's tuned to the morning news. I glance at my watch on the way in. Two minutes until the traffic report. When I step into the room, a phrase from the current story reaches my ears.

Freedom Solidarity Movement.

I go still.

"*. . . a little-known domestic terrorist group . . . ,*" comes the anchor's voice. "*. . . reportedly plotting attacks against government targets . . .*"

I squeeze the mug so tightly the heat radiates through my palms, cuts into them like tiny daggers. I close my eyes, like I can block this out. But I can't shut off reality, and I know exactly what this means.

It means there will be even more pressure for the Bureau to open investigations connected to FSM. With this in the news, it has to happen. It's only a matter of time until someone else finds the record of that email. The slides. Until Zachary is officially under investigation.

The anchor's voice cuts through my thoughts. "*. . . a senior government source has confirmed that authorities are investigating. . . .*"

Jackson. It has to be. He's the senior government source, the one leaking this information. *Jackson did this.* That swell of anger is back, churning inside me. Does he know I visited Barker? Does he know I'm digging around?

The broadcast feels like a message. A way for Jackson to communicate with me. To warn me, threaten me. After all, if I don't do what he wants, it's all going to be in the press, isn't it?

A sound makes me jump. I spin, and Zachary's ambling into the room. He glances at the screen, then pauses. He's reading the captions, the scrolling text, listening to the report. Then he frowns and looks at me. "It's in the news now?"

"Yeah."

"This could be bad, huh?"

Guilt washes over me. "I don't know."

"You don't *know*?"

"Zachary—"

"Isn't it your *job* to know? To figure this out?"

"You think I'm not trying?" How dare he speak to me like this? After all I'm doing to protect him.

He turns his back to me, and my gaze settles on a dirty plate beside the sink, unrinsed, stained with streaks of hardened pasta sauce, fork and knife dropped carelessly beside it.

I should let it go. My brain tells me to just let it go. But I'm too frustrated. "Clean up your mess."

He glances at the plate, then back at me, his eyes hard. "I made us dinner. I figured you'd clean up." The challenge in his tone is unmistakable.

"I wasn't here," I say through gritted teeth. "I was working, and then I was with Grandma."

"You're *never* here!"

I can't do this. Not now. I should just walk away. "Grow up, Zachary."

"What?"

I shouldn't have said it. But it's out now. "*Grow up.* Stop making such a mess of *everything*." I shouldn't have said *that*, either, but there, I've said it.

"I make a mess of everything?"

"Yeah, you do." I feel a pang of regret as I say it, even through the anger.

"*I* make a mess of everything?"

"You don't think through consequences, Zachary. Quitting those clubs at school. Leaving trash in your room. Leaving the kitchen like *this*. I'm sick and tired of cleaning up your messes."

He blinks at the fury in my voice. I should stop. But I keep going.

"God, Zachary. Going to see Halliday—you have no idea the trouble you've caused. All you thought about was *you*. What was best for you. That's *all* you seem to think about. So clean up the kitchen."

"Clean it up yourself."

"Don't you dare talk to me like that. I'm your mother."

"Yeah?" There's a look in his eye I really don't like right now.

"*Yeah.*"

"Could've fooled me." Then he heads for the stove, picks up the pot, slams it down in the sink.

I access Jackson's file, even though I shouldn't. But there's nothing sensitive.

I find his original processing forms. He passed his polygraph with flying colors. No deception noted. Reinvestigations—same deal. Nothing suspicious. No red flags.

I dig into his financial disclosure forms. His bank accounts and assets are all in line with his position.

The stack of folders on the corner of my desk has never been so high. I eye it occasionally, know I should be digging in, but I just can't force myself to do it. The misconduct in those cases pales in comparison to what Jackson's doing.

Midmorning, Parker knocks politely, enters with a large binder. "Sorry to bother you, Chief. How's your mom?"

"Better every day. Do you need something, Parker?"

"I'm hoping you can take a look at this." He extends the binder. "Op plan. For the Daniels case." He shifts his weight from one foot to the other. "It's in your pile there." He nods toward my desk. "But I know you've been distracted. . . ." I see color rise to his cheeks, the realization that he's said something he shouldn't have.

I take the binder from him and watch as he searches for what to say next, how to recover.

He clears his throat, fiddles with the badge at his hip. "Happens to everyone. It's just . . . it hasn't happened to you before, you know?"

"Right, Parker."

He nods toward the binder in my hand. "I just need you to sign off on it. I've bumped the op twice already, and the others are starting to get pissed."

Shit. "I'll get to it right now."

Half an hour later, I bring the binder back over to his desk, signed and approved. Garcia leans back in her chair as I make my way through the bullpen, watches me.

"Need something, Garcia?"

"You look beat, boss."

"Rough week."

"That's what sick leave's for, no? Take more time. Delegate some of these tasks. There's plenty of us that could help."

The bullpen's gone quiet. Everyone's listening. And everyone's pretending not to.

"It's under control, Garcia."

She shrugs. "Whatever you say, boss."

I retreat back to my office. And through the window, I watch my agents exchange glances, exchange words, their eyes darting every so often in my direction. *Dammit.*

I open the first folder in my stack, force myself to start reading, to pay attention. I have to do this. I have to stay on top of my work, my responsibilities. I can't have everyone talking about me, speculating about me.

I get through a handful of files. Garcia's mortgage fraud case. An op plan that Flint put together, a controlled-drug buy run jointly with DEA. A new case that Wayne's about to open, an Assistant Special Agent in Charge accused of embezzlement.

Marta hasn't called back. Midafternoon, I dial her work number, her direct line. Three rings, then voicemail connects. "Call me back," I say. "Please, Marta. It's important."

I pull out the file, the unlabeled one, from the back of my desk drawer. I skim the notes I've made over the years. The field reports from the incident in the row house—at least the scraps that aren't classified. The press releases on Jackson's achievements, his promotions. There has to be something. Something I'm missing.

But by late afternoon, I've found nothing. I'm feeling desperate. He's covered his tracks too well.

I catch myself staring at the framed picture of Zachary on my desk. His senior picture, my favorite one. He's smiling, but it's a small and oddly adult smile, not the wide grin he sports in most of the other shots. This one's reserved, and in it I glimpse the shy, fleeting smile he had as a little boy.

My gaze drifts from the photograph to the calendar on my desk, the daily planner. *Zachary's school, 5 p.m.*, I'd scrawled on today's date, the evening section. There's some sort of ceremony today, honor society awards. Zachary told me about it two weeks ago. *Not sure I'll be able to make it*, I had told him, mentally calculating the time I'd have to leave the office, the work I'd miss.

I *am* working. But I'm not accomplishing anything. There's not a single thing that proves Jackson is behind this. Not a single thing that proves my son's innocence.

I look back at the picture of him, that adult smile. Suddenly I'm filled with an overwhelming need to see him. I toss the folder into my work bag and head out.

The high school auditorium is bustling when I arrive, clusters of parents and noisy siblings and extended family. I'd expected a smaller crowd, a quieter one. But maybe this is what all these ceremonies are like. I realize, with a sinking feeling, that I don't know. I haven't been here enough to know.

I take a seat toward the back of the room, along the center aisle. When the kids file in down that aisle, I want Zachary to see me, to know I'm here. For some reason, that seems incredibly important right now. I haven't spoken to him since our blowup this morning. One that wasn't even about the dirty dishes. It was about my frustration, and his.

I watch the families as I wait, all talking and smiling and laughing, and suddenly feel so lonely I nearly weep. Zachary never had that, the big boisterous family. It was just the two of us, mostly. It used to feel like a family, to me at least. I hope it did to him, too.

But it doesn't anymore, not really. We're so distant, so careful around each other. That, or we're fighting. Our little family is on the verge of collapse. Watching the others around me, I know I've failed him.

And for what? The greater good? That's how I always justified it to myself. That my job was important, that I was helping people. That sure, I wasn't always there for *him,* but I was making the country a safer place. I was helping victims. I was there for them when no one else was.

I can feel a tear quivering on my eyelid.

I take a breath, look down at the program in my lap, flip through it. The names are listed alphabetically; I scan until I find Zachary's. Highest honors. A sense of pride fills me. Then my mind flashes to the last time I saw his name in an alphabetical list—the case file system. I'm trembling and I can't control it. I close the program and grip it so tightly it tears in my hands.

On the hour, the lights dim, and the chatter quiets. I glance behind me, toward the bank of doors at the rear, wait for them to open, for Zachary to walk in. Instead, applause draws my attention to the front of the room. I turn with a sinking feeling to see the kids filing onto the stage from the wings.

Why did I think they'd come down the aisle? I'm frustrated with myself for getting it wrong, getting so much wrong.

Zachary's on the stage. He's in a blue button-down shirt and khaki pants, chatting with the boy beside him. I see him look out into the auditorium, scan it briefly, but he doesn't see me. Of course he doesn't; I'm all the way in the back. Other kids are finding their families in the crowd, waving, laughing. Zachary doesn't give it another glance. In his mind I'm at work, where I said I'd be.

But he doesn't look upset. He's smiling, laughing at something the boy beside him just said. Happy. And why shouldn't he be? He's about to graduate from high school. He has his whole life ahead of him, all the opportunities in the world, all these doors wide open. My heart aches with regret.

The kids take their seats and Zachary's in the middle row, hidden from my view. The principal starts speaking, and he has one of those slow voices, slow and monotone. I want to listen, want to pay attention, but I can't keep my thoughts from drifting. Because all those doors aren't really open for Zachary, are they? If I can't take care of this situation, doors will start slamming. And I can't let that happen.

Why's this happening *now*? That's the question at the forefront of my mind, the one I can't push away. Because it's been almost two years since that day in the row house. Two *years*.

Snippets of the principal's speech are connecting, working their way into my racing mind.

. . . *limitless possibilities* . . .

It doesn't make sense that one day, out of the blue, Jackson would decide to plant evidence in my son's bedroom. Something would have precipitated an action like that. Something big.

. . . *the long-awaited day* . . .

A tingle of excitement starts to run through me. What if I'd finally gotten close to the truth, close to finding proof that he's dirty? What if in these searches, I'd actually come across something important, and didn't even know it?

I reach into my work bag, pull out the unlabeled folder. The woman beside me frowns. I flip through to the end of my notes, start working my way up. The last search was a few weeks ago. I was digging into the sleeper agents who'd been arrested, updating myself on their cases, searching for any developments.

. . . *their lives can be whatever they make them* . . .

My gaze zeroes in on one note, halfway down the page: *Al. Pe.—said framed, pled guilty.*

And then it zeroes in further on that single word.

Framed.

I remember the search. Alina Petrova. She was one of the twenty-five arrested in that nationwide roundup of Russian spies. She was adamant, from the beginning, that she wasn't a sleeper, that she was a dissident. *I'm being framed,* she was quoted as saying, on more than one occasion. Others said it, too, but Alina was the most outspoken. The most fearless.

Then she went quiet. When she went to trial, she pled guilty. Admitted she'd been spying for Russia. And disappeared from the headlines. I tried in vain to find updates on her after the trial. Alina was never heard from again.

I'm dimly aware that the principal has finished speaking, that someone else has taken his place, someone who's reading off names. The kids are rising at the sound of their names, grinning and blushing as they walk across the stage to a smattering of applause, the occasional hoot and holler, almost like a miniature graduation ceremony.

My eyes are still on the notes, though. What if Alina was set up, like Zachary? What if she wasn't really a sleeper?

That would explain how Jackson could be working for the Russians *and* disrupting a sleeper cell. It wasn't really a sleeper cell at all. It was victims set up to take the fall.

And what if they threatened Alina, blackmailed her, did something to convince her to plead guilty, and to stay quiet?

Barker wouldn't admit to being manipulated, but maybe Alina would. Maybe she's key to finding the proof I so desperately need.

The sound of Zachary's name pulls me back to the present with a start, and I'm disoriented. I look up to see him striding across the stage, all the way at the front of the room, so far away from me. Why didn't I move closer?

I set down the phone and clap thunderously, like the sound can somehow let him know that someone's here for him, that he's not a school-event orphan, like he's been too many times in the past. I watch him, grinning as he shakes the principal's hand, accepts his certificate.

And as he sits down to silence, not giving the audience another glance, I wish I'd done one of those obnoxious shouts. I wish I'd snapped a picture of him crossing the stage, because isn't that what parents are supposed to do? I didn't do anything the way I should have.

I look down at the notes in my lap. I reread that sentence, the one that connects the dots. Then I look back up at the stage. Zachary's sitting, gone again from my sight. I try to catch a glimpse of him, but I can't, not from here, from so far away.

Impulsively, I stand up. I'm not going to sit here and feel sorry for myself, berate myself for my mistakes. I walk up the aisle toward the front, until I can see Zachary. I slide into a row near the front, and make eye contact, offer him a smile.

His face registers surprise. And then color rushes to his cheeks like a sunburn; he grins back.

Chapter 40

I wait impatiently in an interview room for them to bring her in. It's a small room, square and windowless, just four white walls, a metal table, and two metal chairs, all bolted to the floor. And it's freezing, like all these rooms are. I wish I'd brought a jacket.

While I wait, I check my phone. Nothing from Zachary, nothing from Mom. And still nothing from Marta. No return call. I dial her cell again, hold the phone to my ear. Before the first ring, there's a voice. But it's not Marta's; it's a recording. *Mailbox full*. I press the end button. A swelling sense of worry makes it hard to breathe.

In the distance I hear a buzzer, very faint. The clang of the door. There's a clock on the wall, and I can hear the loud *tick* of each second passing. I watch it, the hands going around, time vanishing in the most visible way, and I think of Zachary. I imagine a future in which I must come to a place like this to visit him, and I shudder. Then I force myself to stop looking at the clock, try to tune out the hammer blow of passing time.

Finally, a key scrapes in the lock. The door opens, and she's there.

I recognize her from her mugshot, but only barely. She looks older, and haggard, scarcely more than skin and bones. Her face is gaunt, her hair streaked with gray. Her jumpsuit hangs off her; it's probably the smallest one they have, and it's still huge.

She sits gracefully across from me, back erect. Her expression is unsettling. It's defeat, I decide. She looks defeated. The guard who led her in withdraws, shutting and locking the door behind herself, and then it's just us. We watch each other, the clock the only sound in the narrow room, which reeks of bleach.

Finally, I clear my throat. "Ms. Petrova, thank you for meeting with me."

"Alina," she says. She has an accent; it's faint, but it's there.

I nod. "Alina." I pause, gather my thoughts. "I want to cut right to the point. You were adamant that you were innocent. Then you pled guilty. Why?"

She holds my gaze, unblinking. Then she shrugs. "Why do you think?" she challenges.

"I have an idea, but I need to hear what you have to say."

Her lips tighten.

I try a different tack. "You said you were being set up. Why did you believe that?"

She regards me steadily. Then, just as I'm sure I'll get nothing from her, she says, "I resisted. Spoke the truth about Putin, about his government. Did it under an assumed identity, of course." She shakes her head, like it had all been a mistake.

"You think the Russian government learned your real identity?"

"They know everything. When they don't know, they hack in and find out." Her eyes mock me.

"Why did you change your mind? Why did you plead guilty?"

She shakes her head again, lips in an unyielding straight line. I wait, but she says nothing.

"Are you being treated well here?" I ask, shifting tactics again. I look at her thin frame, and suddenly I mean it. My concern for her is real. "Are you getting enough to eat?"

"They give me enough food."

"And you eat it?"

"When I must."

"Why only then?"

Distrust flickers in her dark eyes. "You just never know. They have . . . ways. When it comes to food . . . you never know what is safe, do you?"

She's living in fear. So afraid of them coming after her, she doesn't even eat. God, how awful.

Studying her face, the sincerity that's there, the dread, I know this woman is not guilty of anything. And in the instant that thought crosses my mind, I see Zachary in this very spot, in his own jumpsuit, his own life ruined, just like Alina's. The thought absolutely terrifies me.

"Someone got to you," I press. "Someone convinced you to plead guilty."

Her face tightens again.

"Someone threatened you," I insist. I pull a small photograph from my bag, the headshot of Jackson I printed from the Bureau website. I slide it across the table toward her. "I think it was this man, right here."

She glances down at the photo, and I wait, my heart pounding. She looks up. "It was not him."

"But it was someone." My mind's racing. It wasn't Jackson, but someone had threatened her. "Who was it, Alina? What did he say? Did he threaten you?" I ask, more urgently. I'm getting to her. I know it; I've experienced it in interrogations countless times before. She has to admit it. She has to say something.

"Not me," she insists, visibly frustrated, and what I hear is *That wouldn't be enough. I'd take my chances.* And then there's one of those interminable breaks of time where no one breathes, no one makes a sound, where all the air seems sucked out of the room. That moment balanced on the razor's edge of truth or lie.

"They know where every member of my family is." Her voice is a whisper. *"Everyone I love."*

"Alina—you need to say something."

She shakes her head.

"You need to tell the truth, Alina."

"The truth is a very dangerous thing, Agent Maddox."

"The law will protect you."

"The law? The law is nothing against *them*."

"Alina, you've always stood up to them. You've fought for the truth. Stand up now."

Her chin quivers, the smallest bit, and then her jawline tightens. "It is my *family*." She tilts her head up, gives me that unflinching, mocking gaze. "I am *doing* what I *must*. Would you do anything different, Agent Maddox?"

The deputy director of the FBI is working for the Russians.

I'm on the plane home, and I'm struggling to wrap my mind around just how serious this is. The Glock in Zachary's closet was just the tip of the iceberg. I've seen more of that iceberg now. I'm starting to get glimpses of what's below the surface, and it's almost unimaginable.

I can't even begin to comprehend how dangerous that is for our country. Is it possible Jackson is feeding the Russians information? Sharing secrets? I've never found anything to suggest the Russians have benefitted from him being in a position of power. Our collection of sensitive intelligence hasn't diminished. Our assets haven't been harmed. Nothing's happened, as far as I can determine.

But with Jackson on their side, the Russians have tremendous influence. Unfathomable access. And that's enough to make me think I can't wait any longer. I need to tell someone. But who? Who can I trust? And what would I say?

Should I go to Director Lee, tell him his deputy is working for the Russians, framing my son, threatening all these other innocent people?

What happens when Scott and Barker and Alina deny it? I haven't a shred of proof, and Jackson's tracks are covered. If I come clean, if I mention the gun, the slides, it would look like I was making spurious charges to cover for my son.

No one would believe me.

And nothing would happen to Jackson.

Jackson worked Russian counterintelligence. How much did he pass back to the Russian services? He must have been doing that. And now he's the Bureau's number two. Does that mean more access? Not complete access; I know that from my meetings with Barker. But enough to irreparably damage our country, cripple our intelligence-gathering efforts, I'm sure. I find myself wondering again if the CIA has any idea what the Russians are doing, of just how far the Russian government's reach extends.

I need to talk with Marta. I need to reach her. I'll go to her home. . . .

My eyes finally close; I've barely slept in days. I can't keep them open any longer. But I don't shut off my mind. I can't.

Thinking of the CIA makes me think of that woman, the one with Jackson in that row house, years ago. *Vivian.* For the first time I wonder: Was that picture Barker gave me real? Was she truly safe? Or had she stood up to Jackson and suffered the consequences?

I try to push the unanswered questions away. But Vivian Miller is still on my mind. I can't get her off of it. She's the last thing I think about before I drift off.

What happened to her?

Chapter 41

The train lurches forward and the woman tightens her grip on the handrail, shifts her weight to keep her balance. The crowd of commuters sways with the motion, and for a moment her husband disappears from view. She takes a step to her left, and there he is again. At the far end of the Metro car, head down, phone in front of him. He hasn't looked up, hasn't noticed her. Even if he did, he wouldn't recognize her instantly, not with the hat, the glasses, the baggy sweatshirt she's never worn.

She shouldn't be doing this. But at the same time, she can't *not*. His once-rare meetings in the city have become increasingly frequent these last few weeks, and she's on edge. He said he has another today, told her he wouldn't be able to pick up the kids if the schools called. And so instead of driving to work, she took a sick day. Stopped for the hat and glasses and new clothes, drove to the Metro station, waited near the entrance for him to appear. Then followed him onto the train, a safe distance away.

She learned surveillance tactics ages ago. Hasn't practiced in a couple of years, but it's all coming back. And this should be easy.

Red Line all the way in. His office is near Gallery Place. Three more stops now.

The train grinds to a halt at Union Station. The doors open. Her husband looks up from his phone—and then angles through the crowd toward the open doors.

Her heart starts to pound. She elbows her way toward another open door.

The platform is packed with people waiting to pile on. She's going to lose him. She needs to see where he's going.

She scans the crowd, catches sight of him, heading away from her, toward the exit. Breathes a sigh of relief, starts moving toward him, her eyes never leaving his back, ignoring the jostles, until—

An older man steps directly into her path, stops. "Hello," he says with a nod. It's unsettling, seeing him here. They know each other from work, after all, and there's a limit to what they can say in public, how they can acknowledge each other.

"Hi." She tilts her head to peer around him, find her husband's back in the crowd.

A chime rings from the train. The doors are about to close. She continues to search the crowd, realizes with growing panic that she's lost him.

"I'm afraid I can't chat right now," she says. Where could her husband be? He was *just* here. The train inches forward, and her eyes dart in that direction—and then she spots him. Inside the train. In a different car, head down, absorbed with his phone.

"Not a problem," the older man says. His eyes, a clear blue, stay fixed on hers.

She tries to make sense of this. Her husband knew he was being tailed. Stepped off the train to lose her. Hopped back on at the last second. Classic technique.

Or he was distracted, accidentally exited at the wrong stop. Realized his mistake, boarded again.

The older man steps aside, out of her way, but by now it's too late. The train is barreling forward, out of sight.

He offers her a smile. "Nice seeing you again, Vivian."

Chapter 42

Zachary doesn't care where we go to dinner, so I pick a local Chinese restaurant, a place that's safe and predictable. That certainty is what I crave right now.

We sit across from each other in a red padded booth, examine our menus. Zachary is talking about the theme for the senior prom—a masquerade ball. I listen to the excitement in his voice and remember helping him get ready for his first dance, in middle school. Teaching him how to knot his tie. Dropping him off at the gym, decorated with balloons and streamers, watching him dash toward the entrance.

A waitress takes our order, returns slowly with our drinks—iced tea for me, root beer for him. When she's gone, he looks around, leans forward, lowers his voice. "So what's going on with the anarchist stuff?"

"Don't worry about it." I say it almost without thinking. If the Russians are involved, I don't want Zachary to be part of this anymore. I never should have let him get involved in the first place.

"Don't *worry* about it?"

"It's under control."

He leans back against the booth, shoots me an incredulous look. I'm sure he can tell by my face that it's not under control. Not even close. I take a sip of my iced tea and ask him if he's rented his tux.

"Want to know my guess?" he says, ignoring my question.

I shake my head, reach for the sugar.

"It's someone you investigated. Someone's coming after you, like that mobster did back in Chicago. Only now, you're in even deeper shit. And I am, too."

"I told you not to worry about it." The reprimand comes out sharper than I intend it to, but his words were too close to Barker's warning and they stung. *You don't know how deep.*

"And I told you I want to help."

I shake my head. "It's my responsibility."

"It's my *life*." A frustrated look crosses his face, and I feel a wave of guilt.

He's right; I know he is. But this is the *Russians* we're talking about. He doesn't know how powerful they are, how ruthless. And he's only a boy. The more I can distance him from this, the safer he'll be.

He pulls his phone from his back pocket, pointedly turns his attention to that, and I don't ask him to put it away. It's easier than continuing this conversation.

I take a sip through my straw and watch him. His face is impassive, his fingers swiping through screens, opening apps.

Then there's a flash of anticipation. He's reading something on the screen, something that excites him. He blinks, and his face falls, pinched with disappointment.

"What is it?" I have that panicky feeling, the one I get when I know something's wrong and I can't do anything about it. It's like a train is speeding right toward me and I can't step out of the way.

His eyes stay on the screen. Reading, or rereading, trying to comprehend something.

"Zachary, what's wrong?"

"I didn't get into Maryland." His tone is hollow.

"What?" I say, because the words couldn't be more unexpected. He had the grades. The test scores. Far beyond what he needed.

He turns the phone in my direction, so the screen is visible. "Email from the admissions office."

"Does it say why?"

He shakes his head.

The waitress arrives at the table, slides our plates clumsily down in front of us. I thank her, pretending not to watch Zachary. He's turned his attention back to his phone, and I can see him struggling to comprehend this news. Only when the waitress leaves, when it's back to just the two of us, does he look up. "Oh God, Mom. Was it because I quit all the clubs?"

He looks so impossibly young. He has the face of the brokenhearted boy who didn't make the basketball team in middle school, even though he tried so hard, practiced so much.

"No," I reply, and anger starts boiling inside me. It's Jackson, I'm sure of it. I don't know what he did, how he did it, but I know it's him. Maryland was a safety school, for God's sake.

"Is it that anarchist stuff? The email, the pictures I found on that forum?" My son's eyes are searching my face: he wants answers. "Did Maryland find out?"

"No. I don't think so."

"What if I don't get into any of the other schools?" he asks. In my mind I hear that little boy in the car again. *Are we safe, Mommy?*

Only this time, I don't know what to answer. I don't know. And I don't know if it even matters. There's so much more at stake than just college now.

The waitress picks that moment to stop at our table. "Everything okay over here?"

I glance down at our untouched meals. In my mind I see Zachary's face just moments ago, that nakedly crestfallen look.

"Yeah," I lie. Then I look up and make eye contact with my son. "Everything's going to be fine."

Zachary announces he's going to meet up with some friends after dinner. It's a Friday night; I shouldn't be surprised. But it makes me long, just the same, for the days when he was too young to go out. When Friday nights would just be the two of us. Movie nights, usually. I can still hear his high-pitched giggle at the antics of some character. I never quite knew what he was laughing about, never really watched with him, was usually on my laptop, or my mind was still at work.

I wish I could go back and do it over again. Snuggle with him, laugh with him. Really, genuinely laugh. Pay attention. Be there for him.

I head to the hospital. Mom's sitting up, reading one of those cozy mysteries she likes so much, the ones with cats on the cover. She smiles when I walk in, sets her book aside. I kiss her, then sit in the chair beside her.

"You look so much better. How are you feeling?"

"Good, actually. Sounds like they might be letting me out of here in a few days."

"I heard. I'm glad." I think of her heading back to that condo, alone. "You need to come stay with Zachary and me for a bit."

"Oh, I wouldn't want to impose! I'll be fine on my own."

"It wouldn't be an imposition. You're my mother. And your grandson would love it."

"Yeah, but . . ." She shrugs, then offers me a tight smile. And I know we are both thinking about the terrible things we said to each other. "Thanks, honey. I'll think about it."

Mom fingers her book, but doesn't pick it up. I hear a cart roll by in the hall. Someone's dinner, no doubt.

"Where's Zachary?"

"Out with his friends."

"Things okay between the two of you?"

I shrug. "Sure."

She frowns like she doesn't believe me. "And how's work?"

"Fine."

It's the usual exchange. *How's work? Fine.* But this time I can see in her eyes that she wants to say more, that there's more coming. *Don't do it, Mom.*

"How are the hours?"

"What do you mean?" I ask, too defensively.

"You know what I mean. Are you still working around the clock?"

"I work hard." I say it tersely, the kind of tone that should end the discussion. I can tell from her reaction it's not going to succeed.

"Zachary will be leaving for college so soon."

Don't do this again. "What's your point?"

"Just that maybe you ought to take it easy this summer, honey."

It's the endearment that provokes me. Just for once, she could understand how important my job was. How necessary. And after our argument at my house, after I finally told her the truth, she should understand *why* it's so important. "Say what you really mean, Mom. I work too much. I don't spend enough time with my son."

"Well, you don't."

We glare at each other. Two nurses stop outside the door, complaining about the patient in 306, who threw his tray at an orderly.

"It's just that—look, at the end of your life, Stephanie, you're going to regret it. You'll regret that you don't have a better relationship with your son."

"He's a teenager, for pity's sake, Mom. There's plenty of time to get closer."

"You don't *know* him."

"Of course I do!"

She shakes her head. Her fingers are pleating the sheet again. She's going to say something I don't want to hear, and the anger bubbles up inside me. "You don't, Stephanie. And if you don't now, you never will."

The anger's reached a boil now. "Why do you always feel the need to kick me when I'm down?"

"Oh, honey, I'm not kicking you when you're down! I'm trying to help you."

"By constantly telling me that I'm a terrible mother?"

"You're not a terrible mother, Stephanie! I'm not saying that. I would never say that. I'm saying you don't know him."

"And you do?" I hear the sneer in my tone. And I don't care.

She blinks, wounded by my sarcasm. "Yes. Yes, I do. Better than you. When he's in trouble, Stephanie, he comes to *me*, not *you*."

The words feel like a blow, like they physically hurt. "What are you talking about?"

"He does. Like that time he needed money. He didn't go to you. He came to me."

That time he needed money? What's she talking about? I rack my brain and can't think of that ever happening. But I can't exactly admit that, can I?

"Look, honey, I'm just saying you need to work on your relationship with Zach. He needs to feel like he can trust you."

Frustration is making it hard for me to think straight. Could that be true? Does Zachary trust her more than me? Does he love her more than he loves me?

"You need to rethink your priorities."

"I need to go." There's a pulse beating so loudly in my brain that I'm dizzy.

"Stephanie—"

"Quit butting into my life, Mom. Just for once stay the hell out of my life."

The radio is off, and the only sound in the car is the engine hum. There's a storm of thoughts in my head, one I'm trying to sift through, make sense of.

I can't focus on that conversation with Mom. I can't think about it. I can't acknowledge that she might be right, that I might have made some terrible mistakes, ones I can't fix.

And so I think of what I *can* fix, what I *need* to fix.

Jackson. The deputy director of the FBI is doing this to my family, tearing it apart, threatening to destroy it.

I can't forget the crestfallen look on Zachary's face at the restaurant. That bastard Jackson did something to make sure Maryland would reject my innocent son.

It's another message. Another warning. Jackson's letting me know he has the power to destroy Zachary's future.

And of course he does. His people got to the accused sleepers *in prison*. Convinced them to trade a chance at freedom for life behind bars. My life and Zachary's are so insignificant compared to that. So very, very insignificant. If they can do that, what is the limit to what they can do?

It's dark by the time I arrive home. I park and turn off the engine. But I don't move. The Maryland rejection—that was because I visited Alina, wasn't it? The leaked threat was because I visited Barker. Digging around is having direct consequences—ugly consequences—for my son.

How much worse would it get if I actually told the truth? I didn't even want to consider the possibility.

The fact that he has me trapped, that I have no choice right now but to be silent, makes fury blaze inside me.

I force myself to pull the keys from the ignition and get out of the car. Distracted, I trudge to the front door. I unlock it and step inside. It takes a fraction of a second to realize there's no beeping from the alarm system. It's deathly quiet.

Another fraction of a second, and then a voice calls from the darkness.

"Stay right where you are."

Chapter 43

I'm intensely aware of the gun holstered at my hip. Of him, behind me. Close. I can feel his presence. I can picture exactly where he's standing.

"Do not reach for the gun," Jackson says, like he can read my mind. "You are going to slowly raise your hands above your—"

Like hell I will. I pivot toward him, my right hand reaching for my gun and my left arm rising in a blocking maneuver, and I'm stopped, almost instantly, before I can fully turn, before I can grab the gun.

He has a hand on each of my arms, a powerful hold. He anticipated my moves, knew exactly what I was going to do. And it dawns on me, an instant too late: he knew because he was trained precisely the same way I was.

I'm breathing hard. His fingers are digging into me, keeping me immobile. I can feel his strength; I know there's no breaking away.

I look down at his hands on my arms. He's wearing thin latex gloves. There won't be prints on anything.

Just then he yanks my arms back, transfers both my wrists into one of his hands, and slides my gun from its holster. He lets go of my arms, but by then I'm powerless, and we both know it. Without my gun, I don't stand a chance against him.

What do you want? my mind is screaming.

"I thought it was time we spoke face-to-face." His face is grimly serious, the way it was that day in the row house. He's that person now, not the grinning, affable man in his headshot. He looks threatening.

My eyes drift down to the gun in his hand. My mind is spiraling, unwilling to surrender, and then it settles on the butcher's block in the kitchen, all those sharp knives inside. A tingle of anticipation runs through me. A knife's no match for a gun. But I need something to defend myself, and a knife's better than nothing.

He watches me. It's an unsettling look, like he can read me. He's been trained to do that, though, hasn't he?

"What do you want from me?" I ask.

He gives his head the smallest of shakes, an annoyed one, like I don't have the right to ask questions, like he's in charge here, even though he's in *my* home.

He's not in charge. I won't let him bully me into submission. "What do you want?" I ask again.

"Say nothing. *Let it go.*"

This isn't just to buy my silence. I've *been* silent. "What else? I know there's more."

"There's always more," he agrees.

I glare at him, but all I really see is the image in my mind, the knives in the kitchen. I envision the best way to dart to the counter, what he's likely to do in response. Go after me, I know; that'll be his instinct. But I'll have the element of surprise, and he won't have time to think through the smartest response. And that means I'll have a knife before he can draw a gun. I'll be able to take the weapons, restrain him, get the authorities here, let them see he's in my house, threatening me.

My heart's pounding. I need to do this; I need to make my move.

"The knives are gone," he says. "I removed them."

The words make me go cold. He knew what I was going to do. *How did he know what I was thinking?*

"What else do you want from me?" I take a step forward, toward him, toward the door.

He cocks his head. "I need you on my side, Stephanie."

"Meaning?" Another step forward.

This time he takes a step back. "You have an important position. Internal investigations. If anyone raises suspicions about me, you'll shut it down, and you'll let me know."

"You want me to protect you." The words make complete sense.

"Think of it as protecting your son, if you want."

The mention of Zachary makes my stomach hurt. "And if I don't, you'll try to make it look like he's plotting a terrorist attack."

He laughs, softly. "Not *try*, Steph. He'll be convicted. He'll be in prison for a very long time."

In my mind I picture Alina. Rail-thin, in that oversized jumpsuit. The chilly box of an interrogation room where we spoke. But I wouldn't even have *that* with Zachary, would I? We'd probably have to talk through plexiglass.

"We have plenty more on him. And on you, too."

Me? What do they have on me? And more importantly, what else do they have on Zachary?

"The burner phone, the call to the tip line. Interesting decision on your part."

In my mind I see the Suburban, the headlights sweeping toward me. "I had to do something."

"What you *did* was create proof you knew about a plot. Your *son's* plot. Which you aided and abetted."

Aided and abetted. Oh God.

"You can't prove a thing." I picture the Suburban again, the onrushing headlights. There's no way, if he was at the wheel, that Jackson could have seen what I did, captured any proof. He was too far away.

"Oh, but I can." He transfers my gun from his right hand to his left, then reaches into his pocket, pulls out his cellphone. Swipes the screen with his thumb, brings up a picture, turns the phone so I can see it.

It's me, crouched down by my tire, wedging the burner phone underneath.

Shit.

How did he capture that? He must not have been the one driving the Suburban. He must have an accomplice.

He has proof I bought that phone, made that call, destroyed the evidence. Proof that I knew about this plot, kept it hidden.

"You're connecting the dots, aren't you?" He looks amused.

I glare at him. "And if I do what you say?"

"Your kid goes off to college, enjoys his life. You do, too."

This time, in my mind, I see Barker. The photographs on his mantel, the happy family. I try to push the image away. In its place I see Scott, loading frames into the cardboard box. The snapshot of his kids, smiling. They're in Omaha, but they're together. They're safe.

God, I want that. I want with all my heart for Zachary to be safe, and happy, and for life to go on as usual. All I'd have to do is let Jackson know if he's being investigated. Protect him.

"I know who you're working for," I spit.

"*Do* you?" His tone mocks.

It still doesn't make sense, all this effort to set a trap around Zachary, to use him as bait to get me to shut down investigations. It's too complicated.

And it's not just about protection. I know how these people

work. If they got their claws into me, if I agreed to do what Jackson's asking, it wouldn't end there. There'd always be more.

"I could come clean," I say. "About everything."

"Oh, you know better than that."

My gaze flickers to the alarm system beside the door. I've moved closer to it, unbeknownst to him. Close enough to reach the panic button, blinking green.

I lunge for it, press hard. The green light changes to red, and I know that somewhere, someone's calling 911 on my behalf. The police will be here any minute. A tremor runs through me, and I don't know if it's relief or fear. But at least I've done *something*.

"Bad move." The way he says the words—it chills me. "What exactly are you going to tell the cops?"

He reaches for the door handle, then turns, and his expression is cold, ruthless. It's the same warning look he shot me in that row house, years ago. "*No one* would believe you, Steph."

When the door closes, I reach for my phone. Call the alarm company, tell the operator it was a false alarm, that I don't need the police. The panic button served its purpose, didn't it? Jackson left my home. And I proved I'm willing to fight back.

Still, those words are lodged in my brain, running on an endless loop. *No one would believe you.*

Jackson has proof I called in the threat. Which means I had some sort of evidence and didn't turn it in. It's not just Zachary anymore who's in danger of going to jail. It's me, too.

He wants me to stay quiet and protect him. And in exchange, Zachary's future remains bright.

Or I can tell the truth, and know that both of us are going to prison.

He's trapped me.

I want more than anything to protect Zachary. But staying quiet isn't the best way to do it. I know that, deep down. I've always known that, since the day Halliday tried to destroy my life.

If I'm silent this time, Jackson wins.

Chapter 44

Two hours later, I've installed cameras around the front door, inside and out. Covert audio recording devices, in case he spots the cameras. A motion detector that sends an alarm straight to my phone. If Jackson comes back, I'll be ready.

Another listening device is on me, wrapped around my body, under my shirt. I tested it, made sure it works. I'm always going to be wearing it from now on. I know how to find the power button through my clothes, discreetly.

I'm feeling confident. Prepared. Next time I see Jackson, I'm going to get the proof I need. I'm going to get him sent to jail.

He's not going to get what he wants. Not this time.

Chapter 45

Saturday passes in a blur. If not for the cloud hanging over our heads, it would have seemed like any other. In the morning, I went grocery shopping, picked up the dry cleaning, went for a long run. Zachary slept in, spent a few hours working—coding, on his laptop, at the desk in his bedroom. I tried in vain to keep my mind off of Jackson, and the slides, and the fact that my son's future is hanging in the balance.

Sunday morning I drove to Marta's apartment in McLean, near Langley. Knocked on her door. No answer. Called her cell again. Voicemail full. Marta travels a lot, for work. If she's out of the country, she might not have her personal cell. Or she might just not want to talk to me, still. She's tough; I think she's okay. Still, the seeds of worry start to grow.

It's Sunday evening now, and Jackson hasn't come back. I hate that I'm protecting his secret, knowing this awful truth about the Bureau's number two. But with the wire, with this plan, I feel like I'm finally fighting back. He'll be back, I know he will. The Bureau taught me the skills to lay a trap for those who think they're above the law. I'm ready for his return.

It's just a little longer; I'll tell the truth soon.

Zachary and I are having takeout from the Mexican place a few blocks away. Burrito bowls and tacos. He's telling me about a concert planned for August, downtown. That group he likes, that one that's always railing about the police.

"So can I go?" he asks.

"It's in *August*. Can we talk about it then?"

"I have to buy tickets."

"You know I don't like their music."

"And you know I do."

"Fine. But same curfew."

He rolls his eyes, brushes a shock of uncombed hair away from his forehead. My phone buzzes on the table, an incoming text. I glance at it, feeling a surge of hope that it's Marta calling back, finally.

Number unknown.

Have you made a decision?

The text feels intrusive, invasive, like he's back here in my home, uninvited. It's Jackson, I'm sure of it. I have the sudden, disturbing sense that we're being watched. But no one's looking at us, of course; we're safe inside, the blinds drawn, the alarm set.

"Are you okay?" Zachary's face is brimming with concern. I realize he's been talking and I haven't heard a word. And I don't know how to answer his question, because I'm not okay—*we're* not okay—not in the slightest.

"Just a lot on my mind." I watch him take another bite of food. Then I look back down at the phone, at the text.

Have you made a decision?

I don't know. Have I?

I change into running clothes and slip out of the house, start off at a slow jog. The air is cool tonight, but there's no wind. It makes the night seem especially quiet. All I hear are my feet pounding the pavement. I pick up my pace, running faster.

I'm heading north, away from the city, away from the Mall and the monuments. Seven miles, fourteen round-trip. I know exactly where I'm headed.

I pass the sign for Friendship Heights, and as usual, my mind turns to Marta. That sense of worry runs through me again, leaves me unsettled.

I need to track her down, make absolutely sure she's safe.

I run faster. I can feel a tightness in my legs, muscles protesting, warning me I'm running too fast, too hard. There's sweat on my brow, and it's cool against my skin.

I'm in Bethesda now, in that neighborhood I know so well. Vivian's. Without thinking, I take a right onto her street, still running hard. Everything's hushed here. There are cars in driveways, light peeking through curtains and blinds, families tucked away for the night.

I catch sight of her house. Dark, like usual. But there's a car out front, idling, taillights and brake lights glowing. I feel a shiver at the nape of my neck.

A few strides more, close enough to see the shape. A hatchback. Virginia plates.

The same kind of car that drove away from Mom's condo, minutes after her fall.

Chapter 46

The brake lights blink, then the car starts moving. Away from me at first, but suddenly it swings around in a U-turn, headlights washing over where I stand. Instinctively I back away, into a thicket, hide myself there, heart thudding.

It continues on, and I watch it go. It's red. *A red hatchback.*

In my mind's eye I see that security footage from Mom's condo, the man in the dark cap exiting the elevator right after her fall, hustling out into the parking lot, sliding into a hatchback.

And now there's a hatchback in front of Vivian's house.

This isn't a coincidence.

It could be, scolds the voice in my head. The psychiatrist.

It's not, I tell her. And I feel it with every fiber of my being. Mom's fall wasn't an accident. The hatchback being here, that's not a coincidence.

You're getting paranoid, the voice jeers.

I need to see who's driving this car. I need to see where it goes.

I take off, feet pounding the pavement, eyes never leaving the taillights. I'll follow it as long as I can. There's a bigger road up ahead; maybe if the car gets stuck in traffic . . .

I'm at a sprint now, desperate to catch up to it, desperate not to lose it. It's stopped up ahead, at the intersection. There's a steady stream of cars whizzing down the cross street. I'm gaining ground while it waits, getting closer.

A break in traffic. The car turns right. *Shit.*

I'm almost there, almost at the road. If I can just keep it in my sights a little bit longer . . .

A taxi. I see it, out of the corner of my eye. Light on top, lit. I thrust my arm up as I approach the intersection, pray that I'm close enough that the driver will see me—

It veers sharply over to the curb, slows to a stop.

I slide into the taxi, pull the door shut. "Straight ahead," I gasp to the driver.

"Where to?"

"I'll direct you as we go."

This is insane. I'm wheezing, scanning the traffic, desperate for a flash of red. The taxi swoops into the left lane, picks up speed.

And then I see it.

About four cars up, right lane. Red hatchback. A surge of hope bolts through me. *I'm not paranoid.*

The car shoots right at the next intersection. "Right here," I instruct the driver.

We continue to follow behind, traveling at forty miles per hour. Deeper into Maryland. North Bethesda. We're almost into Rockville when the hatchback turns again. Left this time, into a neighborhood.

"Left here. But hang back a bit."

The driver eyes me in the rearview mirror. He knows I'm following the car. But he turns anyway. Slows, so the car is just in our sights.

The hatchback winds up a hill, down another. It's a wooded neighborhood, larger homes, mostly colonials. And we're the only two cars on the street. It's going to spot the tail, for sure. I need to peel off.

"Can you take a right here?"

The driver turns.

"If you could just idle here a moment . . ."

He pulls off to the side of the road, and I strain forward in my seat. Brake lights glow red. The car slows, driving at a crawl. Then unexpectedly picks up its pace again, continues on, until it's out of sight.

The driver's watching me in the mirror again, relishing this game, waiting for the next move. And I don't know what to tell him.

I want to tell him to step on the gas, to catch up to the hatchback. But I'm unarmed. Vulnerable. So's the taxi driver, and it's wrong to put him in jeopardy.

I study the street, that stretch where the hatchback slowed. If I can figure out why it was here . . .

"Can you drive down there?"

The driver complies.

One house in particular draws my attention. A two-story colonial, wide front porch. Minivan in the driveway.

There's a warm glow coming from inside. The windows are bare, no curtains, no blinds, nothing to block the view.

I see a woman, standing in front of her kitchen window, drying dishes.

Just as the car pulls even with the house, she looks up. We lock eyes, just for an instant.

And I feel my breath catch in my throat.

It's her.

Chapter 47

"Ma'am, which way?"

We're at an intersection. I look around, but there's no sign of the hatchback. But maybe, just maybe, I've found something even more crucial.

Two years. I've searched in vain for this woman for almost two years.

And here she is.

She's connected to Jackson somehow. She's the whole reason I'm in this mess, isn't she? It's all because I had this obsession to know if she was safe.

"Ma'am?" The driver's eyeing me again in the mirror. I hear the suspicion in his voice. I've pushed this too far.

"Dupont Circle."

He turns on his blinker.

As I listen to the sound, watch the blur of headlights around me, I think: Vivian's *here*. She's safe.

I close my eyes and take a breath. But all I can see in my mind is that hatchback. I see it pulling out of the parking lot after my mom's fall. Idling in front of Vivian's house. Now *here,* in front of this house.

Whoever's driving that car was involved with my mom's fall.

And now he's tracking Vivian. Spying on her.

And I was wrong. She's not safe after all, is she?

I stare at the chess set in front of me, still untouched, waiting for Zachary's move. But all I can think about is *my* next move.

Vivian Miller knows Jackson. Jackson is the one who resettled her after the incident in the row house; that's what Barker told me. And now she's back. Am I right? Is she in danger, another target, another victim of blackmail?

Or is she working for him, for the Russians?

My brain urges me to wait. Wait for Jackson to approach me again, record a confession, get him sent away. Each time I've dug around, searching for proof, I've dug Zachary deeper into a hole. I don't know Vivian Miller's story. I don't know how she fits into all of this. And without knowing that, approaching her would be a risk.

But my heart tells me she's a victim. That she's vulnerable.

Can I let that go?

Zachary's alarm blares at six. I listen to the shower as I sit at the table, coffee untouched, watching the clock.

Zachary swings around the corner, dressed in jeans and a hooded black sweatshirt. He blinks when he catches sight of me, shrugs, and heads for the pantry. Comes out a moment later, shoving protein bars into the back pocket of his jeans. About to dash. The sadness that hits me makes my eyes tear.

"What do you have going on at school today, honey?"

"Nothing."

"After school?"

"Nothing, Mom."

Frustration ripples through me. "Zachary, Grandma told me you visited last week."

"And?"

"And you never told me."

"So?" he challenges.

"She mentioned you brought *Lila*."

"Yeah? What's your point?"

"Zachary, you won't even *talk* to me about her."

"Why do you care?"

Why *do* I care? Why am I itching for a fight right now? "Because I'm your mother! Because I should know what's going on in your life."

"You never tell me what's going on in yours!"

"That's *completely* different."

"*Why?*"

"I'm your *mother,* Zachary. I should know who you're hanging around with, what you're doing. It's up to me to keep you safe."

"You don't think I feel the same way about you?"

Speechless, I stare at him. What's he *talking* about?

Before I can find words to respond, he stoops and kisses my cheek. A moment later, the front door slams shut.

The name on the mailbox says *Lane*. Not *Miller. Lane*.

There are lights on in the house, but I don't see anyone moving inside.

I ignore the doorbell. Instead I knock, hard. And I wait, breath held. Moments later, she's visible through the narrow window beside the door. We blink at each other through the glass. She looks like she's just seen a ghost. *She remembers me.*

A dead bolt unlocks, and the door swings open.

"Can I help you?" Vivian Miller asks, regaining her composure.

"Steph Maddox, FBI." I flash my credentials, and I can see the wariness return in her eyes. "Do you have a moment to chat?"

She studies my credentials carefully before she looks up and nods. "Yeah, of course. Would you like to come in?" She opens the door wider.

She ushers me into a living room. There's a worn couch against the wall, an overturned toy lawnmower in the corner. I sit down on the sagging cushions of the couch; a doll with a tattered dress is propped up on the opposite chair, regarding me unblinkingly.

"Viv? Everything okay in there?" A man's voice, from deeper within the house. There's a clang of pots and pans. The fridge door opening, shutting.

"Yeah," she calls back. She doesn't elaborate, doesn't mention me. And she doesn't take her eyes off me, either.

A toddler walks into the room, finally draws her attention away. "Chase, thumb out of your mouth," she orders, reaching out for the child. But her voice is tender.

Another boy walks in. A twin? They look around the same age, though this one's smaller. He heads for the toy lawnmower, grabs it, pushes it out of the room. The first boy pounds after him. I hear the lawnmower in the kitchen, along with more clanging.

"Sorry, it's a bit crazy in here," she tells me, with a brief smile. She sits, folding her hands in her lap. She's in a loose cream-colored top and slim black pants, black flats. Her hair is shorter than last time I saw her. "You have kids?"

"One. A son."

"How old?"

"Seventeen." It seems like only yesterday I was saying five.

"You don't look old enough to have a seventeen-year-old."

"How old are yours?"

"Nine, six, and the twins are three."

"Four kids. Wow."

I can see from her face she's used to hearing that.

"Viv, can you—" A man steps into the room. He's tall, with thick dark hair and square features, holding a spatula in one hand. He catches sight of me, stops. "Oh, I'm sorry. I didn't know . . ." He trails off, glances at Vivian quizzically.

"This is Special Agent Maddox," she tells him. "From the Bureau."

He smiles at me, completely at ease. Almost too much at ease, like having FBI agents pop by in the morning is a regular occurrence. "Nice to meet you, Agent Maddox." There's a screech from the other room, and then a girl's shriek. *Dad! Luke's cheating!* "Apologies for the commotion. Mornings are a bit chaotic around here."

"No problem at all."

His smile broadens and he steps out of the room. I hear him refereeing the kids' squabble, tamping down their protests in a calm tone.

"Sorry. Okay." I see no apprehension in her face, no indication she's concealing any sort of treasonous secret. But she's watching me carefully. "What can I do for you, Agent Maddox?"

"Call me Steph." I hesitate. There's more clanging in the kitchen. "We met once before. Years ago. The night—"

"I remember." Her gaze stays even. Her tone, final. The message is clear: *I don't want to talk about that day.*

"Are you still at the Agency?"

"I am."

"Still working on Russia?"

For the first time, something changes in her face. It was a shot in the dark, but I can tell from her expression that I'm right. I keep pressing.

"It's just that . . . Do you know a woman named Marta Marko-vich? She works for the Agency, too, and she's an old friend of mine, and I haven't been able to get in touch with her recently."

"Marta, yes, of course." The suspicion loosens, but doesn't leave her eyes.

"She doing okay?"

"I think so."

"You don't work with her anymore?"

She picks up the doll, smooths its collar down. "I can't really get into that sort of thing. I'm sure you understand."

Right. I know that from my conversations with Marta, about her. Another clang from the kitchen, footsteps, general breakfast-making chaos.

"Is there something I can help you with?" Vivian asks.

"Actually, yes. I want to talk to you about someone you've worked with in the past. A colleague of *mine,* actually. Deputy Director Jack-son."

Does that surprise her? I can't tell. "I know him well."

"Do you have any reason to believe he could be involved in any illegal activity?"

The sounds from the kitchen go quiet.

"Jackson?" She says it almost with a laugh. "Definitely not."

She looks like she's telling the truth. Like there's not a shred of truth to the accusation, in her mind at least.

"I'd trust him with my life," she adds, firmly. "In fact, I have."

She looks completely sincere. And it fills me with confusion, be-cause I remember that night. I remember the look on her face, and on his. The bite of his fingers on my arm—

I hear some sort of utensil against the side of a pan. The fridge door opening again, thumping shut.

"In that row house, the night of . . . that incident . . . you were keeping a secret." I'm not sure where I'm going with this. But I need to understand what it was, what she's hiding. "You were with Jackson. And ever since—" The house seems suddenly quiet. A shiver runs through me. "Ever since, I've been worried about you."

If she's surprised by this, she doesn't reveal it. "I'm fine."

Is she really? I try to read her expression, but all I see is that look of bone-deep fatigue. A woman doing her best to juggle kids, a marriage, a home, and a demanding job. I remember that feeling, from when Zachary was young. Like there weren't enough hours in the day. "Why'd you leave the country? You and your family?"

"How do you know that?"

"Why did you?" I press.

She gives me a searching look, and for a moment I think she's not going to answer. "There was a threat. I can't say more than that."

"And now you're back?"

"It's cooled down." Her tone is clipped. She wants to cut off this questioning, be done with it. She wants me out of her home, not reopening old scars.

I lean forward. "Do you feel safe? If someone's threatening you, if something's wrong . . ." I search for the right words, and settle for the simple truth. "I'd believe you."

She holds my gaze. I can tell from her expression that she remembers our last conversation, every word of it. But she doesn't reply.

I reach for a business card, scribble my personal cell on the back. And then, as an afterthought, my address. "If you think of anything," I say quietly, "or if you're ever in trouble, *find me*."

The kitchen has gone quiet. Vivian sets down the doll, almost tenderly, takes the card from me, then looks toward the kitchen, briefly. The sounds resume again, the rattle of cereal poured into a bowl, a stepstool being dragged across the floor, but when Vivian looks back at me, the confusion in her eyes has deepened.

There's music playing in the kitchen now. "If You're Happy and You Know It." Three kids clapping in unison, someone giggling.

"Take care of yourself, Vivian," I tell her, rising. "And those gorgeous kids of yours."

Chapter 48

I spend a few hours at the office, but I can't concentrate. Can't think of anything but my conversation with Vivian, which plays in a loop in my brain. Vivian *Lane*. She has a new identity. That's why I was never able to track her down.

She was out of the country, and now she's back. Working on Russia for the CIA.

Nothing about our conversation makes sense. She still seemed haunted by that night. But she sounded genuine when she said she trusts Jackson. *Trust him with my life.*

Around lunchtime I leave, drive to CIA headquarters. I need to find Marta. After my conversation with Vivian, I'm even more concerned about Marta's safety. She won't pick up her phone, won't answer her door; if there's any way to find her, to get answers, this is the place to do it. I flash my badge to the armed guards at the security checkpoint and drive into the sprawling, wooded compound.

The afternoon is cool, and I cinch my coat tighter around my waist as I walk from the parking lot to the building. Wind whips in, bringing a biting chill, making me shiver. Will spring never come?

I push through the doors at the entrance and see the famous seal emblazoned on the floor. There's a row of electronic turnstiles ahead, a handful of employees scanning their ID cards and keying codes into readers. And another security station off to the right; I head there, tell the guard I'm here to see Marta. Pull my credentials from my pocket and hold them up for the guard to see.

She gives a curt nod, then turns her attention to her computer screen. A moment later, she picks up the phone and dials. Turns her back to me slightly, and I take it as my cue to step aside, look away.

There's a television in my line of sight, off to the side of the guard post. An image of Wall Street is on the screen, with scrolling text about interest rates and unemployment numbers. I pretend to be fascinated.

The guard hangs up the phone and turns back to me. "Why don't you have a seat. We'll see what we can do."

I thank her and take a seat on a bench along the wall. Facing me are framed pictures of the CIA leadership team. The director, Harrison Drake. Two deputies, one for intelligence, one for operations. The former looks familiar; I remember reading an article about her once, feeling a little nip of envy. Elise Brandt. A woman, barely older than me, already the Agency's number two.

There's a steady stream of people coming through the doors, making their way through the lobby, toward the turnstiles. I watch them, and then I glance at the clock on the wall. With each passing minute, I'm more unsettled. My palms are clammy. I can feel dampness on my forehead.

I turn away and another section of the wall catches my attention. It's a quote, etched into the marble. *And ye shall know the truth, and the truth shall make you free.*

I stare at the words, read them silently, hear them echo in my mind. For the first time, I find myself questioning them. I've always believed that the truth would prevail; deep down, I still do. But it's not so black-and-white anymore. I know the truth about Jackson. And it's done anything *but* make me free. Knowing the truth means I'm trapped.

On the television, a segment on the recent earthquake in Turkey runs. Images of people standing among the rubble. In an instant, their lives crumbled around them. Their world will never be the same.

I look back at the clock, feeling the steady creep of anxiety. I'm losing the upper hand. The element of surprise is gone. And that might not be all. The longer I sit here, the more likely Jackson will find out what I'm doing.

I'm about to walk over and ask the guard for an update when her phone bleats. She picks it up, listens, then glances in my direction, and I know the call is about me. "Yes," she says. "Right here." I don't even try to hide that I'm listening. I watch her, and out of the corner of my eye I see the television screen go red, *Breaking News* flashing in white.

"Yeah," the guard says. She casts another hasty glance in my direction. On the television, the anchor's face appears. *Plot! More Details Emerge.* Fear is starting to simmer inside me.

Another guard walks over to the TV, turns up the volume.

". . . *according to the unnamed government source, terrorist targets include the directors of the CIA and FBI, as well as the Senate majority leader. The majority leader has reportedly requested enhanced security for the named targets—*"

"Agent Maddox?" I hear, and I turn toward the voice with a start. It's the guard.

"Yes?" I get to my feet.

"I'm sorry, but the woman you're looking for won't be able to see you."

Won't be able to see you. Not won't be able to see you *now*. *Won't be able to see you*. Did they get to her, too? Did they hurt her, the way they hurt Mom?

This was a mistake. Whatever it means, this was a mistake.

"Vivian Miller, then. Sorry, Vivian Lane. I need to see Vivian Lane." Maybe *here* she'd tell me something about Marta. Maybe *here* I'd know if she's really, truly safe.

"I'm sorry, but you're not authorized to be here. You're going to have to leave."

Not authorized to be here? More strains from the news bulletin reach me. "*. . . CIA director . . . FBI director . . . Senate majority leader . . .*"

"Agent Maddox?" the guard repeats, and I blink, refocus on her face. And it might be my imagination, or it might be my training, but I can see the hand at her side rising ever so slightly, like it's getting into position to draw her gun quickly, should the need arise.

"Yes, I'm sorry," I mumble, turning, gathering my bag, completely unsettled now. "I'll be going."

My eyes light on the quote on the wall again as I walk past it. *And ye shall know the truth . . .*

If only I didn't. If only I never saw Jackson's hand on Vivian's back, never let it haunt me the way it did. If only my past hadn't convinced me there was something more there.

I start walking quickly toward the exit, like I can't get out of here fast enough. The place suddenly feels dangerous; everything feels dangerous.

That breaking news. Naming the targets. It wasn't a coincidence that it happened while I was here, waiting. While the guard was on the phone.

It was another warning, and I suddenly realize it might be the last one. Because what else can Jackson release? All the other pieces are there now, out in the public. The identity of FSM. The threat of violence. The targets. It's a solid plot. The only piece that's missing is Zachary's name.

I push my way outside into the icy air, desperate to be out of that building. And as I do, I see a black Suburban pull away from the curb, where it had been idling, close to the entrance. As it passes by, I catch a glimpse of the man in the backseat.

And I'd swear it was Jackson.

Chapter 49

The rest of Monday drags by, then most of Tuesday, too. I spend a few hours both days at Mom's bedside. Mostly we watch television together, or chat with Zachary when he stops by. Conversation between the two of us is stilted, awkward.

I don't try to contact anyone else, don't do any more research. I'm convinced that doing so would be reckless. That my activity's being monitored. That nothing's private, nothing's safe. Will there be more warnings? Or is the next step releasing Zachary's name?

Yesterday morning, I dug through my desk drawers until I found the picture Barker gave me, the one of Vivian. I placed it in front of me on the desk and stared. And irrational as it was, it made me angry. This is all because of her. If I'd only let it go, none of this would have happened. My son would be safe.

I've continued to wear the recording equipment, review the tapes from inside the house, check the security system almost obsessively. It's surveillance, really, like those countless, mindless hours I've spent sitting in cars over the years, watching houses, waiting for someone to appear. Patience is the nature of the job. Be patient, and the criminal will slip up.

But so far, no one's slipped up. I haven't seen Jackson again, and I haven't heard from him. I look at my phone compulsively, the text. *Have you made a decision?* Sometimes I touch the screen, bring up the keyboard, imagine typing a response, telling him I'll do it. It would be so simple.

We did Chinese takeout last night, Zachary and me, then we sat on the couch together and watched TV—that competition show with the obstacle course. "Gonna be weird not living here anymore," he said, out of the blue, catching me off guard. "I mean, if I get into any schools," he adds miserably.

"You will," I say. And then, more gently, "It's going to be weird for both of us." What I really meant was, *I'm going to miss you, too.*

Pizza delivery tonight, followed by chess, finally. He moved his rook, just like I thought he would. And I took it. Then he moved his queen, sacrificed her, because it was the only way to protect the king. And so we were at a stalemate, once again.

At least I'm putting up a good fight. I haven't lost yet.

Zachary says good night and the dull thump of bass begins reverberating overhead. I open an IPA, drink it while I sit in the living room, staring at the chessboard. Why don't I know what the next move will be?

When the bottle's empty, I drop it into the recycling bin, open another. I sit back down on the couch, and my thoughts turn to Scott. I close my eyes and picture him here, beside me.

What would have happened if I'd let Scott interrogate Zachary that day? He'd have seen the truth, that Zachary wasn't involved, that my son had never heard of FSM. And then, maybe, we'd have been in this together. Fighting this, together.

God, how I wish I had someone on my side. How I wish I wasn't in this alone.

Inexplicably, my thoughts turn to Vivian Miller. To her smiling husband, spatula in hand, corralling the children for breakfast.

I take the last sip of beer and bring the bottle to kitchen, drop it in the recycling bin. It clatters against the last one, almost violently. Drowns out the thumping bass from upstairs, if only for a moment.

What if it's not too late? What if I talk to Scott, tell him everything?

What if we can fight this together after all?

It's unseasonably cold in Nebraska, wintrier even than D.C., three or four inches of crisp, fresh snow on the ground. I rent a car at the Omaha airport and drive to Scott's house, the address I found in his personnel file.

It's a boxy house, two-story, roof glistening white. The lights are off, the driveway shoveled and empty. I sit idling in my car and watch the street, watch the house, wait for Scott to appear.

At twenty past five, a black sedan approaches, pulls into the driveway.

I step out of my car just as Scott's stepping out of his. He's in a long wool coat, his breath crystallizing in front of him. He goes still when he sees me.

"We need to talk, Scott."

"I told you I don't want to be part of this."

"Just hear me out."

A snowplow rumbles onto the street. Scott watches it briefly, then turns and heads toward the front door, his boots crunching the snow. I follow, and he doesn't try to stop me.

He slides his key into the lock, and I focus on his hair again, that streak of gray I first noticed that night he arrived at my door to question me about Zachary.

My eyes drift down to his left hand. It's bare.

He catches me looking. Meets my gaze, holds it. Then, without a word, he opens the door, gestures for me to step inside. I do, apprehensively.

He follows me inside, flips on the lights, shuts and locks the door behind us. I pull off my coat and hang it on a hook beside the door. The house screams bachelor pad, short-term rental. It's sparsely furnished, the living room nothing more than couch and television, a cardboard box doubling as a coffee table. Kitchen appliances look decades old; the countertops are bare. He's been in Omaha more than a week, but you'd never guess from this empty house.

Scott looks at me like he's trying to figure out what to say. Finally he holds up his left hand, looks at the spot where the ring should be. "Feels weird without it. . . . It's been over for a while. The move to Omaha . . ." He shakes his head, quirks a smile. "That was the nail in the coffin."

"I'm sorry, Scott," I say. And partly, I am. I'm sorry for the role I played in it. Sorry he's hurting.

"Said she wasn't leaving her job, wasn't pulling the kids out of school." He sinks down into the couch, a threadbare one. "So who is it, Steph? Who's doing this?"

I need to say the name, even though everything's telling me not to. "Jackson."

"The deputy director?"

"Yes."

He's watching me, frowning. But there's something else on his face now, a strange mix of emotion. Curiosity and anger. Frustration.

But the doubt is gone. And my heart starts to race. I'm so relieved I have to bite back laughter.

He believes me.

"Why?" Scott wants to know.

I can do this. This is why I came here.

I think back to that conversation, all those years ago, when things ended between us. *I can't be with someone who won't open up to me. Who won't trust me.*

I trust Scott; I do. More than I've ever trusted another man—another person—in all my life.

So I tell him everything. The whole truth. From the very beginning to the very end.

By the time I'm done, I feel like a weight has been lifted from my shoulders. I feel freer than I have in days, since this all began. In *years*, really.

He's listened, asked a few questions, nodded. But I can tell from his expression that he believes me, as insane as this all sounds.

I'm not sure he's ever meant more to me than he does right now.

But whatever weight I've lifted from myself, I've placed on him. I can see it. His eyes are haunted; his voice is hollow. "Shit, Steph," he says when I've finished. "I wish you'd told me about Halliday. A long time ago."

"I wish I had, too." God, I really do. Life might be so different right now if I'd never kept that secret.

"Is he part of this?"

"I don't know. I mean, it's got to be Jackson. But the timing . . . it's just too much of a coincidence."

His eyes rake my face, a gaze as intimate, somehow, as a caress. "So what do we do now?"

The words bring a smile to my lips, one I don't try to stop this time, can't repress.

We.

Scott and I talk through our options, what few there are. Try to figure out our next move. How we're supposed to stop a corrupt FBI deputy director, one who's working for a foreign adversary, one who's already proven he has the reach to affect our lives, personal and professional.

The answer isn't clear, not in the slightest.

At around seven, I realize I'm starving. He suggests Thai, says there's a great restaurant downtown. "Panang curry and pad Thai?" he asks, with a smile.

I smile back, feeling wistful. How different my life might have been if he'd stayed in it. We could have been a family, the two of us and Zachary.

We still could.

I catch myself looking down at his left hand again.

"Beer, too?" he asks.

"The hoppiest you can find."

He grins again, and this time I swear *he's* the one who looks wistful. *He's* the one who looks full of regret. And the realization fills me with anticipation. With *hope*. And it's strange, because I don't even remember the last time I felt this way.

He grabs his coat and leaves, and I call Mom. She's asleep, but I speak briefly to her doctor. They'll be sending her home very soon. I'll need to convince her to stay with Zachary and me. I don't tell her I'm in Omaha. Then I call Zachary, let him know I'm spending the night here, will fly home in the morning. "You in for the night?" I ask him.

"Yep."

"Did you eat? Doors locked?"

"Yeah, Mom."

"Give your grandmother a call. And call me if you need anything. Love you."

He mumbles an *I love you, too.*

I turn on the television, mute the sound. There's a commercial on, for life insurance. An older couple strolls along the beach, smiling and laughing, while text below urges viewers to *Call today for a free quote!*

Scott's married. It's a line I won't cross, ever.

But he won't be married forever.

I turn my thoughts back to Jackson, and our options. Trying to figure out our next move. I raise the volume on the TV to keep myself awake. I'm half listening when a phrase cuts through my thoughts.

"*. . . Vice President Sam Donnolly was asked about the threat this afternoon. . . .*"

The threat?

The screen changes, and footage of the vice president appears. He's standing on a factory floor, at what looks to be an impromptu press conference. An off-camera question is audible: "*The majority leader called for more robust protective measures. . . . Are you saying it's not necessary?*" The camera zooms in for his response.

"*I've seen the intel,*" Donnolly answers, "*and frankly I think it's a load of malarkey.*" Bulbs flash around him; the sound of the shutters is audible. He pauses dramatically, a born politician, looks around, then his gaze settles straight on the camera. "I give the American people *my word* that this attack will not happen."

Somehow, hearing him say it gives me another surge of hope. Because he's right; this chatter about an assassination plot is nonsense. The press is blowing it all way out of proportion. I see it, Donnolly sees it. Soon everyone will see it. The truth will come out. And the truth is that the FSM plot is bogus.

Chapter 50

The next thing I know, light is streaming through the windows, glittering off the fresh snow.

The television's on, but now it's one of those morning shows. Cheery hosts, a brightly colored set, lots of chatter about the snowstorm that hit the Midwest.

Shit. How long did I sleep?

I struggle into a sitting position, look around for Scott, but I'm alone in the room. I fumble for my phone and check the screen: 7:34 A.M.

Dammit, Steph.

The house is quiet; Scott must still be asleep. All I can hear is the TV and the whoosh of the furnace. I get to my feet, wander into the kitchen. Look for coffee, don't see any. He was never a coffee drinker, was he?

My stomach growls. Curry and pad Thai—I'm hungry enough that it sounds good, even for breakfast. I open the fridge to find the leftovers.

There's a carton of juice, a bag of deli meat, an unopened package of sliced cheese.

No Thai leftovers, no beer.

Concern starts to creep through me, but I tamp it down. He said he was hungry, didn't he? He finished the food he brought home.

I look for the trash can, peer inside.

No food containers. No beer bottles.

Still I try to reason with myself. The restaurant was closed, because of the snow. He came home without dinner.

I walk quietly upstairs. Peek through one door; the room's empty, not a single piece of furniture. Then another—the bathroom. There's a third door, closed. I listen, hear nothing.

I tap softly, push it open, just enough to see inside. Scott's bedroom, I think. Queen bed, unmade, sheets askew. There's a biography of J. Edgar Hoover open on the nightstand.

"Scott?" I call cautiously. "Are you here?"

Silence.

"Scott?"

Downstairs again, I open the door to the basement. I flip on the light, peer down the stairs. The faint smell of mold wafts up at me. "Scott?"

His car's not in the driveway. There are no tracks in the snow. Unease is running through me. But there's got to be an explanation. Scott was here, and had to leave. He's already at work.

I find my phone, pull up his number, dial.

Four rings, then voicemail. I end the call.

I pull up another number. Zachary answers on the first ring.

"Hey, Mom."

"Hi, honey. Everything okay there?"

"Yep."

"Okay, good." *Be careful,* I have the urge to say.

But he tells me he overslept and he's going to be late for school and ends the call.

My unease is spiraling into something more. But it shouldn't be. Zachary's fine. Scott's just at work.

I walk back upstairs, into the bathroom. Start the shower, turn it as hot as it'll go. Undress, test the water, still not hot.

A thought hits me. If he's at work, I can reach him there.

I pull a towel off the rack, wrap it around myself. Head back downstairs for my phone. Search for the number for the field office, call the main number. A woman answers. "Special Agent Scott Clark, please," I say.

"I'm sorry," comes the reply, crisply. "Agent Clark's not here."

"Can you transfer the call in?"

"Who's calling, please?"

I end the call. Dial his cell again.

Straight to voicemail this time.

Something's wrong.

I navigate to my email, the work one. Not even sure why; it's instinct, really.

Scan the subject lines, and then my eyes stop.

A heartbreaking loss.

Sent nineteen minutes ago by the head of the Washington Field Office.

I double-click, read the words. My hand is trembling. Everything inside of me is screaming this can't be what I think it is, what I know it is.

It's with a heavy heart that I'm forced to report the tragic death of an agent who was, until recently, one of our own.

This can't be.

. . . one-car accident last night . . . snow . . . road conditions . . .

Please, God, no.

. . . Special Agent Scott Clark . . .

My eyes stop. My heart feels like it stops, too.

Scott.

Chapter 51

I'm reading the words, but it's not real. This is all a bad dream, some terrible nightmare.

. . . icy road . . . died on impact . . .

No.

This isn't happening.

. . . no witnesses . . . investigation ongoing . . .

Not Scott, no.

The phone falls from my hands. Panic and nausea cascade through me in waves.

In my mind I see him. Back when we were first dating, when we were young and ambitious and ridiculously in love. I see him with Zachary, playing baseball at the park, always hitting those pop-ups he knew my son could catch. And last night, before he left for food, the teasing grin on his face, the light in his eyes.

I'm the one who got him into this. Who dragged him back into it, pleaded with him to help me, flew all the way out here to Omaha. I'm the one who got him killed. If I hadn't said I was hungry, he'd never have gone out.

I realize too late that my legs are giving out, buckling. I collapse to the floor, sobbing uncontrollably.

Scott. My Scott. Dead.

While I was here, sleeping, Scott died. The police found his body, notified his wife, the Bureau, and the whole time I was sleeping. I feel like I'm going to vomit.

How can this be happening? How can Scott be gone?

Jackson did this.

The thought is a spark at first, one that catches and spreads until it's a raging firestorm.

Jackson did this. Because I told Scott the truth.

Because he was willing to help me.

After an eternity, I struggle to my feet, cinch the towel tighter around myself, swipe the tears from my face. The shower's still running. The bathroom door's half open. I push it wide, and I'm met with a wave of steam, like a sauna.

The first thing I see is the mirror.

All steamed up, except for a message:

Z'S NEXT

Chapter 52

Steam is already starting to fade the words, condensation dripping through them like blood, blurring them, even as I watch. In moments, they'll be nothing. The message will vanish.

I bolt toward the shower, lunge for the faucet. The gush of water stops; the house goes quiet, except for the drip of the last drops swirling down the drain. I strain for any sounds of the intruder who left this threat.

My gun. My gun's in the living room, on top of the mantel; that's where I left it last night. Is it still there?

I fumble for my clothes, yank them on. Then I step out of the bathroom, heart racing, ears still tuned for any whisper of sound in the house, any way of knowing where this person is.

I creep downstairs, stealthily. My Glock's on the mantel, still there. I quicken my pace, reach for it, check to make sure it's still loaded. Grip it tight in both hands.

The back door. It's wide open. I walk closer, feel the chill surge in from outside.

I look out, gun raised. There are footprints in the fresh snow, leading away, into the woods.

The icy air cuts through my clothes, and I can't stop shivering. Whoever was here is gone.

Z's next.

I'm in the car minutes later, on my way to the airport, foot pressed down on the gas, much too hard. The roads are plowed, but slippery. I text Zachary. *Call me.* My phone rings seconds later.

"I need you to be extra careful today," I tell him. I know I'm scaring him. But I'm so far away from him right now, and I know he's in danger. I know what these people are capable of.

"What's going on?"

What am I supposed to say? Violence? Murder? "You were right. It's like Chicago, only worse."

He swears softly. A week ago, I could have scolded him for using that word. "It's him, isn't it? Halliday?"

It might be, at least partly. But the truth—the depth of this—is even more terrifying. "Zachary—it's complicated."

"Are you in danger, Mom?" He asks it bluntly.

I picture Scott's car, that black sedan, crumpled and twisted. I squeeze my eyes shut, try to force out the image, but it won't go away. *Am* I in danger? "I'm concerned about *you.* So you need to promise me you'll be careful."

"He can't get away with this—"

School. D.C.'s an hour ahead of Omaha; Zachary's at school, and they'll know exactly where he is. Fear hits me like a body blow. "I need you to skip school today."

"What?"

"Leave school." I'm racking my brain for some safe place for him, and in my mind all I can see is my mother. "Go to the hospital. Stay with Grandma today."

"Really, Mom?" His voice wavers with fear. I'm scaring him.

"Zachary. Do as I say."

"I love you, Mom." I can picture the worry on his face. But it's not his face now. It's the face of that lonely, scared child, in that rearview mirror all those years ago.

"I love you, too, Zachary."

The weather snarled air traffic in Omaha, delayed my flight home by hours. I'm finally back. It's cold in D.C., but blissfully free of snow. I head straight to headquarters. I'm not going to wait any longer for Jackson to approach me. I'm going to do something I should have done days ago. I'm going to go after him.

He killed Scott. *My* Scott. He took Scott away from me. He hurt my mother, and now he's threatened my son. I won't be terrorized any longer.

I stride into the lobby, past the security guard, take the elevator up to his floor. I swing open the door to the anteroom and his secretary looks up from her desk. Surprise flickers across her face, then confusion.

"I need to see him," I say brusquely. I don't wait for her to reply, but cross the anteroom, toward the closed door to his personal office. I'm there before she can respond, and I swing it open.

The office is empty.

"He's not here," bleats the secretary, trailing after me. I breathe deeply, needing to slow my pounding heart, and glare at the vacant desk, like my anger can somehow make him reappear. Then I turn on my heel.

"Where is he?"

Her look changes instantly from confusion to fear. Not surprising; I'm certainly acting unstable right now. She returns to her desk, turns her attention to some papers in front of her, shuffles through them. Pauses, reads something.

"Agent Maddox, right?" she asks, without looking up.

"Yes." She knows damn well who I am, and she can report me to security if she wants. I'm going to get the recorded admission, and I'm going to come clean, and it's going to happen today.

"The deputy director's due at the Grand Ambassador Hotel this evening. Charity dinner—" she begins, and I'm out the door without listening to the rest.

The Grand Ambassador is a stone's throw from the White House. It's a storied nineteenth-century landmark turned modern luxury hotel. There's a wide circular drive in front, and I pull into it now, bring the car to a stop along the curb. A valet greets me just as I'm opening the door. "FBI," I say quietly, discreetly flashing my badge. He glances at it and backs off.

I can't stop thinking about Scott. Picturing his sedan, crushed. Fury is making it hard to breathe. I know I need to think clearly, but I can't.

The bank of glass doors leads into an oversized atrium, one with marble floors and crystal chandeliers and heavy gold drapes framing huge windows. There's a tall clock tower in the center. A reception desk and a grand piano off to one side, a sitting area off to the other. At the far end of the room is a set of huge double doors, the entrance to the ballroom.

I scan the room, don't see Jackson. There's just a scattering of people. I eye each individual as I stride through the room, as if any one of them could be a threat.

I make my way quickly to the double doors at the back of the atrium. There's a gilded sign in front. I recognize the name; it's one of those events that always draws a handful of cabinet members, some senators and representatives, and the people willing to shell out big bucks to mingle with them.

A harried-looking man in a tuxedo hurries past, a tablet in his hand like a clipboard. One of the organizers, no doubt. I stop him, show my badge.

"Is Jackson here?" I snap. "The deputy director of the FBI?"

He looks first at my badge, then at my face, blinks. "Jackson? No."

He scurries away and I walk back into the center of the lobby, then over to the sitting area. I take a seat on a small tufted bench that offers a clear view of the front doors, all the way through the atrium and down to the double doors of the ballroom.

More people are coming, dressed to the nines. But all I can see in my mind is Scott. His grin. His arms around me, the way it felt to rest my head against his chest. Watching Zachary race toward him, giggle with him, ride on his shoulders.

Died on impact.

There's a window behind me, covered with heavy shimmery curtains. I pull one aside slightly so I can see out. The view is of a service door, the concrete landing in front of it, surrounded by white rails. Two men stand outside, kitchen staff by the looks of them. Both in black pants and shirts, white aprons over top. One has a cigarette, dropping ash, the other holds a cup of coffee. They're leaning against the rails, huddled against the cold, chatting.

I turn away from the window and scan the lobby again, focusing on the area near the entrance. Still no Jackson. I lay my hand on my shirt, discreetly feel the recorder underneath. I'm ready to go. When he arrives, I'll get an admission. And I'll take it directly to Director Lee, tell him everything that's happening. Zachary will be in the clear. Mom will be safe. And Jackson won't hurt anyone again. He'll be locked up for the rest of his life.

Men in tuxedos, women in rainbow-colored gowns, warm coats

over top, arrive. They float through the atrium back to the ball-room, chattering and smiling. The man with the tablet greets them, ushers them inside.

On the hour, a woman in a long dress of black lace takes a seat at the grand piano, starts playing show tunes. More guests pour in. There's still no sign of Jackson. My nerves are starting to fray.

A silver-haired man with a security detail arrives. He looks vaguely familiar; a member of Congress, I think. Then another congress-man. A senator from Tennessee. The number of people in the lobby grows. More arriving guests, more hotel patrons stopping to watch the spectacle. I glance at the clock in the center of the atrium, then settle my gaze on the bank of glass doors. He has to arrive soon.

More dignitaries. Some saunter through, smiling and nodding to the onlookers. Others walk resolutely, their heads down. In be-tween arrivals, I'm watching the accumulating clusters of hotel guests in the lobby, the gaggle of reporters gathering near the clock.

I glance again out the window behind me, but the landing is empty now. The kitchen staff are gone, no doubt preparing to start serving dinner. Time crawls by, and Jackson still hasn't arrived. I take out my phone, wonder if I should call his secretary, try to pin-point exactly where he is.

Then I glance back at the doors, and my heart stutters. A familiar face is there, walking into the atrium, holding his wife's hand. The director of the FBI. J. J. Lee, accompanied by three men in crisp white shirts, suits, one in front and two behind. The group moves briskly through the lobby. Lee flashes a smile at one of the senators.

I'm on edge now, completely so. This isn't the first time I've taken down someone powerful, but this feels different. My eyes dart from face to face, looking for anyone suspicious, anyone who might be doing surveillance of their own, someone who's watching me. Ev-eryone seems innocuous, but I don't let my guard down.

I glance back out the window behind me, and what I see makes me take a sharp breath.

There's another man outside now. Same black uniform, no apron. He's leaning against the railing, staring off into the distance, taking a drag from a cigarette. And his face is familiar; I know him.

Dylan Taylor.

He blows a lazy stream of smoke from his lips, taps some ash off the end of the cigarette. Hunches his shoulders against the cold, but otherwise looks at ease, calm.

There's a tingling sensation at the back of my neck, a strong instinct that something is terribly wrong. It feels like all the pieces are there in my mind, but they're not in the right order, haven't snapped together, refuse to make sense.

Dylan's a waiter. Surge staffing for special events. Hotels. Works Thursdays. It shouldn't be strange that he's here; it makes sense. So why does it feel so wrong?

He drops the cigarette, grinds it under his heel, then walks back inside, the service door slamming shut behind him. And then the spot where he had been standing is empty, and it seems almost like he was never there, like it was all a bad dream.

My mind is still struggling to process what I just saw, what it means, if it means anything at all. Maybe it's nothing, maybe it's a coincidence. But in my experience, something like this, it *means* something. It's part of something bigger. Everything's part of something bigger.

I pull my attention back to the present, and I try to focus. Jackson. That's why I'm here. Jackson is arriving any moment now. My gaze goes to the bank of glass doors.

There's a figure standing there, one that's such an expected sight, and at the same time *not,* because he shouldn't be here, he doesn't belong. But he's *here,* looking around, awkward and out of place, in a heavy hooded sweatshirt and jeans, a backpack slung on one shoulder.

My whole body goes cold.

It's Zachary.

Chapter 53

He's standing still, looking around like he's searching for someone. His hair falls across his forehead, skimming his left eye.
He adjusts the backpack on his shoulder.

I don't understand. My mind is struggling to connect the dots,
or maybe protesting against the picture that's beginning to emerge,
insisting that it can't be true.

Zachary, here.

Dylan Taylor, here.

I'm moving closer to my son; I didn't even realize I'd stood,
started walking. He pulls out his phone and frowns down at it.

I'm nearly to him when he looks up again, catches sight of me. I
see recognition light his face, just for an instant. Then confusion
flashes across it. "Mom?"

I take hold of his arm and move to the side of the lobby, toward
the reception desk. I search his face, my hand still gripping his arm,
not letting go. His eyes are round; his confusion has deepened. He
looks worried. But is there anything more there? Is there guilt?

Zachary, in the same place as Dylan Taylor. What the hell is
going on?

"What are you doing here?" I ask, too loudly. A woman in a frilly pink dress looks up and scowls. "Why aren't you at the hospital?"

"Meeting someone." He's instantly defensive. "Chill, Mom."

"Who?"

My heart is pounding. He's here, in the same place as Dylan, the same place Jackson's supposed to be.

It's not a coincidence.

And then, as I watch him check his phone again, realization hits.

Someone lured him here. Someone wants Zachary here, in this hotel, at this very moment.

I tear my eyes away from him, look around the lobby. I don't even know what I'm looking for. My gaze skitters over random faces, ones that seem like maybe they're watching us, even though I know they're not. I look for Jackson. I don't see him.

"Mom, what's going on?"

Two women in sequined dresses and fur coats walk through the glass doors, laughing. Just behind them is a small cluster of people. Four of them, dark suits and flexible earpieces, surrounding a silver-haired man and woman in the center, matching their pace, walking in step, like a protective box. I catch sight of the silver-haired man's profile; it's CIA director Harrison Drake.

Director Drake is at the ballroom doors now. My eyes are locked on him, the back of his black jacket. The image of Director Lee walking through the lobby flashes through my mind.

And then I'm walking again, running, without even realizing it. *Mom?* I hear Zachary call after me. But I'm moving quickly through the lobby, toward the ballroom doors. Director Drake disappears into the ballroom. Same place as Director Lee.

I'm in front of the tuxedoed man now, the one with the tablet. "I need the guest list," I say.

He nods, then hands the tablet to me. I scan the list of names on the screen, heart pounding. And then my eyes stop.

There it is.

He's on the list. Senate majority leader Shields.

All three of the targets, here, in one place.

The fragments of information swirling around in my brain slam together in that very moment into a single, awful truth.

There's going to be an attack, and they're going to frame Zachary for it.

There's a small square box in front of Shields's name. Unchecked. The senator's not here yet.

And if I can keep him from arriving, I might buy us time.

I thrust the tablet back at the tuxedoed man and pull out my phone, find the FBI operations center on speed dial, place the call, hold the phone to my ear.

"FBI Special Agent Steph Maddox," I say, when the call connects. "I need the Senate majority leader's security detail. It's urgent."

There's a pause on the line, and I rush through the lobby, elbowing my way through the guests, back to Zachary, the phone still pressed against my ear. People are staring at me. I see him there, ahead of me, where I left him, watching me.

I need to get Zachary out of here. He's in danger now, more danger than I ever thought possible.

"Leave," I say, when I reach him.

"Mom—"

"You need to leave. *Now.*" I tighten my grip on his arm, start steering him toward the door. He braces himself at first, resisting, then he moves.

"Mom, I don't understand—"

"Honey, just trust me on this one. You need to leave." There's desperation in my voice; I can hear it. I'm sure he can, too.

We push through the doors, out into the cold air, to the wide walkway in front of the hotel. Everything looks normal. Valets, a stray luggage cart, cars idling on the curb. It doesn't look like the scene of an imminent attack.

But it is, isn't it?

All three targets will be here.

"What's going on?" Zachary asks again, and I realize he's staring at me. And I feel tremendous guilt, because surely he can see my fear, the fear I've always tried so hard to mask, to let him think everything's okay, even if it's not, to protect him.

Emotion wells inside me. He's too young to face this. "I'm sorry, honey."

"For what? What is it, Mom?"

"Dammit, Zachary, just do what I say," I snap.

At that, hurt crosses his face, a pain that looks all too familiar. How many times have I been short with him? How many times have I not taken the time to explain?

It's not that I won't, I think. *I can't.*

"This is Shields's detail," comes a voice in my ear.

"Zachary, don't argue with me this time. Just *go*." I turn on my heel and stride back through the glass doors, saying a silent prayer that Zachary obeys me. "What's your ETA?"

"We're three minutes out."

"Turn around."

"Ma'am?"

"*Turn around.* Do not approach the premises. Repeat, *do not approach the premises.*"

I end the call and drop the phone back into my pocket. Fear is coursing through me. I can feel the eyes of bystanders on me as I elbow through the lobby, but I don't see them. I don't see anything except those double doors at the back of the room. The doors that lead to the ballroom where Director Lee is sitting, and Director

Drake, and countless members of Congress and a host of innocent people who have no idea what's about to happen.

I'm almost at the double doors. I see the tuxedoed man near the registration table. "Who's in charge of security?" I snap.

"Who?" I bark, almost a shout now, when he doesn't answer, and he starts to stammer as the color drains from his face, but I don't have time to wait. The clock's ticking. I turn abruptly and reach for the door handle. It doesn't matter who's in charge. We need to get those people out of there. I'll make the announcement myself, for God's sake.

I'm pulling the door open when I hear the first screams.

Chapter 54

I'm too late.

I try desperately to process what's happening on the other side of the door, what's causing those screams, what sort of danger there is. But I can't tell; I don't know.

I draw my gun. It doesn't matter what's going on inside. Whatever it is, I need to get in there. I need to help.

I swing the door open and see chaos. Women in gowns and men in tuxedos, panic on their faces, heading in my direction, toward the doors, the beginnings of a mass exodus.

I step forward, try to see around them, through them. I strain to hear any other sounds that can tell me what kind of danger lies ahead—gunshots, shrieks of pain—but all I hear are those screams, those panicked screams, coming from deep within the big room.

When the wave of people reaches me, I stand still and let it part around me. People are pushing, tripping over high heels and long gowns, desperate to get away. A woman in bright red sees my gun and yips in terror, spinning away from me.

The screams stop, and a wail takes their place. I start moving, pushing my way through the crowd, like a fish headed upstream, trying to see past the fleeing mass, the terrified faces, heading blindly in the direction of the thin, piercing wail that doesn't stop.

I can make out two clusters toward the front of the ballroom, a few tables apart. Circles of people, crouched down, each surrounding something—or more likely, *someone*—on the floor. I know these circles; they're the kind that surround victims.

Victims. Oh God, they've done it, haven't they? CIA director, FBI director, Senate majority leader . . . those were really targets.

Shields isn't here yet, but Drake is, and Lee—

I head for the nearer circle, stepping around an overturned Chiavari chair. There are two men standing on the edges of the group, jackets off, holsters exposed, guns trained in my direction. Instinct, and all my training, tells me they're on my team. Members of a security detail.

"FBI!" I shout as I approach.

They hesitate, but don't lower their weapons. I'm close enough now that I can see the fear on their faces, the uncertainty.

I move closer to the circle. There's a man on the floor, in a tuxedo. Another man crouching over him, blocking my view of his face, pressing on his chest, doing CPR. Others staring with horrified looks, some with hands over their mouths. Someone is weeping inconsolably.

A woman lets out a wail. I can finally see the victim's face. There's blood smeared under his nose, trickling from the side of his mouth. His green eyes are vacant.

Director Lee.

The room feels suddenly like it's spinning. I back away, one step, then two.

The director of the FBI is dead.

FBI director, CIA director, Senator majority leader. Director Drake's in the middle of that other circle, isn't he?

The woman's wail intensifies. I run to the other cluster.

A man sprawls in the center of a throng of stunned people. Blood spatters the crisp white front of his tuxedo shirt. Over him, a woman bends, attempting CPR.

I'm dimly aware of a shout, nearby. *". . . intended victim . . . Get him the hell out of here!"*

There's a silver-haired man being rushed toward a service door at the far end of the room, agents on all sides. Director Drake.

Drake's alive.

I turn. I look back at the cluster of people, confused.

Intended victim.

Someone else is in this circle. Someone who wasn't meant to die.

I take a step forward, then another, and for the first time I see the face of the victim in the middle. Blood dribbles from his nose and mouth.

A face that I know well, because it has haunted me for years.

Halliday.

He's dead; this monster is dead.

And he deserves it.

The thought is overpowering. I see him as a young senator, my boss, his hands on my arms, gripping tight. . . .

I blink quickly, pull myself back to the present, to the victim in front of me, sprawled at my feet. Guilt tears through me. How could I even think that? No one deserves to die this way.

Halliday was murdered. It doesn't matter if he deserved it or not. *He was assassinated.* Just like *Lee.* The director of the FBI is dead.

I taste bile in my throat.

This means Jackson's in charge of the Bureau. He's the acting director.

A Russian agent is now the head of the FBI.

I feel my legs buckle. I reach out a hand and steady myself on a table.

The Russians are in charge of the FBI.

And there's a killer on the loose.

Sounds come roaring back, and movement. There's commotion in the room, confusion, panic. Halliday's pretty wife is hysterical. I focus on what I can see. A tablecloth that's been ripped off a table, twisted on the floor. An overturned vase, its flowers trampled underfoot. Broken champagne glasses littering the carpeted floor.

Drake and his detail have disappeared through the service door, into the kitchen. *The kitchen.*

My mind flashes to Alina. I can see her small frame; I can see the terror in her eyes. *You just never know. They have . . . ways. When it comes to food . . . you never know what is safe.*

These men were poisoned.

My feet are moving. I'm running for the kitchen door. I reach it, shove it open, blindly. There's more commotion on the other side, people shouting.

And there, sprawled on the tiles, near the ovens, is another body. Dylan.

There's an ominous ringing in my ears. I back out of the kitchen, grope for my phone, pull up the number with trembling fingers. I've never been more terrified in all my life.

Dylan was a server here tonight, wasn't he? He was one of the people bringing around those trays of canapes, those flutes of champagne. And they killed him.

They're eliminating all the loose ends.

They're going to kill Zachary.

My son's next.

"Mom?"

Relief washes over me at the sound of his voice. "Zachary, are you okay? Do you feel sick or anything?"

"No? Why?"

He's fine.

They haven't gotten to him yet.

"Where are you?"

"On my way home."

"Lock the doors. Do not eat or drink a thing."

"What's going on?" I can hear the bewilderment in his voice.

In my mind, I see Mom, being pushed down those stairs. Scott, being run off the road.

A jolt of anger slams through me, and then all I can think about is Jackson. *He did this.*

"Just do as I say."

There's an agent approaching, long gun in hand. Part of Lee's security detail, a guy I recognize from headquarters. "Where's Jackson?" I shout.

"Jackson?"

"Where is he? He's supposed to be here."

"He wasn't scheduled to be. Just Director Lee."

I struggle to process this. The secretary lied to me.

Jackson lured *me* here, too.

I look back into the room, at the two clusters.

Zachary was here. At the scene of three homicides. How long before the authorities realize that?

The gun planted in his room. The FSM email, the extremist forum. Now this. *It will look like my son is responsible.* How long before he's arrested?

The thought sickens me, but at the same time—miraculously—it centers me.

If he's in jail, he's vulnerable. I picture Alina again, barely skin and bones, too frightened to eat. And then I see the writing on the bathroom mirror. Z's NEXT.

I'm moving even before I realize it, this time out into the lobby. I see the bank of doors, the place where I caught sight of Zachary. I replay the scene in my mind. I can see myself rushing toward him, pulling him aside, talking to him. Calling Shields's security detail. Pulling my son out of the hotel, out of harm's way.

All before the first screams.

All before anyone knew there'd been an attack.

My eyes dart to the ceiling, to the corners that house the security cameras. Six, in here alone. Discreet, but I can see their shape, their lenses.

That footage would be enough to place Zachary here at the scene. To convince a jury that I had foreknowledge of the attack. To make us both look complicit.

I need to get to that footage before the rest of the Bureau does.

Chapter 55

The lobby is chaos. I scan the room, and finally I see the man with the tablet, over near the base of the clock tower, looking panicked. His hair is rumpled and his bow tie is gone. I wade through the swirling crowd in his direction. He notices me when I'm almost to him, and his eyes widen.

"I need the security footage," I say.

"Footage," he repeats. Then he nods quickly, assuredly, like he finally has a purpose, and he's relieved to have it. "This way."

He leads me up a shabby flight of stairs, down a corridor. Punches a code into a reader, pushes his way into a small room.

There's a long desk, four screens arranged in a row, live footage from different security feeds. A laptop off to one side; a wall of recording equipment.

He drops down into a swivel chair, rolls close to the computer. Brings the screen to life, starts typing commands. As he does, I watch the screens. One's showing the commotion in the lobby; another, the ballroom, now with paramedics present, and stretchers. A few uniformed police, too, but they're milling about helplessly. The

Bureau should be there in full force by now, establishing order, but I don't see any familiar faces, don't see anyone in charge of the situation.

The typing pauses, and I shift my gaze to the laptop. A new window has popped up, some sort of message.

Come on, I urge fretfully. *Faster.*

He hesitates, closes the box, starts typing again.

I need this footage. I need to pore through it, and I need to find *something* before the Bureau ties the attack to my son.

Once the authorities have this, once they spot Zachary, and *me,* I'll be out of time.

The typing stops again. The same window pops up. Apprehension starts to creep through me.

He gives the screen a long look, then swivels toward me. Somehow I know what he's going to say before he says it.

"The cameras . . . they're not recording."

"Are you sure?" I demand, but even as I say it, *I'm* sure.

Of course they're not recording.

Whoever did this, whoever did this dreadful thing, of course they'd need to eliminate the evidence, the proof that they were here.

"I'm sure," he bleats, bewildered.

It's a relief, in a way. At least a temporary one. It means there's no footage showing Zachary was here. No footage showing that I acted moments *before* those first screams.

But the Bureau will put the pieces together eventually. They'll find that email to the recruiter, and they'll geolocate Zachary's cellphone. They'll know he was here in the hotel before the murders. They'll realize exactly when I made that call to Shields's security detail.

They'll tie us to the attack eventually.

But the person who really did this? Without footage, his tracks are covered.

My eyes are back on those screens, darting from one to the next. Live feeds, but not recording. Whoever did this, he was here. He was on these screens. And we don't have it recorded.

There's the ballroom, those two dense clusters. The lobby, jam-packed with people. The doors at the front, people heading toward them, *out* them.

There's no perimeter. People are *leaving*. Oh God, what a disaster. No one's in control here, no one's preventing witnesses from leaving.

And then I see it.

A figure, on the screen.

Dark cap, head down, just like the guy in the surveillance footage from Mom's condo.

I take a step closer, peer at him intently, my heart beginning to pound.

"Can you zoom in on this?" I say, pointing to the man.

I can dimly hear typing in the background, and then the man grows larger on the screen. I still can't see his face; nothing but that cap.

He's close to the bank of glass doors, heading outside. About to get away.

"More," I urge.

The man on the screen raises his arm to push the door open, and I see it.

A tattoo, a familiar one.

Two knives, crossed in an X.

Chapter 56

There's no perimeter down there, no one stopping anyone from leaving. He's going to get away.

Gun at my side, I race down the hall, down the flight of stairs, back into the lobby, into the mass of people milling about, and I try desperately to catch sight of him.

I snake through the crowd until I'm at the doors, and I'm shoving now as I push through them. I'm outside now, and I still don't see him. I'm scanning the parking lot, eyes settling on anything that moves. He couldn't have gone too far. He's got to be here somewhere.

Then I see it. At the far end of the lot, pulling out of a row, heading for the exit.

A red hatchback.

I watch it for one stunned heartbeat, then two.

Then I spin on my heels and run for my cruiser, parked along the curb. I slide in, start the engine, look over at the exit. The hatchback's turning south, onto the main road.

I press down on the gas.

I pull out of the lot, onto the street, same direction. I can't see the hatchback anymore, and I need to get it back in my sights.

I must stop this monster, get the proof I need.

I pass one car, then another. Strains from my car radio reach me. *". . . the FBI director . . . a senior senator . . ."*

Taillights, up ahead. It's the hatchback; I can tell. I ease up on the gas, keep my distance. Can't let him know I'm here.

". . . a botched attempt . . ."

If he knows he's got a tail, he could be leading me into an ambush. Some sort of trap. But what choice do I have? I can't let him get away.

". . . speculation that CIA director Drake was another intended victim . . ."

Drake. The question I had in the ballroom comes rushing back. The CIA—was that supposed to be in the Russians' hands, too? If Drake had died, who would have been named acting director? In my mind I see those portraits on that wall at Langley.

And the Senate. Shields was supposed to be here tonight. He was supposed to die, too. Who would have been positioned to be the next majority leader? Good God. Have the Russians really infiltrated Congress, and the CIA, the same way they've infiltrated the Bureau?

We're on streets that are growing less congested, more wooded—and darker, too. I drop back, so that I can only just barely see the taillights. I pull up a map on GPS, monitor the roads, the direction we're headed. I don't know this area, not as well as I need to.

Brake lights blink ahead.

". . . transferred to an undisclosed location for their protection . . ."

The hatchback slows; I slow. Then it turns right.

I look at the map. It's turning onto a dead end that backs to the woods. *A dead end.*

I silence the radio, cut my lights, make an abrupt right, onto a street that I was just about to pass. This one backs to the same woods. Through the trees I can see the hatchback, just barely. The illumination from the headlights, mostly. He stops about midway down the road, just behind another car, one that's mostly blocked from my line of sight.

He cuts his lights, too, and then everything is dark.

I park along the side of the road. Grab my surveillance bag from the backseat, take out my camera, the one with the telephoto lens, sling it across my chest. Pull my Glock from my holster. Then I turn off the overhead light, inch open the car door.

I'm going in on foot. I have to see who's in that other car, what they're doing.

I push through the trees, heart pounding, cold cutting through my clothes, hand tight on my gun. Naked branches slice at my face, but I don't slow. I can't go too near; don't want them to hear me, or see me. Just near enough to see them, photograph them.

Dead leaves crunch under my feet. I flinch. Near enough now; any closer and they'll hear me. I crouch, aim the camera in their direction, zoom in as much as I can.

Damn it. It's too dark.

I rise and start walking again. Closer now. Each footstep feels like it echoes.

I look through the camera again. This time I can see two figures, but they're indistinct. I press down on the shutter anyway.

Aim at the cars, what little of them I can see. *Click. Click.*

Doubt I got anything useful. A little farther, though, and I think I can get a shot of the figures, a clear one. I start walking again, off to my left, stepping softly through the brush.

Then I freeze, aim the camera again.

There. The man with the tattoo.

I zoom in as much as my camera will allow. Pan to the man across from him—

His head's turned ever so slightly away from me. If he'd just turn—

He looks over his shoulder.

Click.

And then it's the back of his head again. Dammit.

He opens the car door and slides inside, shuts the door.

I aim at the window, but it's tinted. I can't see a thing.

I hear another car door opening, then shutting.

Engines starting, first one, then another.

Headlights blaze on. I thrust myself against a tree, shield myself from view. Frozen as one car pulls a U-turn, speeds off. Then the second.

I step around the tree, watch as they head off on the main road, in the direction from which we came. The second car's a small blue sedan. A Corolla, I think.

My cruiser's too far away. Following them is useless.

I look down at the screen of the camera, press the arrows until I get to the photo I'm looking for, the one where he was looking over his shoulder. If I clicked at the right time, maybe—

It's a perfect shot. Head-on, his features startlingly clear.

Vivian's husband.

I can't tear my eyes away from the image on the screen.

It's him. The man I saw that day in her home. *With her children.*

He's involved in this. With Jackson, with the attack, with *everything.* Is *she*?

I turn off the camera and start walking back toward my car, utterly shaken.

No. She can't be. The way she looked in her home that day, the way she reacted . . . She was confused. Afraid, even. I'm certain of it.

At least I think she was.

But if she's not involved, she's vulnerable. She's living with the enemy, and she has no idea. Is her husband working for the Russians, too? Are they using her? Are they a *threat* to her?

What am I supposed to do now?

Run. The compulsion enters my mind, sticks there. Echoes in my head with each step.

We could do it, couldn't we? Pick up tonight, leave town, *disappear*?

God, the thought is tempting. It would keep Zachary safe. We've done it before; we could do it again.

But this is different. This is worse. This enemy won't let us just go.

And Mom's in no condition to travel. I can't leave her behind. I can't risk what they'd do to her.

Besides. The Russians are in control of the FBI. Almost seized control of the CIA, the Senate.

I can't let that happen. I can't run; it wouldn't be right. I have a sworn duty to uphold the law, to protect my country.

I'm nearly at the street when I hear another sound, one that stops me in my tracks, freezes my blood to ice.

A gun being racked.

Chapter 57

I hear the crunch of leaves. Footsteps, coming toward me, from behind.

My Glock's in my right hand, at my side. This person approaching—does he see it? If he doesn't, he will, any moment. I use the sound of his footsteps to picture exactly where he is.

And then I swing toward the sound, raise my gun.

"Shoot me and your son dies," says the voice. I find him in my sights. His hands are at his sides.

I don't shoot. It's a split-second decision, one drilled into me during years of training. If there'd been a weapon pointed at me, I'd have pressed the trigger, even before the words registered.

But there wasn't, and so I didn't. And that briefest of pauses is enough for his words to reach my brain. *Shoot me and your son dies.*

I watch him through my sights. My finger's on the trigger. Blood's pounding in my ears. He raises his right hand, and now I see the gun in it. He's drawing on me.

Shoot, Steph. You need to shoot.

But my finger doesn't move. *Your son dies.*

"You know this goes beyond just me, Steph."

He has the gun in both hands now, barrel pointed directly at me. He's aiming at me, I'm aiming at him. Standoff. His face looks calm, too calm.

"Drop your weapon, Steph."

I don't. I will myself to press the trigger. To shoot him, to kill him, to eliminate this threat.

It wouldn't, though, would it?

Your son dies.

He starts walking toward me. I keep him in my sights, keep the gun trained on him, my finger on the trigger. He's in front of me, only steps away.

"Don't be foolish, Steph. I've gone this long without killing you." Jackson levels his gun at my heart. "Don't make me do it now."

I drop the gun. It lands in the leaves with a quiet thud.

He keeps his gun trained on me. His face is expressionless. "Get in the car." He tilts his head toward the road.

Numb, I start walking. I can hear him behind me, close.

There's my car, through the trees. A black SUV, too, parked farther up the road. I stop.

"Move," he urges. I can feel the barrel of his gun bite into my spine, and I start walking again, because I know now.

They finally decided it's safest to just get rid of me. Like Scott.

I've gone this long without killing you. Don't make me do it now.

If he wanted me dead, he'd have already done it, wouldn't he? Or he'd have had someone do it for him. He wants something else.

What?

We're nearly at the car now. I'm still wearing the wire. I just need to power it on. . . .

I picture the device, under my clothes. Feel it against my body. I need to press that button, through my clothes, and I need to do it without him seeing.

He's going to kill me.

The thought is there, echoing in the darkness.

He opens the driver's-side door with one hand, the other still gripping the gun. "In."

Every muscle in my body feels like it's resisting, like it's screaming at me not to do this. It's too dangerous. It would mean stepping into an enclosed space with a killer. A traitor.

But I need proof. I need this, more than I've ever needed anything.

"Get *in*."

I make my muscles move, climb into the car. As I slide over onto the passenger seat, I turn my body away from him, press the record button through my clothes.

He slides behind the wheel and slams the door—an instant later I hear it lock. I look over at him. Same hard look he had in the row house that day so long ago, and in my home when he confronted me there.

He throws the car into gear and pulls away from the curb.

We drive onto the main road. It's empty, and dark. I'm waiting for him to speak. To incriminate himself. To get the proof I need. But he says nothing. The only sound is the whir of the engine, and the faint strains of the radio—news coverage of the attack, reporters speculating endlessly on the murders, reports on the lives and careers of Halliday and Lee.

"What do you want?" My voice sounds like it belongs to a stranger.

He keeps his eyes on the road, his lips set tight. He's heading south, toward the river. There's more traffic here, more lights. I'm memorizing every road sign, mapping out the route in my mind, trying to picture exactly where we are. Exactly how I can get away, when the time is right.

"Tell me," I insist.

He turns the volume up on the radio. It's the Senate majority leader. *"The vice president promised the American people there was no threat. He should tender his resignation immediately. . . ."*

I watch Jackson's profile, wait for him to say something, *anything.* I'm ready. I just need a confession, and then I need to escape—

We're snaking through Southwest, through the commercial district. The radio host's voice reaches my ears. *"A blistering attack on his own party,"* she's saying. *"Unprecedented . . . they need a scapegoat, someone to blame. . . ."*

Jackson turns the volume down, and silence slams down on us. He slows to a stop. It's a lonely road, one that flanks the water.

There's no one here at this hour. No people, no cars. I can see the river just on the other side, dark, black, glittering.

It's the perfect place to dump a body. He brought me here to kill me.

He puts the car in park and reaches for his gun.

Zachary. Images of my son flash through my mind. All the stages of his life, all those fleeting, lost moments. As a newborn, his tiny pink hand closed stubbornly around my thumb. A toddler, taking those wobbly first steps. Flying high on the swings, a grin lighting his face. Riding off proudly on his bike, away from me. And as he is now, on the cusp of adulthood, striding across that stage to shake the principal's hand, his future wide open before him. And I remember holding him tight, as if I could never let him go, outside the ballroom.

No. I'm not going to let this happen. I shift in my seat so I can kick the gun out of his hand, but as soon as I twist he grabs my leg, twists it so painfully I gasp.

"Relax," Jackson says. "I'm not going to hurt you."

My leg's immobilized, the gun in his other hand, out of my reach.

"As long as you don't make any rash moves," he adds, and the pressure on my leg loosens. His hand hovers over it a moment longer, like he's waiting for me to make a move, but I'm obediently still.

I'm perfectly still, just like he wants me to be—for a second, then two, then . . .

I swing my right fist toward his face, connect with his cheekbone, with everything I've got. He yelps like a wounded dog. And I'm already on top of him, grappling for the gun, trying to pry it out of his grasp—

Crunch. I double over, wheezing, curl around myself reflexively. His fist caught me square in the stomach. He pins me back against my seat, and I'm trapped there, gasping for breath, blinded by pain.

He reaches for my camera, pops open the bottom, takes out the memory card, snaps it in half. It's a sickening sound.

Doesn't matter, though. I know what I saw. I know *who* I saw.

"Give me the recording device, Steph."

"I . . . don't have one," I lie.

"You do." His eyes are hard, and there's no doubt in his face, none whatsoever. I have the chilling sense, once again, that he's a step ahead, that he always will be one step ahead. "You can give it to me. Or I'll strip you down and find it myself."

I stare at him and I know I don't have a choice. I wish I had a second device. But the way he's watching me, with that intimate, penetrating gaze, I have the feeling he'd know about that, too. That it wouldn't matter how many devices I'd brought; he'd have somehow known.

I hesitate a heartbeat longer, then reach under my shirt. I hand the device over, fury and frustration brewing inside me.

He takes it from me. Powers down his window, launches the recorder into the river. It lands with a sickening splash. By the time the window is sealed shut again, the air in the car is frigid.

He holsters the gun. Puts the car into drive, pulls away from the curb. I watch the road in front of us, but I'm not seeing a thing. I'm trying to anticipate his next move. Desperate to figure out *mine*.

Jackson begins humming, softly. Some tune I don't recognize, one that sounds somehow ominous. A shiver runs through me. I focus on my surroundings—we're crossing the bridge into Virginia now. *Where's he going?*

The streets grow familiar. We're in a neighborhood, one I've been to before.

He turns onto Dylan's street, and I see it. Cars, everywhere. Police cars, marked and unmarked. Lights flashing.

Jackson pulls to a stop along the curb. The house is ahead of us, and throngs of agents in raid jackets mill about.

He reaches for something that's tucked between his seat and the center console and I freeze. He pulls it out, hands it to me. "Open it."

I do as he says, knowing I'm about to die.

It's a stack of photographs, black-and-white. The top one is Zachary. Outside the lobby of the hotel, shot from a distance, a telephoto lens. I recognize his posture, the way his backpack's slung carelessly on his shoulder.

Jackson's people have pictures. Someone was there at the hotel, waiting, photographing, gathering evidence. Was it the man with the tattoo?

I know how bad this is, what it means.

"I just want to give you a taste of what we can release."

I turn to the next picture. Zachary's half-turned, looking over his shoulder. His face is clearly visible.

"This isn't proof of anything."

"Are you sure?" he taunts, softly.

It's almost hard to do it, to flip to the next picture. I don't want to see it. But at the same time, I need to.

Another picture. Zachary and me, near the bank of doors, in a heated conversation.

A close-up of me, pointing away from the hotel, clearly telling Zachary to leave. The panicked look on my face is unmistakable.

"What exactly were you doing tonight, Steph? Because it sure looks like you knew what your son was doing there."

The third photo. Me again, running toward the hotel.

"Time stamp shows that's just *before* the first 911 call. How did you know?" He's toying with me, like this is all a game, some dreadful game. "And of course there's your call to Senator Shields's security detail. To the tip line. Your visit to the late Dylan Taylor. *How is that all going to look?*"

He's right. It will look like I'm just as guilty as my son.

"Time's up, Steph," Jackson says.

I wasn't able to get us out of this. *Time's up.*

"If we release those photos, it doesn't matter what you say. No one would believe you. *No one.*"

Those words. Those *words*. The same ones he said to me when he broke into my home. The ones *Halliday* said to me, so many years before. The ones I *believed*, the ones that forced me to put up walls that changed my life.

Everyone I care about is in danger. I picture Scott in my mind. The deadly slick of ice beneath his wheels. Mom, face bleached with pain. *That's* what happened when I told the truth. I close the folder. Then I reach out and place a hand on the door, steadying myself.

"It doesn't have to come out. It's up to you."

Scott's face fills my mind once again. And Director Lee's. I see the Russian flag, imagine the people behind it, the ones orchestrating all this.

I squeeze my eyes shut to block out the images.

I feel Jackson turn toward me. I open my eyes, and he nods toward the folder in my lap. "Keep going, why don't you?"

I look down at the folder. And I open it, because the temptation is too much, because I need to know.

This photograph is shot from a distance, darker than the first ones. It's a location that's unfamiliar, some sort of street corner. Zachary's there, and a taller man, his face obscured. They're in the middle of a handoff, the wad of cash clearly visible in Zachary's hand.

"That's your son buying the poison used in the attack."

"Bullshit!"

He laughs softly.

I stare harder at the picture. It's definitely Zachary. Knit cap, hooded sweatshirt. The Taurus is parked out front, on the street. A street sign's visible. Walnut and Carver, I think. Northeast D.C. Surely it was doctored? I can't be certain. But I'm certain it's not what Jackson says it is.

Fear is paralyzing me, the terrifying realization that I under-estimated what these people are willing to do to get their way.

I turn to the next picture, because I have to see everything they have.

The exterior of Dylan's house, again at night. Front door open, Dylan inside. Zachary, on the porch.

"Zachary's fingerprints are all over that house," Jackson says, and the fear is all-encompassing now.

I don't understand this. None of this makes sense.

Did they plant my son's fingerprints in Dylan's house? How long do I have before they claim they have evidence?

Jackson puts the car into drive. I take one last look at the house as we pull away from the curb. Agents, everywhere.

Are there really prints?

There'd be no record of Zachary's fingerprints in the Bureau's system. Not yet, anyway. But if he's arrested, that would change.

"Keep going," Jackson says.

I turn to the next picture. This one's brighter, clearer. It's Zachary. I recognize the location; it's the landing outside the service door of the hotel. *What's he doing there?*

And there he is, Dylan Taylor. They're in the middle of a handoff. A paper bag this time.

The picture looks real. It looks genuine. It would convince a jury, wouldn't it? Dylan and Zachary, at the scene of the crime, together. Exchanging *something*.

Were they really?

No. They couldn't have been. This is fabricated, all of it.

But it's *good*.

Oh God.

I stare sightlessly out the windshield, dimly aware that we're on the route back to D.C.

"At noon," Jackson tells me, "the evidence against Zachary will come out. Acquisition of poison, intent to kill U.S. government officials. Three homicide charges. First-degree murder, cut-and-dried. Unless you agree to work for us."

He reaches for something, and I have this dizzy fleeting hope that it will be a gun. If it's a gun, and he kills me, they'd leave Zachary alone, wouldn't they?

It's not a gun. It's a cellphone. He hands it to me.

"Call the number programmed, Steph. Tell them to take care of it, and the prints will be erased from the Bureau's system. Those pictures will never come out."

They want me to call so they'll have a recording of my voice. My voice, requesting a crime, committing treason. So they'd have proof to destroy me, if I ever dared cross them.

And they'd be turning me over to a handler, someone who'd give

me more tasks in the future. This isn't all about staying quiet, protecting Jackson. I'd be theirs, and they'd ask for more.

But they have Zachary's *fingerprints*. I know what that means. Fingerprints are everything. Fingerprints mean a conviction.

We're turning into that wooded alley now, the one where my
cruiser is parked. Jackson eases to a stop beside it.

"I know you love your son, and I know you wouldn't betray him,"
he says.

Betray my son for the greater good. Or choose the one person
most important to me in all the world, and betray so many others.

"Noon," Jackson says again. "If you haven't made the call, those
pictures go to the press."

I hear the click as he unlocks the doors, and I know I'm free, but
I know, too, that I'm more trapped than I ever have been.

I slide back into my own car, shut and lock the door behind me. I'm
shivering uncontrollably. The SUV drives off, and then it's just me,
alone.

Noon tomorrow.

How can I do anything, *prove* anything, by noon tomorrow?

I reach for my phone on the passenger seat, to check the time.

Three missed calls.

All from the hospital.

I unlock the screen, dial the missed number. All I can picture in
my mind is Mom. They've told her about Zachary. They're never
going to leave my family alone.

"This is Dr. Green."

Dr. Green. The young one, the pretty woman who suggested
Mom had been pushed down the stairs. "It's Steph Maddox. I'm
calling to check on—"

"Ms. Maddox," she interrupts. "I'm so sorry."

Does *she* know about Zachary, too? Did Mom hear this slander about Zachary and then blab to—

"Your mother went into cardiac arrest. It happens sometimes, after internal injuries like she sustained. We did everything we could..."

No.

"... but we weren't able to save her."

Chapter 58

In the dead of night, little is visible through the windows of the penthouse apartment. The Potomac is inky black; Washington, cloaked in darkness. Only a handful of sites are visible, illuminated like beacons.

Jackson takes off his jacket and lays it on the back of a low, stiff couch. His holster is visible at his hip; his badge catches the light. He walks to the window and looks out for several moments, then turns.

"I showed her the pictures," he says.

Wes stands off to one side of the room and watches him. His tie's loosened around his neck, his shirtsleeves rolled up to his elbows. "And?"

"I don't think she believes it."

Wes says nothing.

Jackson runs a hand through his hair and starts pacing in front of the windows. "We shouldn't have been in such a rush. This would have happened eventually. Me as director."

"Stop worrying."

"What if she comes clean?"

Wes picks up a glass from a nearby table. He raises it to his lips, the ice clinking the only sound in the room, the only response to Jackson's question.

"It's all under control," Wes says.

"I don't see how. This is all so—"

"The boss knows what he's doing."

"Doesn't make sense. The other two *targets* are—"

"Untouchable now. Protected. *Think*, my friend. Think *ahead*."

The two stare at each other. Finally Jackson sighs and looks back out the window, down to the icy river below. "What if she tells the truth?"

Wes crosses the room, stands beside Jackson. He looks out at the city, at the illumination shimmering in the distance. "She won't. She'd never do that to her son."

"She might. Greater good and all that."

The two men stand side by side, silently, staring out at the city below.

"Would that be the right call?" Wes asks.

"Probably. Don't you think?"

Wes walks to the couch, sits. The chessboard's in front of him. The play is further along now; they made the moves he thought they'd make. He gives the board a hungry look, his eyes roaming from piece to piece. This game, it's all about thinking ahead. And the only piece that matters, in the end, is the king.

Chapter 59

There's a low rumble of thunder in the distance, heavy clouds in the sky, as I park my cruiser along the curb in front of my home. A biting chill to the air, the kind that makes me wonder if the clouds will spill rain, or it'll freeze and start spitting ice. The promise of spring feels like it's been snatched away.

Mom. I sink down onto the bottom step and hold my head in my hands. It's throbbing now, a pounding headache.

Oh, Mom . . .

My heart hurts. It's like a piece of *me* has been ripped away.

How is this possible? How can she be *gone*?

I can see her smile. Her arms, open wide to me, enveloping me in an embrace. Giggling together at the dinner table, just the two of us. Back when we were close. Before Halliday, before I put up that wall. The one I never had time to tear down.

Time is precious, Stephanie.

Why didn't I listen? Why didn't I *talk* to her, when I had the chance? That accident—it should have been a wake-up call, an opportunity to set things right between us. And instead, I pushed her away, right until the end. Said terrible things, things I didn't even mean. Now there's no taking them back. There's no apologizing. *Time's up.*

She's gone, and Scott's gone, and Zachary's on the verge of going to jail—or worse. I've never felt more alone, more hopeless, more *terrified.*

I hear footsteps and look up, and there's a woman walking toward me on the sidewalk, heavy jacket over pajama pants, a fat dachshund waddling at her ankles. That new neighbor, three doors down. She's peering at me with a concerned look on her face and I realize I'm sobbing. I struggle to my feet and stumble up the steps.

The buds on the cherry tree near the front door are round balls now, lighter pink in color. A sliver of silky petals is peeking out from a few of them. Tricked by that early blast of spring weather, unprepared for winter's last stand. I want to tell them to stop, to wait, because it's too cold now, and too wet, and they'll never survive.

How is this happening?

Mom.

Scott. *Zachary.*

Z's NEXT.

Jackson has somehow created those fake pictures. Zachary's *fingerprints* are in the possession of the FBI.

Jackson has forged enough evidence to make sure my son goes to prison, and stays there.

And he has enough to make sure that I'm in prison, too.

I unlock the front door, check the alarm, punch in my code. I swipe my tears away and hesitate on the threshold a moment, listening. It's quiet.

I need to tell the truth about Jackson. But every time I acknowledge this, I have a vision of Zachary in a prison jumpsuit. Of Alina, too terrified to eat. *Zachary would never be safe in custody.*

I need to keep him out of jail.

But at what cost?

I reach into my pocket for the phone Jackson gave me. All I have to do is make the call. Find the number that's preprogrammed, press send, ask them to take care of it. Agree, in essence, to work against my country. To work for *them*. Seal my own fate, preserve my son's future. His *life*.

Upstairs, Zachary's bedroom door is closed. I rap my knuckles against it, softly, and when there's no answer, I open it a crack. How is it possible he's asleep? He's in his bed, the sheets tangled around his long legs. I sit gingerly on the edge of his bed and watch his chest rise and fall, the way I have ever since he was an infant.

What if we never have the chance to grow closer, just like Mom warned? I never set things right with *her*. What if history repeats itself?

Tears sting my eyelids. I never should have shut Mom out. I should have opened up to her, bridged the divide between us, apologized for all the hurtful things I said. I should have told her I loved her.

Images from earlier in the night flash through my mind. The blood gleaming on Director Lee's shirt, his lifeless eyes. The wails of his wife. His widow. I squeeze my eyes shut, but I can't force out the images. They're etched in my brain; I'll never be able to get rid of them.

Zachary stirs in his sleep, rolls over onto his side, toward me. I study his face, and I can see the boy who used to be in this bed. The one I'd read bedtime stories with, who'd wrap his arms around my neck so tightly when he whispered good night. The one whose forehead I'd feel when he was sick, the one I'd cradle in my arms when he'd had a nightmare.

It seems like those days were yesterday, and a lifetime ago. Everything has changed since then; nothing's the same. Nothing can ever be the same again.

I reach over and touch his cheek, the spot where I used to leave good-night kisses. His skin is warm. I have the strange sense that it could be the last time I see him in his bed. The thought sends a torrent of fear ricocheting through me. Fear and desperation and *anger*. This isn't fair. None of this is fair.

I make my way down into the living room, collapse on the couch. There has to be a solution. There has to be some way to share the truth without endangering Zachary. But *how*? I have no idea how deep this goes. Yesterday I never would have dreamed that the CIA and Congress were infiltrated, certainly not to this degree.

I don't know what to do. I don't know my next move.

I try to channel the psychiatrist, try to call her into my mind, but she won't come. The chair where she sits is empty. I'm all alone, with no one to talk to, no one to turn to.

Zachary's future is entirely in my hands.

I stare at the chessboard. We're never going to finish this game, are we?

I have the strangest urge to throw something, to break something, just to see it shatter.

I settle for overturning the chessboard. Pieces fly everywhere, clatter to the floor.

Noise, upstairs. I go still.

Zachary's door opening. Shit, I've woken him.

He pads downstairs. He's in basketball shorts and a long-sleeved T-shirt, and there's a crease on his right cheek, from his pillow. He looks at the scattered rooks and pawns, then squints at me. "You okay?"

"Yeah." I avert my eyes, though slightly too late. An awkward silence hangs between us. *I need to tell him about Mom. I need to tell him his grandmother's dead.*

He sinks down on the loveseat, stretches his long legs out. "What happened tonight?"

It's impossible to concentrate. I want to cry for my mother, for myself. But I *have* to think, to focus on the danger at hand. Zachary's all I have left. I have to protect my son, and *then* I can mourn my mother. "What have you heard?"

"There was an attack."

I nod.

"Some VIP died—that's what the news kept saying."

"Three people were murdered."

"Three?" He blinks. "I went to bed before I heard the details." He reaches for the remote, turns on the television. It's tuned to a local station, and it's breathless coverage of the attack, even more frantic all these hours later.

There's video footage of the exterior of the hotel, the flashing lights of dozens of first responders. I force myself to watch. The screen switches to cellphone pictures pulled from social media: a sobbing woman in a ruffled gown, terrified men in tuxedos, a sheet-draped stretcher being loaded into an ambulance. Director Lee's picture pops up on the screen, beside Halliday's.

Zachary's gaze is locked on the screen. His face is pale and stricken.

He didn't know Halliday was one of the victims.

Shit.

Halliday's his father, monster or not. He was in my son's life, however briefly, and now he's gone. He's lost his grandmother and his father on the same day.

"Zachary—"

"How did they die?" He's still staring at the screen, in shock.

"Some kind of poison."

Zachary lifts the remote again, changes the channel. More praise of Lee's career, then an ad for antacids.

"Must have happened right after I got there, huh?"

That's why he thinks I made him leave. He has no idea I put the pieces together just before it happened, that *he* was a key part of the puzzle. "Yeah, I think so."

"Terrible," he murmurs.

The station replays the vice president's remarks vowing there would be no attack. There's a profile on what little is known about the Freedom Solidarity Movement. Repeated mentions of missing CCTV footage. Dylan Taylor's picture pops up on the screen. An old one—his hair's buzzed short, and he's grinning broadly. *Possible Terrorist?* reads the caption.

The screen switches to a live shot outside the hotel, a sea of cameras and reporters, floodlights illuminating the area. The reporter on the scene launches into a spiel on the investigation into Dylan Taylor, the hunt for accomplices. FSM associates are being rounded up and questioned. No arrests yet.

Noon tomorrow.

"Jesus, Mom, what is it?"

I shake my head, because I can't get words to form. "I'm sorry," I stammer.

Fear flares in his eyes. "Do they think it was me?"

Not yet. I shake my head.

"Then what?" Confusion clouds his features.

"Just . . . everything."

"Mom, dammit, for once, tell me what's going on!"

His fury startles me.

His features soften. "Oh my God—is it Grandma?"

My throat grows so tight I don't know if I'll be able to respond. *Grandma.* In my mind's eye I see the big bear hugs she used to give him. The smile that lit her face whenever she saw him. God, she loved my son.

"She passed away, Zachary. She had a heart attack. They couldn't save her." I say the words, but in my mind I'm picturing her at the top of those stairs, a faceless man behind her, pushing. They tried to kill her. *Did they succeed in the hospital?*

Does it matter? Either way, *they murdered her.*

Guilt washes over me. Tears burn in my eyes.

"She *died?*" His voice is a whisper.

"She loved you very much, Zachary." A tear spills down my cheek.

"I loved her, too."

"I know, sweetheart. And *she* knew that, too."

He buries his face in his hands, and his shoulders begin to heave. I have this urge to hug him, to comfort him, but I stay seated. *Mom would have hugged him.*

"She was always there for me," he weeps, lifting his tear-stained face.

Mom's accusation rings in my head. *Your work is your life. Zachary comes second. He always has.*

I stare at the picture on the television screen, the anchor's mouth moving. And then my eyes drift down to the overturned chessboard. A game, just a game. Trying to protect the king, above all else. But it's my son who's the vulnerable piece, and the danger he's in is *real.*

The television screen goes abruptly blank. The *Breaking News* screen appears, those big bold letters, the distinctive chimes.

The anchor appears. "We're going live to the Naval Observatory," she intones, "where the vice president is about to speak."

The screen changes again, a close-up of an empty podium in a nondescript room. The vice president walks up to the podium, head bowed, his wife by his side, his hand in hers. He looks up at the cameras. There are dark circles under his eyes, which are wet with unshed tears.

"My fellow Americans," he begins. "Tonight . . . tonight a horrific terrorist attack took the lives of two great patriots. I stood before you last week and pledged that no such attack would take place, and for that I am truly sorry."

His voice falters. He pauses and wipes a tear away. "I've decided I can no longer in good faith serve as your vice president. I am heeding calls to step down. I have submitted a letter of resignation to the president. And he has accepted it."

There are audible gasps from the pool of reporters.

"It has been the honor of my life to serve you." He puts a hand over his heart and looks directly into the camera. "Thank you, and God bless America."

He reaches for his wife's hand and steps away from the podium. His face has aged decades in a week, and I understand it perfectly. I see my own emotions reflected in his expression. I see the tremendous, overpowering, all-encompassing guilt.

The anchor begins stammering, struggling to figure out what to say. A panelist jumps in, speculates that this only would have happened if the president requested it, attributes it to the majority leader's influence.

I tune out. All I can think about is that look on the vice president's face. He didn't see a threat, and he told the truth. I didn't see it either, *because it wasn't real*. It wasn't a threat from an anarchist group. It was a threat from the Russians. Using extremists as cover.

The threat didn't exist. He spoke the truth, and now he's forever disgraced, his career in ruins.

"I didn't even get to tell Grandma the good news," Zachary says.

It takes me a moment to realize he has spoken. "What good news?"

"I got in. *First-choice* school."

An overwhelming sorrow fills me. But I force a smile at him. No matter what happens next, we don't have much more time together. And suddenly I desperately want things to be as normal as possible.

I want to sear every detail of every precious moment with him into my memory.

"Berkeley," I say softly. To think I was once worried about how far away he'd be. Now I'm worried about his freedom, about his *life*.

"Georgetown," he says.

"Georgetown?"

He looks sheepish. "I want to be closer to home."

I want to be closer to home. I'm not sure he's ever said words that mean more. God, how much I would have loved to hear him say that a week ago.

I join him on the loveseat and wrap him in a hug. It's an instinct really, and one that seems to catch both of us by surprise. He's tense at first, but then he puts his arms around me and hugs me back tightly, and I sink my face into his shoulder.

"My job," I confess, because I need to tell him what's going on, but I don't even know where to start. "I never thought it would affect you the way it has."

"What your job *did* was prove that there are good people in the world. People who do what's right. That the good guys always win. Isn't that what Grandma always says?"

Tears blind me. "You're more important to me than anything in the world," I tell him, loving him for his innocence. "And I'd do anything to protect you. You know that, right?"

He gives me a smile, a sweetly wistful one. "I'd do anything to protect *you*, too, Mom." He stands up, stoops to kiss the top of my head. "I know you don't believe it, but I would."

I watch him head toward the stairs, disappear from my sight. He doesn't look back. And I sit alone in miserable silence, overcome with grief and guilt.

Make the call, agree to work for the Russians. Protect my son, betray my country. Betray everything I believe in, everything I stand for.

Or tell the truth. Assume that no one will believe me, not without proof. That Zachary and I will both end up in jail. Assume there's a very good chance he'll never make it out alive.

I take out the phone, the one Jackson gave me. All I have to do is call the number programmed in it, and Zachary will have a future. It's the *only* way Zachary will have a future.

I've never felt more hopeless in my life.

And then I hear the knock at the door.

It's them, isn't it? The police. Coming to arrest my son.

I'm supposed to have until noon tomorrow. Jackson *told* me I'd have until noon tomorrow.

They can't be here now.

If they're here, time's up.

More knocking, more insistent this time.

I drop the phone, force myself to stand, to walk to the front door.

I look through the peephole, and the sight shocks me.

I turn off the alarm, unlock the door, open it. I stare at the woman there for several moments. Then Vivian speaks.

"Can we talk?"

Chapter 60

Wordlessly, I usher her inside, close and lock the door behind her. As I reset the alarm, she takes two steps into the foyer.

"What's going on?" I demand. In my mind I'm back in those woods, watching the man with the tattoo. Snapping that photograph *of her husband*. He's part of this. *Is she?*

She glances around the room at the scattered chess pieces, then at me. Her face is drawn, dark circles under her eyes. She looks haunted, scared. "Could we step out back?"

I grab a jacket from the coat rack and lead her out to the back deck.

It's frigid out, and it's that eerily still sort of night, where there's no breeze, no traffic. Everything's hushed and motionless.

"After you left my house," Vivian begins, once we sit across from each other at the patio table, "I couldn't stop thinking about what you said. What it all means . . ." She shakes her head, like she's banishing an unpleasant thought. "You mentioned Marta. . . . Well, I talked to her."

"You did?" My thoughts are spinning, unable to process this. Where is she? Is she okay?

Is Marta working for the Russians?

"She's out of the country," Vivian says, like she can read my mind. "No access to her cellphone. She said—"

She glances around, then leans forward. "She said that if you have suspicions about Jackson, they're justified. That she trusts you, that it doesn't matter if we don't have proof. That we need to look into it, fully. So I did."

She believes me.

"We have an asset," she continues quietly. "Someone highly placed in the Russian government, highly reliable."

Justice Ranger. I flash back to sitting in O'Neill's with Marta, hearing her mention a new asset, an important one.

"He's in the U.S. right now. I went to see him. I showed him a series of pictures, and I included Jackson."

"Did he recognize him?" My heart is thumping in my throat.

She nods. "Took a long hard look, said he's seen him before. In Moscow, years ago. Sources have been telling us there's a high-level plant in the U.S. government. But until now we haven't known who it is."

Until now.

"Jackson's working for the Russians, Steph."

Oh, thank God. Vivian knows the truth, too.

"It's not proof that would hold up in court," she cautions.

"But it's something." It's enough to make people listen. "So what now?"

"An official debriefing. The source is on his way to a safe house. Director Drake's headed there, too."

On his way. This is happening, and it's happening *now.*

"We need to figure out if this goes deeper than just Jackson," Vivian continues. "How much leverage the Russians have, how many people on the inside."

"Yeah," I murmur. In my mind I'm picturing the other intended victims. Drake, Shields. They've got people on the inside, in the Agency *and* the Senate. Of course this goes deeper than Jackson. A hell of a lot deeper. "They've got leverage all right."

"That's what I'm afraid of." Her dark circles look even more pronounced. I think of her husband, and for the first time I wonder if she'll be completely surprised by the truth, or if she suspects he's not loyal. "I want you in that debriefing, Stephanie. I need you to tell us everything you know. Will you come with me?"

She believes me. But her husband's entangled in this, and now she knows the truth about Jackson.

She's in danger. And I'm the one that caused it. I'm the one that dragged her back into this. What role does her husband play in this conspiracy? What kind of threat does he pose? To her? To *her* children?

"Yes." Of course I'll go. I'll tell them everything. And it's going to change her life forever. "But I need my son to come with us. He's part of this, too."

I want them to see the truth in his eyes. And I want him with me. I need to keep him safe.

She nods like it doesn't surprise her. "I'll wait in the car."

Together, we walk back inside. She heads out the front door, and I walk up the stairs, into his bedroom.

"Zachary," I say. He stirs in his bed, but doesn't wake.

My mind flashes back to that day, years ago. The sleepy boy in the backseat, as we headed out of town.

Mommy, are we safe?

We left our home that day, never returned to it. All to escape an enemy. Did we ever really escape?

And now. Now the enemy's even deadlier. Mom and Scott are dead. Are we going to have to run again? Will we ever return?

I head into his closet and look around. I spot the place on the lower shelf where I found that gun, an eternity ago, when all of this started. There's a duffel bag on the floor. I'll pack a few things for him, in case we can't come back.

I reach for the bag, and I have this vision of packing our bags, all those years ago.

Mommy, are we safe?

"Zachary," I say again, louder this time.

I grab a couple of pairs of jeans from the shelves, a couple of shirts.

I can hear the rustle of his sheets. He's waking up. Finally.

I unzip the duffel, and a quick glance inside tells me it's not empty; it needs to be cleared out before I start packing. I reach in and pull out a hooded sweatshirt, then a knit cap.

There's more underneath, at the bottom of the bag. An ATM card. *Mom's* ATM card.

He needed money, Stephanie. Her voice fills my head.

Beside it, a scrap of paper, Zachary's scrawled writing. *Walnut/ Carver.*

In my mind I see that photo Jackson showed me, the stack of cash being exchanged on that street corner. *Walnut and Carver.*

The apprehension has morphed into a sickening sense of dread.

I hear Zachary's voice in my mind. *I'd do anything to protect you, too, Mom.*

He can't get away with this. We should make him pay.

No.

"Mom?" His voice, right behind me. I turn, and there he is, towering above me. He looks from me to the bag, the items spread in front of me. Clothing, address, ATM card. He looks fragile, like a deer frozen in headlights. When his eyes land back on me, they're naked with guilt.

There's a ringing in my ears. None of this is real, it can't be. Because I see the look on my son's face. I know the look.

"Zachary," I breathe. "What did you *do*?"

Chapter 61

"What did you do?" I say again.

He reaches out for me, like he wants to be held.

"It was you." My heart feels like it's clenched in someone's fist. This isn't happening. It can't be. "I trusted you. I *believed* you." I don't even know why I'm saying it, why it matters.

"Mom, I—"

"People *died*." I wait for him to deny it; I *need* him to deny it.

"It was just supposed to be that bastard Halliday," my son says.

In my mind I hear my mom: *You don't know him the way you should.* And Scott: *You don't know him as well as you think you do.*

The ringing is back in my ears. I think I'm going to faint.

Zachary did this.

My son is a killer.

"*Why*, Zachary?"

"He deserved it."

"It wasn't just Halliday—" I whisper.

"I don't know what happened, Mom! Dylan—he must have screwed up."

In my mind I see those photos, the ones Jackson gave me. He

knows Dylan. *Knew* Dylan. I picture the boy sprawled on the floor of that kitchen. "Tell me what happened. *Tell* me, Zachary."

"When I did that DNA test, I found . . . other family members. A half brother. Dylan."

I'm going to vomit.

"I looked into him. Halliday, too. You know, online. Did some . . . digging."

Hacking. Not like it matters, really. Not when you compare it to his other sins.

"What I found . . . I knew . . . I knew what he'd done to you. His campaign . . . He was doing research. On *us.* Dylan, too. He was using a private investigator."

In my mind I can see that search term on Zachary's laptop. *DC private investigators.* The pieces are falling into place. "You hacked in to see what he was doing." My voice sounds chillingly calm.

"The guy was *following* you, Mom. Following us. And I saw Halliday's emails. He thought you were a *liability.* They were making plans to discredit you. To ruin you."

Why didn't he *tell* me? Why couldn't we have dealt with that, *together*? "Zachary—"

"I had to do something. So I started meeting with him. And I—"

Oh God. "The gun—it really was yours?"

He shakes his head, adamantly. "I met with a dealer, but I didn't buy."

"You were going to *shoot* him?"

"No!" He sounds astounded that I would suggest it. "It was for protection. To protect *us.*"

Relief staggers me, but is swiftly extinguished. This wasn't protection. This was murder.

"Last week, someone contacted me. Dealer's friend. Said he'd gotten some . . . drugs."

I never should have said anything to him. Never should have let him know what was happening. "So you bought the poison. With your grandmother's money. And Dylan?"

"When I saw his name on the encrypted forum—*DTaylor*—I knew. That Halliday was setting us up. Trying to destroy my life, and Dylan's, and yours, too. I couldn't let him get away with it, Mom. Especially not with everything he'd *already* done to you."

There's a pleading look on his face. He wants me to understand, needs me to understand, but how can I understand this?

"So I got in touch with Dylan. And he was really scared. The FBI had been to his *house*, Mom. He wanted to help. Knew Halliday was going to be at that charity dinner . . ." He shrugs, miserable. "I brought him the drugs, at the hotel. . . . And somehow things just went wrong."

Someone made this happen. Someone coordinated it. Someone played him—and played *us*.

But Zachary was part of it. Zachary tried to kill Halliday. One count of first-degree murder, two counts of—

"I made a mistake, Mom."

"This is more than a mistake, Zachary."

"I'm going to jail, aren't I?" I flinch at the terror in his voice.

Are we safe, Mommy? The question reverberates in my brain so loudly that I'm dizzy.

I squeeze my eyes shut and breathe deeply, and I'm back in that car, watching him in the mirror, listening to my own whispered promise.

I'll always keep you safe.

I meant it. I always believed I'd do anything to keep him safe. But *this*?

If I turn my back on the truth now, it's all been for nothing. All those years of trying to do the right thing, at all costs. To be the champion of those who were wronged. To speak for those who dared not speak.

But how could I turn my back on my son?

I look at the phone, the one Jackson gave me.

Then I look at this frightened young man across from me. This criminal. My son.

And I know what I need to do.

Epilogue

Jackson's at home, asleep in bed, when the encrypted phone rings.
"It's over," an unfamiliar voice says. "Rendezvous point. Immediately!"

He springs out of bed, suddenly wide awake. Slides his feet into athletic shoes, throws a coat over his sweats, tucks the phone in his pocket. Heads straight for the door, swings it open, sprints down the hall and flights of stairs, exits the building through the rear.

Once outside, he bows his head against the cold drizzle and walks quickly. His hands are in his pockets, his shoulders hunched against the rain.

Streetlights cast ghostlike pools of light; the light catches the mist, illuminates it until it's a haze. Each time he passes through one, he's visible, then he steps back into the darkness, and he disappears from sight.

A car approaches, the first one he's seen. Its headlights cast a beam of light over the street; its engine cuts through the quiet of the night. Jackson tenses, but the car passes, and then all is still and dark once again.

There's a dumpster up ahead, a big blue one. It's set just off the road, in a service alley, and its lid is open. Without slowing his pace, Jackson takes the encrypted phone and in one swift movement throws it into the dumpster. It clangs against the side, and clatters to the bottom.

He knows he's not alone even before he sees anyone. Some sixth sense, all those years of training. And his pace slows, then grinds to a halt, just as he hears the sound that confirms his suspicion. Someone racking a gun.

His own gun's at home. He closes his hands into fists at his sides, and he waits.

A man steps from the shadows into one of the pools of light. Jackson's eyes settle on the pistol in his hand, at his side. And then on the tattoo on his forearm. Two knives, crossed in an X.

His mind flashes back to that restaurant. The man with the tattoo, approaching the table. Wes giving him the smallest nod, barely perceptible.

And in that instant, everything becomes clear.

He was set up. Betrayed. Sacrificed for the greater good.

The man raises the gun, and Jackson closes his eyes. He takes a deep breath, focuses on the sweet scent of the rain, the way the cold lands on his skin like ocean spray.

And then everything goes black.

The gunman stands over the body. He watches blood trail into rivulets of water, an almost inky blackness. Watches the rain pelt Jackson's skin, his lifeless eyes. Then he holsters the gun.

He extends his forearm. Grabs one edge of the crossed knives. Slowly, carefully, peels the image from his skin, until his arm is bare. Crumples the design into a ball, holds it tight in his fist.

Then he rolls the sleeve down to cover his arm, turns, and strides away.

• • •

Across the river, in the penthouse apartment, Wes stands in front of the picture windows, looking out over the city. There's a steady drumbeat of rain, the occasional flash of lightning in the distance. His gaze settles on the part of town where he knows Jackson has an apartment.

Had an apartment.

He glances down at his watch. By now, it should be done. And it had to happen. Protect the king, at all costs.

They knew Steph Maddox suspected Jackson, had for years. Under any other circumstances, they would have just eliminated her. It's certainly what Jackson wanted, *begged* for. She was a threat to the operation. But that secret—that *secret*.

They learned it from Halliday, from hacking into his research, doing their own digging. *Watching* him, just like they were watching *all* the likely presidential candidates. The election would turn out in their favor, one way or another—that much was a certainty.

They found out about Steph. Knew Halliday was vulnerable to blackmail. Knew he was *theirs*.

And that meant keeping Steph around. They might need her later, to intimidate Halliday. They couldn't kill her, so they had no choice but to co-opt her.

They watched her. Watched her son. Learned about the DNA test. The *hacking*. An intriguing prospect, really, because it made *him* valuable, too. They watched the kid meet with a gun dealer. Knew he had a secret of his own. All secrets are leverage.

And that's when the idea was born. A way to make sure Maddox would work for them. They would threaten her son's future. Intertwine him so closely with Jackson's rise to power that she would be unable to stop it without betraying the person she loved the most.

They already had a plan in place to eliminate the FBI director, get

Jackson into position. They just inserted Zachary into it. And added a second target.

Second because the others—the ones they leaked to the press—were decoys. "Intended targets" who would be insulated from charges of treason, forever, if the truth ever did come to light.

All it took was dangling the drugs in front of Zachary at the right moment, just before that charity dinner, and the rest fell into place. He and Dylan made exactly the moves they anticipated. All *they* did was ensure that a spiked cocktail made it into the FBI director's hands. And then Dylan's.

It all would have worked out perfectly if Steph had kept her mouth shut. But when she wouldn't let it go, they had to adapt. And once she shared her suspicions with Vivian, they had no choice.

His own tracks are covered—he's sure of it. The gunman is one of Moscow's finest, unknown to U.S. authorities. CCTV cameras all over the city have caught him tailing Jackson, and Steph, too, his tattoo always visible. The authorities will zero in on that tattoo.

They'll reach the conclusion that it was a mob hit, because that'll be the easy answer, the one with proof. By then the gunman will be long gone, back in Moscow. And if Steph ever does decide to come clean? They'll make it look like she ordered the hit, used connections she made on the job in Chicago, all those years ago.

It wasn't his idea, of course. His handler, the man the Americans call Justice Ranger, came up with it. He thought of everything. Wes can just picture how those pale blue eyes will gleam when he hears of the operation's resounding success.

He walks over to the chessboard. Looks at Zachary's pawns, Steph's pawns. So many pawns in this game. Then he moves Zachary's knight, sets it up to be sacrificed.

All the pieces are in position now. The board is just as it needs to look. Steph can't tell the truth without her kid going to prison, and she's not going to do that, is she? They own her. It's not the same as having the director, sure, but they can continue to move her up the ranks. Just like Vivian. Exposing Jackson as a Russian agent—that's going to be a huge coup. Enough to make her chief of the Counter-intelligence Center, most likely. Unwittingly married to one of their own, someone who can manipulate her when the time is right, can use their *kids* if he has to. And then there's the asset, the one who will have the full trust of the Agency, and the Bureau.

He reaches for Steph's queen, moves it to the far end of the board.

"Checkmate," he murmurs.

The phone rings, a steady buzz. Wes looks at the screen, and a smile flickers on his lips. He's been waiting for this call. There wasn't any question in his mind, or anyone else's, that it was coming.

He takes a steadying breath, presses the green button. "Wes Shields."

He listens.

"Yes, Mr. President." A pause. "Absolutely, Mr. President. I'd be honored." A long pause this time. Wes's gaze is still centered on the same point in the city.

"Oh, the Senate will get by just fine without me, sir. They'll find a new leader." A chuckle, then Wes grows serious again. "I'll strive to serve the office of vice president with integrity, sir."

A moment later, he presses the red button on his phone, sets it down carefully on the end table. Then he looks back out the window, sets his gaze on a speck of illumination in the distance.

The White House.

Acknowledgments

A novel is truly a team effort, and I'm fortunate to work with an incredible team. Huge thanks to all the wonderful people at Ballantine, especially Kate Miciak, Michelle Jasmine, Quinne Rogers, Kim Hovey, and Kara Welsh. Thanks, too, to the great crew at the Gernert Company, particularly David Gernert, Anna Worrall, Ellen Coughtrey, Rebecca Gardner, and Will Roberts, and to Sarah Adams at Transworld and all those who've worked on editions around the world. I'm so grateful to the core group of editors and early readers—Kate, Sarah, David, Anna, and Ellen—who shaped and strengthened this novel.

I'm also fortunate to be surrounded by great people at home. I've written about characters who have complicated relationships with their husbands and mothers and sons, but thankfully, it's purely fiction. My relationship with my own spouse, and my mom, and my little boys are all wonderfully *un*complicated, and for that I'm extremely lucky. A big thank-you to my whole family, immediate and extended—and especially B, J, and W: Love you!

About the Author

Karen Cleveland is a former CIA analyst and the *New York Times* bestselling author of *Need to Know*. She has master's degrees from Trinity College Dublin and Harvard University. Cleveland lives in northern Virginia with her husband and two young sons.

Karen-cleveland.com
Facebook.com/KarenClevelandAuthor

About the Type

This book was set in Legacy, a typeface family designed by Ronald Arnholm (b. 1939) and issued in digital form by ITC in 1992. Both its serifed and unserifed versions are based on an original type created by the French punchcutter Nicholas Jenson in the late fifteenth century. While Legacy tends to differ from Jenson's original in its proportions, it maintains much of the latter's characteristic modulations in stroke.